Looking For Amateurs

By Nicholas Dodge

I0629892

Nick Dodge
Looking 4 Amateurs

Summary: A college drop-out decides to give up
everything for the chance to enter the porn industry as
a cameraman and editor. Once he finds his
opportunity, he's lunged headfirst into a world of sex,
drugs, and even human trafficking. Can he overcome
his own insatiable dreams of fame and fortune, or be
consumed by them?

Uploaded in the U.S.A.
First edition, February 2026

Table of Contents

Looking For Amateurs

WHEN I WAS A KID, I thought I'd be a firefighter or a police man. Not a police "officer", but a "police man", it was very specific. The dream of a boy growing up to be someone of power and authority, capable of stopping the bad in the world, I guess that all became a fair dream sent away on residing tides and coming storms.

Most people might say that this was all a waste of time, standing outside of a clothing store when I should've been seated in my English Literature 122 classroom learning. Little do most people know, I was learning.

From the start and a year back, I had promised my parents I would attend a community college. So long as they let me stay at home rent free. And it worked.

Unlike the Bachelor of Arts degree, I was quote-end-quote working towards. I knew very well where an art degree would get me, oh Hell, it could've been a God-damn master's degree, and I'd still be flippin' burgers at the damn joint up the street. But the ways in which the tomatoes would be centered to the onions, as well as the composition of lettuce to the sesame seed buns would be artistic as fuck.

Instead, I was here, wasting my time holding up a cheap cardboard sign like some young destitute on the street corner. Sometimes passersby would hiss, some would remark, others spat down to my shoes and hid their children's eyes from me.

But most walked on, without a sigh, sorry, or stare, while plugged into their static screens of sociability. It wasn't my black cap partly twisted to the corner of my medium greased hair crawling out from the brim like thin weeds out of the sidewalk. Neither was it my Ray Bans, scratched so badly along the front of the lenses that you'd probably mistake them for some cat toy otherwise. Nope, it wasn't the ashes from my fag nor the wife-beater that hung lower than my pubescent ball sack.

No.

It was the sign I held that read:

Looking 4 Amateurs
Get Paid
2 Get Laid

Damn straight and nothing else about it.

I didn't mind the dirty looks or people's vicious snarls, they were nothing compared to the death threat messages, hate ridden tweets or the "*kill your-self*" comments on the internet. Although, standing alone there was one thing that would've made this day much more exciting. Having my fucking business partner and longtime friend here to help me edge these girls on.

However, I got a lot of thinking done on my own. Like how the Hell hasn't this store's management come out and talked to me about leaving the premise yet?

Then he finally showed, walking down the sidewalk like some young chump hyped up on one too many energy drinks. Or maybe one too many beers.

The guy wasn't just a fish; he was a sperm whale in a sea of liquor. A guy just like me most nights, I suppose. It's something lacking luster that still leaves me afraid from time to time.

Never mind, I take it back, I'm not afraid, because I *admitted* it.

"Wha'sup man?" He came up to me with his right-hand wavering in the air, waiting for that nice slap to send it back down to Earth like some wishing star falling.

"What's up? I've been here for over an hour man. Don't tell me you actually showed up to Miss Mankey's class again?"

Frankie's history teacher had a slight hunch in her back, which caused her slouched posture. So, Frankie and I gave her the nickname "*Miss Mankey*", it always put us in a good mood when we said it. Did I mention my friend's name was Frankie?

Regardless of where he was the bastard ended up showing, apparently piss drunk by the strut in his steps. "It's fucking two thirty man and you're al'eady wasted? What's wrong with you?"

"Hey, you know how I am with girls."

"I know how you're *not* with girls." That didn't make him happy. I could see a touch of red in his cheeks, so I made quick to apologize to the grunt. He really was like a sort of henchman, if his price tag was cut by half on account of an accidental dent in his skull, lowering the base price.

Yeah, Frankie had more loose fat than muscle, but the guy could lift twice what I could. Though he wasn't fat, he only weighed one-eighty-one, where I barely reached one-thirty-six on a good day. So, I usually made the decision to stay on Frankie's good side.

9

I offered the lug a fag and that seemed to calm him down. He complimented the sign before striking a light and taking in too big of an inhale before choking violently into the air. He pointed a finger, but I didn't say a word, I already had my fun for the day. I told him the store wasn't working out, that the teenage-lingerie store was the way to go. But he hushed me up in his puff.

You see, Frankie might be a drunk fucking idiot most days, but he had a heart of gold somewhere, probably in his gullet, and a fine way of making sense of things in the most naïve ways possible.

"Nah man, you see that?" he slurred to me as he pointed across the way, past the fountain that stained an otherwise acceptable outdoor mall with its putrid green water flowing. His fingers were a bit off, but I followed them the best I could to a group of young girls heading our way. "See man, all the young things come out. For them this place is their drug dealer. But you can't buy your Gucci and Armani without a little green." He said, nearly in *slo-mo-tion* while tapping his pointing fingers now to my sign. "Gotta' pay to get paid. Getting laid is just a bonus."

"You better be right man." I spoke, still feeling the weightlessness of my wallet feathered lightly against my ass-cheek. "Cuz' this was the last hundred I had in my checking."

"What you do with the rest?" He asked and I thought back. It only took me but a second to see in dreamy colors and rewired timeframes shifting through my brain before I realized I had smoked my last gram just the other night. I recall watching Conan O'Brien off YouTube and thinking it was funny at the time. Yet now, for some stupid fucking reason I thought that that last hundred was going back to another few hits down the line. At this point the weed might had been the better option.

But here I was . . . outside of a clothing store with a sign that read:

"Looking for amateurs, get paid to get laid? You're fucking kidding us, right?" The blonde bitch with the red leather bag strapped around her chest like a damn ACU vest with missing pieces, spoke to us as if she were a PETA protester. All day I had listened to people make a mockery of what I was attempting to do, that is, live the American Dream. However, when it came down to it, a pair of ripe ovaries always withstood and demolished the ego of an almost equally young male.

So, there I stood, with my testis tangled and my tongue tied just the same (although, my testes were not tied to my tongue or vice versa, because that may be considered strange). I opened my mouth to reply, but unlike a text in which I could have thought through I instead unleashed a slight slip of acid reflux and allowed my bowls to bury me in a new grave.

They laughed as they held their breath, called me gross and walked off in quite a hurry. The hurry was never fast enough, given these situations. Then, when I looked back to Frankie, I noticed the fucker was too piss-taken by the shake of these girl's asses in the background to defend me.

"Frankie!" I yelled in an instance. Hearing his name yelled like that shook the damn ape's composure. His eyes widened, the girls must had stared back for half a second before continuing along, recording the events for their TikTok's as they went.

But I didn't care, didn't give two shits externally. It was only my pride after all . . .

"Frankie, where were you man? You're supposed to be my wingman, and this is where it gets me? Getting laughed at by a couple of tween prats!"

"That's your own damn fault man, and this was your idea! I thought you were good with the ladies, unlike *me*." Man, he got a big smile after saying that line, and I hated him just a bit more for it.

The day passed on, little by little with no initial progress to be had. Oh, there were plenty of girls. Most of the time they were too busy looking down on their phones to even recognize their steps. The guys that walked by weren't much better, though they stopped by to talk more times than not.

They'd always be asking "*You need a male lead?*" or "*Can you pay me to get laid?*" as if our business was some sort of perverted joke to them. One even stumbled by, looking as plastered as Frankie to my side, who somehow found himself slouched against the wall of the building. He'd come up and take five fucking minutes to read the sign, followed by a questionnaire. Then perhaps back to the sign as if studying some hieroglyph.

I could go all day ranting on about that asshole, but then I would have never gotten to the good part. Or maybe we should call it the bad, the dirty, and the discrete? Because that's exactly what this girl was. We saw her coming from a mile away, but by the time she made it to us we were still surprised by her impact.

The girl had a god-damn miniskirt barely tied around her thighs, bright blue tank, and a pair of B-52 bombers perking from her chest. The way her long, dark brown hair swayed with the gusts sometimes was enough to get me hot and bothered without the sun or shine. Lollipop red lips stared into my heart and soul as they talked, but I wasn't listening. That was until her fingers snapped.

"Hey jerk-off, you're not quiet breast level with those pretty green eyes of yours yet, but you're getting pretty damn close." As she spoke, I sort of wished that every girl would speak to me like that. It was some sort of passion in play.

"My partner is just observing the merch." Frankie slyly started, finally defending me like the world's greatest wingman.

"Uh, right . . . You interested then?" I asked, trying to recover from the sudden heat flash I seemed to be experiencing.

"Interested? Yeah, I'm interested. Interested to know when you'll answer my question." Her voice sounded irritated, like the call of a caged bull.

And I was the rider or, I was hoping to be. "Ah yes, the question. Let's see . . . we provide transport to the studio" (*what else was I supposed to call my parent's basement?*), "where you'll be interviewed to see if you're the right match for our company. Then, given that you've passed your interview we'll begin by-"

"Hun," she cut me short, one finger to my mouth nearly pressing in and onto my tongue. Heaven has nothing on the beauty of a woman's resolve. "I just asked how much, that's it. You don't need to give me the spiel, it's pretty obvious what you guys are out here for."

Wow, and just like that we had our very first film star. I started to formulate high hopes and hearings, or simply to be heard by her. It was . . . hard to explain. Like a rat chasing the scent of cheese through a maze, no real reason except to get what you desire. I was pretty damn certain though that I desired her, and this situation was my maze. Though it would be short lived, I'd blow her away in the bedroom, and that would be enough. At least the alpha males online told me so, *I think*.

"What's your name?" I asked, the silence growing awkward between us three.

"Abby. So how much?" She was anxious, maybe desperate. I was too, so I cut the chase and whipped out my wallet.

"One-hundred dollars." I said, pulling out the five twenties and presenting them as if they were a bouquet.

She looked at the money, then began to giggle. "You think two-hundred's gonna' cut it?" She replied. I couldn't believe it; she was amused yet not taken. "Boy, I've done this shit before. Since high school . . . or was it middle school?"

More pondering ensued, which left me to wonder if Frankie and I were cut out for this. Then it hit me, the price had doubled. "Woah, woah-woah honey, two hundred? I said one."

At this point she burst out laughing. "Oh, God. You two must be the street-side amateurs of the porn world. The deal is you pay me half now and half later. But a hundred in total? You're fucking kidding."

"Listen, listen . . ." I needed to keep her here, to bide me some time. Frankie, sure as Hell wasn't listening anymore, he added his two-cents at one point and called it quits, the freeloader. "Two hundred total, two-fift'ay depending on your success." I was playing a Royal Flush without the damn King, Queen, Jack, or Ace.

But she was a ten, so I didn't have a choice.

"Heh," she sighed with a smile, "seeing as I'm a bit behind on rent this month, sure. What the Hell, what's a good time without risk?"

With that, I thought to myself: *Anytime*.

"So, why don't you follow us back to our cars and you can get a ride, free of charge?"

She gave a quick laugh, it made me feel more like the amateur than the guy holding up the bloody sign. "I'll drive myself, thank you."

With that we were off, Frankie was in the seat next to me. He must've been coming off the buzz because he started to wake up from his dreary-eyed state. Abby was right behind us, following in some semi-beat-up Buick or another, bright blue with rust spots along the hood. You would think if she were bluffing, she wouldn't have had me by the balls the entire time we talked.

Then again, you'd also think she'd be driving something better if she'd been doing this sort of thing already. Whatever the case we finally hit home, like a slugger in Yankee's stadium or something. I would turn to Frankie at every red light or so and ask, "Hey man, you ready? You up for this?"

"Well . . ." he'd drone off, "I haven't seen your ass naked since we were kids and fucking playin' in the pool and shit. Remember when, at that birthday party . . . Gena's or some shit and you had that huge crush on her and all?"

"Yeah, and we were playing chicken, I had her on my shoulders. Man, her crotch was so warm up against my neck."

"Man, we were like ten. That's pedophilic dude."

"Whatever, we were playing chicken in the pool, and you had the nerve to de-pants me right outta' my bathing suit. You threw it into her backyard, and I dropped her straight back into the pool to get them. But then her family dog went and grabbed them, and I was standing nude in her yard. Then her father walked out with the cake . . ."

"They never let you back over again!" Frankie laughed, then I began to laugh.

– 2 –

Dousing Rod

I THINK WE DIDN'T STOP LAUGHING until we reached the neighborhood, as I took a few corners onto my street. Then I saw my parents' house and knew by the empty driveway that they were still at work. I checked my phone; it was a bit after three. We would have a little more than two hours to shoot before my mother got home and my father shortly after. It seemed like a lot of time. But then again, I assumed I wouldn't last more than two minutes tops, so time didn't make a difference. Not with a girl like Abby on my bed.

We pulled up and she pulled in behind us. Everyone was outta' their cars and Abby had locked her purse in her Buick before swinging her keys around one finger as she pocketed them. She gave us this smile, a fake smile that hid what I could only assume was nervousness. Her step, however, was still the most confident I had ever seen in a girl's stride.

"You ready?" I asked, as if there was any way of turning back now. She nodded and asked which one of us she'd be fucking. I opened my arms but kept my hands below my waist, presenting my body like a trophy. For what it was worth, it was at least a bronze medal for sure.

Inside my parents' home, we eventually walked down the steps to the basement. I thought I heard Frankie slip down a step behind us, but I paid no attention really. Abby was between us, following me and leading Frankie who readied his phone.

"Really, you're gonna' film us with your phone?" She asked, though it was less a question than it was a complacent remark.

"Uh, yeah. It's got twelve megapixels and shoots at a nineteen-twenty by ten-eighty aspect and-"

"Ok, ok fine." she said, as we entered through the doorway into my room.

God, even though I cleaned up, it still looked like a mess. Band posters were strung across the white walls; I had some Playboy magazine's creeping out from the bed frame (which I gave a gentle kick to send them back under). I had some twenty-inch LCD television, flat screen hooked to a number of gaming systems and one small window which leaked a shred of light in from outside. Some of the drawers from my dresser had been left open this morning when I got dressed, with pairs of clothing dripping out along the edging.

"Welcome to the studio." I said, as if it were anything impressive.

She laughed, she was always laughing or giggling or some shit. It put my ego in place, lined it up execution style along whatever wall I might have been silhouetted next to. "Nice room." She replied, and I think I saw a bit of blush in her cheeks before she turned to face the window. Even in that beam of light her radiance seemed to disperse across my bedroom.

And that smell of perfume she wore, the kind you get as a Christmas gift, I hoped that it wouldn't leave.

"I can get my father's DSLR camera, if you'd rather we use that?" I said, as Frankie opened his mouth, about to argue with me.

But she spoke first and in the kindest words I had heard from her up to this point, she said "Yeah, that would be great. Just so I know your friend here won't be watching it from his phone during his lunch breaks."

That seemed to put Frankie off, as I ran out into my father's office that resided next door to my bedroom. I scrounged around his belongings for a bit until I found the camera, carefully putting things back in their place. My father could be meticulous at times, a very organized man. He was a mechanic, so I suppose it only made sense. Like a tool cabinet, everything had its place. Though, it was fucking annoying sometimes.

I ran back and found the two silently sitting on my bed, neither facing one another nor speaking. I had to break the ice, although it seemed as if I was chipping through an iceberg. The deeper I went, the more ice there was to break. I got out my phone and texted Frankie very quick-like: *"man lighten up we got a girl hear we gotta do this thing stop being so awkward."*

Frankie looked over at her and smiled, asked her how long she'd been doing this sort of thing. She said it had been a while but assured us she wouldn't cry like the first time. "*Cry*?" I asked, she said the first time is always somewhat traumatic, but it's only natural. I told her we wouldn't hurt her or nothing, and she walked over with her hand right up against my cheek. It was a cold sweat blistering against my skin, but I was sure that my hands were no different.

"You're real sweet," she said, "but it's never because of what you do. I can tell this is your first time doing this too, by the way you spoke to me, by the way you two stood outside with knees buckling. I just hope you're oh-kay in the end."

"Wha-that I'm, ok? I'll be fine." I told her.

"I'm sure you will be." She smiled and stood. At first, I wasn't sure what was happening, it had been a few years since I last got laid. Maybe that's why I was so miserable.

You'd watch these studs or these ugly fucks; fat, thin, fit, or anywhere in between. It didn't matter who they were, they were scoring it with some fine female specimens, and there I was jerking off to their success. But I caught on quickly to her movements, hands gripping at the bottom of her shirt as it came up and over her head. It was all done spectacularly in one quick motion, like pulling a sheet from underneath a set of fine dinner ware and not having a single glass nor fine China plate move out've place.

Then my head clicked back and I shoved the camera into Frankie's arms. He was as surprised as I was and jumped the second I handed him the camera. I hope he had at least caught her taking off those short-shorts, one leg moving out from the opening at a time. She wore a cute pair of pink panties with no logos or sassy writing like: *Hot Stuff* or *Caution*. They were mismatched by her plain white bra, which cradled her breasts in a way that made me feel like a child.

"Well, we gonna' do this or what?" She smirked; she knew by her tight tummy and flashy thighs that she could have any man on two knees.

Funny thing, I thought as I began to sluggishly remove my shirt and jeans: How does a prayer position on two knees, a proposal, or knees down during oral pleasure exist in the same stance? Guess it didn't matter, it was just a passing thought.

I kept my socks on, a little chilled by the bitterness of my basement. I saw her eyes glancing down and she covered her smile. I was hoping to see my junk, large and erected for her as I too looked down. But there was just the small bulge from where my flaccid member lurked, too shy to wake up and give this girl the courtesy she deserved.

I turned around quickly and told her it would only be a minute as I grabbed Frankie and took us both into the hall. I kept my voice low, as I wasn't sure if the camera was still filming us. But I really didn't care, I was frantic, "Frankie, shit man."

"What? What the Hell is the matter with-"

"I can't get it up Frankie, look!" I pointed downward. I poked a hand down there and started strangling the damn thing in an attempt to get it hard.

Frankie shook his head and hushed me up. "Look dude, I brought some of these, just in case." And from his pocket he revealed a handful of pills, three to be exact.

"What-the-fuck is this shit?" I scrambled, at least now my dick was loosened up, but still nowhere near hard. Time felt fleeting, I was worried we would keep her too long and she would give up, take our money and call this a bust. Then I'd be one hundred in the hole and spend another day as a reborn virgin.

"Clam down." He said to me as his warm hand strutted up against my shoulder. "These 'ere are enhancers, they'll get it up in a matter of minutes."

"Minutes!" I accidentally yelled; she must have been having fun listening to us babble from the hallway.

"Listen, take 'em, get in there. We'll buy some time till you get it up and then it's off to fuck-fest for us."

"Us?" I questioned as I grabbed the pills and dry-swallowed.

"I mean *you*, now get the fuck back in there."

He pushed, I pulled, eventually we walked back in with Abby kicking her feet from the edge of my bed. How could something so innocent be prepared to do something so dirty? I guess the answer lied somewhere inside the American Dream.

"So, how you feelin'?" I asked.

"Not quite wet yet, you might have to eat me out first."

"Do we start with a story or something?" Frankie began, and that only pissed me off more. "Bad babysitter, study partner, foreign exchange student?"

"Frankie she's fucking white like the two of us, how foreign could she be?" I replied, though it wasn't any use.

"Swedish people are white, so are Germans, Austrians . . . can you do any accents?" Frankie asked, I couldn't believe where this was going.

"Hmm, I could probably make one up." She replied, as I fiddled with myself through my boxers as the two discussed the next Golden Globe screenplay.

This was turning into a disaster, had I lost it? Was I incapable or had those few years of not getting screwed finally screwed me over? Before I could even turn back to see whether she had left us or whether Frankie had found a notepad to write on, I felt a sudden impact along my bed. Looking over and then standing in utter shock, I saw Frankie on top of Abby. My fucking-fuck partner and *fuck*!

What the Hell was going on anymore?

He already had his hand halfway up her bra and the other underneath her panties. All I heard were wet sloppy suckles along her neckline and her body squirming as her eyes laid shut. It was like watching ecstasy react with the nerves, the fireworks lighting off in one's head. Then Frankie removed his hand from her bra and proceeded to push the camera over to me.

"Do it." He whispered, as I watched Abby become engulfed by his forceful hands digging deeper below her waistline.

I picked it up and noticed it was already filming, had been filming this entire time. Which was fine, that's why they make editing software so cheap these days, for moments such as this. There I crouched, nearly naked as I watched my friend strip, followed by Abby. They crawled around my bed like two dogs in Spring-time merriment (*I would have to change the sheets after this for sure*).

Then slowly but surely it began to happen, hands gripped and I watched two bodies fuse into one violent string of moans and motions. Then out of nowhere I began to realize, looking through the viewfinder at every angle I shot, that my boxers began to rise at the front. And my boner pointed me towards them like a dousing rod discovering water.

– 3 –

Movie Studio 69

THE FIRST TIME my naïve eyes took a glance at pornography was at the itty-bitty age of eight. My best friend and I were playing in a box fort or some shit in my parent's basement one afternoon. It was all pretty innocent, till I heard him call across from the room. I stuck my head out of the top of the two-story castle expecting to fight off a dragon or a Viking warrior. Instead, I saw his hand calling me over, he was staring up at something or another stacked high along my father's shelf.

I tumbled my way down to the bottom floor (if I recall I brought the whole top floor down with me). Then, snaking myself out of the pile of boxes, I noticed a rather large magazine in my friend's hand. The moment he flashed the cover to me I knew that something had changed. I felt a stir underneath my gullet, like some wicked punch or'a couple too many sodas down the throat.

She was a blonde babe, deep brown eyes gazing through me. Her breasts were large, larger than I had ever seen, and they were fully exposed with the rest of her body. She had her legs crossed to cover her crotch, which by this age I never really gave any thought to. I knew boys had pee-pees and girls, well . . . I just thought it was a flat surface and nothing more nor less to it than that. But these magazines were starting to prove otherwise.

But after gazing through the pages, I learned that there was a lot more to the female body than I expected, more than I should have known by then. But that was that, and there wasn't any more to it than such. It's no wonder I never put up a bother about it.

I was exposed to these girls, whose nipples were pins sticking out from the cushions and whose legs were carved out of oiled stones, smoothed, and *sharpened. They glistened, more so than the holographic prints on my favorite playing cards.*

There was something mystical about them, some mystery being bound. The only women I ever really knew were my mother and my little sister, up till this point. We had discovered a treasure and by looking through that magazine's contents, we learned more than we ever previously knew. Little did we know that one day it would drive us mad.

That lady, on the front cover. I didn't know her name, where she went to school, if I saw her on the playground, or was invited to her birthday party last year. I didn't know if her parents knew mine, if she was my babysitter, a neighbor across the way. I didn't know a thing about her, and yet . . . I didn't need to.

"You still mad at me bro?"

"You're damn-fucking right I am. Whose idea was this again? -Oh, yeah- It was mine!" I yelled at Frankie, who was washing up in a second round of beer.

"Keep it down man or my mom's gonna' hear you." He uttered between burps and gags.

"Fuck yo' mother man and fuck you. Fuck your mother for having you."

"That's harsh bro."

"Stop calling me bro, man. We had a plan. I haven't gotten laid since . . . since fucking Courtney during my junior year. And then you had to go and take this from me?" I pouted and babbled as I attempted to navigate through the cluster of crap that was Frankie's mother's desktop. It was a typical mess for a fifty something year old woman, divorced and working day and night. There were folders scattered all about the screen, some by date and others by some precarious numbering system.

Some were called *Family Pics*, *Vacation 2003*, *Hubby*, *Jacks Grad*. It was kind of cute, in a sense, like looking through a virtual catalogue of someone's most precious moments. Those moments and several tax filings and *How-To-For-Dummies* online saved guides. "So, where we saving this shit after it's edited?"

"Oh, now you wanna' talk." He spoke, walking over to me with a fresh brew in hand.

I guess I could forgive him, for now.

I slid the chair to the side to make room as I leaned back and cracked the can open. The fizz began to pick up and around the rim, so I had to slurp the bubbles down quickly while Frankie looked around for the folder he had apparently created. He was no rat in a maze; he was the observer and had located the folder in less time than it took me to swallow. "Here . . ." he pointed with the mouse cursor. I looked over and read: *JacksTaxes2022*.

"Last year's tax folder? That's golden." I said, giving him the betterment of doubt. "At least we know nobody'll be lookin' through there anytime soon. Do you actually file for taxes man?

"Yeah, just not very well." He smirked.

"Well, I guess it's time we edit this bitch. How long before your mother comes around?"

Frankie checked his phone for the time, then came back to face me, eyes staring at a loading bar to his editing program. "Well, it's six of three right now, so my ma'ma just started drinkin'. She probably won't need to online binge shop until about seven-thirty, so we got'us some time."

Time, Frankie says. I wanted to tell him that while he would be sittin' on his ass playing mobile games on his phone, that I had over half an hour of Abby and him fucking around (*literally*). Half an hour that I need to cut the greatest moments of, adjust the volume so the audience could hear every subtle moan, sharpen the resolution so you could see every inch of hair along Frankie's ass-crack.

"Hey Frankie, you ever think about shaving?" I spoke as if to a painted wall drying.

"I did." He droned from the corner with another beer out of who knows how many.

"I meant the other side."

It took him a moment, but he eventually figured out what I was talking about. "Oh," he'd begin in exasperation, "no." and that was that.

Again, there I was, staring at a nut sack bagging against a nice, puckered asshole that I could have only dreamed of touching. It was memorizing, like watching a pendulum bounce. But instead of a hard clank, you heard a wet slap. It might have been gross taken out of context, but that was sex. Wet, sloppy, and disgusting out of context.

How was it that the human race found something so obscene to be so entrancing, euphoric, and divine? It felt like a sin just thinking about it. This endomorphic discrepancy between turn ons and turn offs. Watching a blooming flower get conceptually penetrated by a stick.

God, the mind dives into weird spaces while finding the best crop between your best friend's thighs and a girl's collar. And simply watching her, frame by frame, just made me fall harder for her. It wasn't quite jealousy. I've seen probably hundreds of women, girls, grannies, you name it. I've fallen in love, in a sense, with many of them, but never could have imagined knowing one face to face.

Before she took off, she provided us both with her number for the next time we had a job. Oh, and to pay her dues, which we still owed by the time the video had been released for a month. It was nearly eight, Frankie had been holding his mother off for as long as he could. I saved the file to his "*Tax*" folder and told him to send it to me tonight and I'd take care of it from there. In Frankie's mind, he had done enough work today; in my mind, getting this video up was just as good as getting laid.

Soon, his mother had barged in, sliding off the walls and stumbling over to the computer. Thankfully the job was finished, Frankie sent me home with the last of the beers and he must have called it a night from there. I was only a few minutes away, so I chugged it before getting home in case my parents were still awake to see me bring it in. Then entering my house all lights were out, and my parents' door shut. I rushed down to the basement to finish my work.

The video had been sent. I had been able to cut it down to a nice ten minute short. I left some of the more sensual kissing at the start. Though not before long did I have the live action begin. I must admit, I took a couple of turns watching it myself, acting out the scene and putting myself in Frankie's place. In all honesty, it was the shortness of breathes and the dilation of Abby's eyes when they opened that really got me going.

I found about ten different porn sites, although, in actuality, I could have submitted to hundreds. Yet every time I'd have to create a username, a password, connect the site to my bank account, agree to licensing and other bullshit. Like those updates you just check the box that says *agree* on and continue forth.

By the time I was done it was nearly midnight. I didn't know where the time had gone. All I knew was that my eyes were sore, my libido diminished, and my mind racing for what was in store. She'd probably be an online idol by tomorrow morning, and Frankie and I would be proud producers in the industry. That was the thing I guess, you didn't need the sharpest quality or the greatest script. Hell, you didn't even need the prettiest of people anymore. Having Abby seemed like a bonus in that way.

I slept and dreamed of something terrifying. The dream I had would be lost in the morning for sure, but as I dreamt of it, everything about this reality of mine seemed to diminish.

There I was, being swallowed up by a black spiraling void. It was empty, bleak, an oppressive chasm of no return. No matter how long I struggled, grabbing at the nothingness that surrounded me I kept on falling. I wasn't sure if I was falling downwards or upwards, from across the universe or between nerves inside of my brain.

All I knew was that when I awoke, I was falling out of my bed.

That hard, sudden hit that jutted you from your sleep. The scare was worse than the blunt impact after the fall. It was sure to leave a bruise. But it got me up and out of bed. I didn't waste any time brushing my teeth, styling my hair. I ran straight over to my desktop and forced it awake, the screen flashing into my eyes. God damn that light hurt, from one too many beers from the night before.

Typing in the websites, my hands were almost shaking from the anticipation. I was expecting to see thousands —no— hundreds of thousands of views and comments on how hot the leading lady was. That and the great angles that were captured. Every inch of skin and, in all honesty, I was ready to watch it again myself.

Then I saw the numbers on the first website and choked. Double digits, 52 views. I was in shock and awe. What the Hell went wrong? I even chose a good thumbnail detailing the overall feel of the video: Frankie hovered over Abby with her seductive head hanging off from the bed sheets.

Switching over to the next website there were barely thirty views, the next had a mere forty-four and so on. All double-digit-downers that seamlessly depressed the living Hell out of me. I thought that a penis inserted into a vagina was all that I needed to give the world a good five-minute relief session. Like connecting two Legos, except that didn't really make a structure and a structure is what people were looking for. I had been proven wrong in a matter of thirty minutes.

Five minutes for chopping my own morning wood.

So, I called Frankie, hoping that he was awake and had some insight. The phone rang, rang, rang, and no answer. All except for Frankie's stupid-ass voicemail message:

"Hey, hey you there . . . can't hear you . . . breaking up . . . ha-ha gotcha'ya!"

Yeah, real fucking funny, I'm on the floor rolling, pal. And I called again, then I called some more. Eventually he answered with his usual, weary sort of slurred mumbled speech that plagues him, along with a hangover every morning. "Mmphm, ye-uh, h'is Jack."

"Frankie, the videos are up, but there's no views, Frankie . . . No. Views. What the Hell did we do wrong?" I yelled, scrambling for words, attempting to form a coherent sentence. But nothing seemed to fit together. "What do I do Frankie?" There I stood staring down at the screen, the minimal amount of views still haunting the digits of pixels on my computer screen. Frankie hummed and scratched his throat, careless, apathetic, and seemingly still asleep. "Frankie, c'mon man!" And after that an idea must have hit him.

"Did you tag the videos? Did you look at the metadata?" Suddenly his voice was clear, a goddamn whistle and I was the dog. Another thing about Frankie, which I might have mentioned before, was that the guy was dumb. But he was the smart sort of dumb, I mean he was knowledgeable in some surprising respects.

What I'm trying to say is a person ain't so stupid when they can fish a friend out of an ocean too deep to swim in. Mobilized again, I let Frankie walk me through the process.

We began to discuss all sorts of popular tags: *teen, fuck, sex, amateur,* **couple** (that word seemed to bother me), *orgasm, cum.* Then I started to suggest other tags for maximum exposure: *slut, anal, milf, orgy,* **daughter** (that word also seemed to bother me), *oral, deepthroat.* If porn was a study in school, I'd already have my master's degree.

We summarized, and I submitted these tags to each one of the ten or so video sites I had uploaded to on that night before. It was a real pain, having to go through that many sites again and *not* get distracted. Not just by the breasts and the pussy lips puckered, but by the fact that I still wasn't getting enough.

Hold up - getting *enough*?

I wasn't getting anything . . .

School was in less than an hour and I was less motivated than ever to attend for one more day. Once those tags got searched and our video was featured on the front pages of <u>Recently Uploaded</u>, I'd have no need for school. I'd have all the money I could need.

What education promised is what selling sex bought out. Why attend an hour and a half long class, three to four times a day when it took a fraction of the time to take a picture of penetration in-action for the same end result? Wasn't it always true that my parents wanted the best for me?

A good job so I could afford a nice home in a nice home in a splendid neighborhood and eventually retire from my savings. This would do that and more, like redefining The American Dream all over. And Frankie and I were just a couple of entrepreneurs working the system. Supply and demand, baby.

But I knew I was getting too far ahead of myself. Class was less than half an hour away now and I thought I should at least show up, for moral reasons. To make myself feel better about myself, I was doing a service to the college by being there. I was their marketable student, and they didn't have to even pay me. In fact, I pay them to fill those classrooms and keep their business stable.

To ignore the activists who haggle everyone outside of the front doors; to appease the dean and make them feel as though they hold significance within their jurisdiction; to ensure that knowledge always carried a $10,000.00 price tag per semester with a limited shelf life.

But moreover, I had hopes that Stephanie or Briana would be there, second to last row where I like to sneak a peek every now and again. Thank God for girls.

– **4** –

Better "*Things*" to Do

IT WAS AN HONEST THING in elementary school. Curiosity killed the cat they say, but few people know the whole saying. I recall my friend and I hanging out with two girls from the neighborhood. They were both in our Third-Grade math class with us and our parents' figured boys and girls need to meet up someday. That we needed to know that cooties weren't real and that a peck against your cheek would burn the flesh from your bones. I suppose the second wasn't intended, but the notion of it was.

So, there we were, the four of us kids, just playing board games and sitting around talking like you'd do at the jungle gym at that age. Just innocence, compliant in our naivety with a lacking parental guidance. What was the worst thing that could happen? Well . . .

My friend had reminded me of those stacks of magazines my father kept in plain sight, the likings of which had been invisible beforehand. He was still curious, as curious as ever. And sure, I had taken glances times again, there and there over days.

When I wasn't busy building Legos or training my pocketable monsters on my gaming handheld. Not while I was building my castles or slaying my oppressors, saving the planet or capturing creatures. But in the shadows of the night or while my parents were busy at work or watching soap operas, I would sneak a peek at them again.

What was the worst that could have happened?

We were.

We took them down and showed them to the girls. They became as intrigued as we had been months ago, by the bareness and absurdity that was the human figure. Memorized, my friend looked to me and I looked back. He took me out into the basement hallway and said "Hey, just follow my lead." I assured him I would, although a churn in my stomach aroused and I became petrified. He practically steered me back in with them.

They were still glancing over the photographs, then over themselves, feeling their chests and examining one another in private. My friend then asked them both "Do you two want to play a game?"

At first, they were hesitant. He explained that the game was simple. "We'll show you ours if you show us yours." And that's when I felt pale and sick.

I had never exposed myself to anyone but my mother, father, and perhaps the babysitter on one occasion. An occasion that I never could recall but had been discussed by my parents and I in revelations. After a while they agreed and we were first. Ten seconds, that was the limit. Afterwards, it would be ten seconds for them, simple. So, my friend placed his hands around the loop of his pants and looked over to me, "Ready?"

I wasn't sure, but on the count of three I let them drop, and there we stood. My best friend and I with our pre-pubescent wangs hanging out.

Stephanie must have taken the day off, but luckily Briana had shown up. She was a few chairs away from me, so my view was limited. But that tended to make the experience much more exciting. I could see the thin crease in her jeans depicting that sliver that separated her butt cheeks, like the crescent of the moon. And much like the night the classroom was dim as we watched a presentation on social standards between the male and female sexes.

It wasn't all too interesting, at least from what I could tell when I tuned in every now and again. But if I wanted to stay awake, I had to keep my focus on something worth the wake. Like the perfect roundness that formed on either side of her fold . . .

Then I heard a song play, a song that I knew was from my phone. An industrial rock single by a 90's band that I had torrented as a ringtone just a few weeks ago. God-damn it was loud, the presentation paused as my professor glared over to me. I probably looked like a fucking ape trying to pull the thing out of my pocket.

Finally, I got it out, the name on the phone was Abby. Suddenly my professor's deviant glare was just a white wall in the background. I left the room to answer it, along the way I saw some 90's-looking faggot giving me the "*rock'out"dude*" gesture, or whatever that shit was. Then in the hallway I pressed my cheek to the phone as if telling secrets, and heard her voice speak out "*Hello?*"

Sometimes the hardest words to say are those that begin and end a conversation, fear of the present, fear of the future.

"He-hey, hey . . . what's going on Abby?" Why was it that even a voice in silence could speak such fathoms and catch one's own mouth biting at their tongue?

"Hey, just wondering when . . . well, when will our next shoot will be? I'm kinda' in need of some extra cash and . . . how's the first video doing?"

I didn't want to tell her how I fucked up something so simple. It is, after all, the little things that grow into huge catastrophes. I was afraid that, due to my lack of attention to the mega-info or whatever it was, that I had royally fucked any chance of that video having made it to the big leagues. Or at the least, the *bigger* leagues.

"It's uh, it's going well. Just starting to pick up traction and . . . I can call and ask Frankie if he's up for another round?" I didn't know what to do. I was too afraid of offering up my own self to her, to even consider making myself into a lead actor. And with Frankie at the helm I figured I would keep it as such. But then . . .

"Well, what are you doing later?"

Holy-Jesus-fucking-shit in a bird basket in September, my God. Not in a million years did I ever think that this would happen.

"I-I-I . . ." I apparently have aphasia. "I'm not doing much, just . . ." I looked back into the classroom window and assumed my debts had already been paid. "I just got out of class, actually. Are you available right now?"

Please say yes.

"I'm free, yeah. But . . . can you do me a favor? Can we just, I don't know, just sit and talk about this for a bit maybe?" Her voice became something I did not recognize. It was soft and sincere, she had lost a certain edge to herself, an edge that had cut deeply before had now become blunt.

"Um yeah, that's fine." *It wasn't*, "Wanna' meet at the mall again?" I was decomposing from the brain to the spine and through my balls.

"Sure, I'll meet you by that coffee shop at the corner, say in like fifteen or so?"

It was the best I was gonna' get. I agreed and ran out to the parking lot, ignoring the crosswalk signs and the angered horns that honked during my jaywalking. I passed some kids flirting, those awkward giggles and slight passing touches against arms and hips. I whiffed in a puff of smoke from the car parked beside mine, a different set of kids blowing Mary Jane inside their Mustang.

I said "Hey, you mind if I take a hit?" and they didn't care, already blazed out of their minds. I took a huff and knew I would need it for this meet up.

But as I sat in my car, seconds before closing that door I heard my name being called out from nearby. I got out and examined my surroundings, first looking back at the stoners, none of which were feminine fatal. Then over the car, I saw her, a lovely creature I had not set eyes on since . . . well, forever.

"How are you!" It wasn't a question.

"Kim, my God, I haven't seen you since . . ."

"Elementary school, I know! It's been a long time. Glad to see you. And call me Kimmy, Kim's so formal." She smiled, "I'm surprised I even recognized you, really!" It was incredible, just looking at her, seeing how the human body changes over the years.

She was gorgeous, in a different way than Abby was. She was that cute sort of gorgeous that when it catches your eye you can't see anything wrong with the world. It wasn't just the innocence that hung off from her blouse like sewn roses working in the frill.

"Yeah, I barely recognized you either. I'm actually about to head out to . . . meet a friend." I guess I could consider Abby a friend.

"Oh, well I won't keep you in that case." She smiled, then came the awkward laughs and moments where butterflies flittered. We both knew we wanted to say more, but we couldn't. Then she looked over into the other guy's car as another large puff of smoke released from the crevasse of the windshield. "Disgusting, don't you think?"

I stayed silent to the question. Then, in a heated panic I figured: **Screw it**. "So, uh, did you want to trade numbers? Maybe we could, you know? Catch up sometime."

She gave into a moment, which kept me on my toes. "Yeah, that would be great, actually. You know, after high school I kind'of lost touch with a lot of people. It would be nice to just, reminisce." She cuffed her hands behind her back.

Yet I felt like the prisoner. We exchanged numbers and went on our way. I felt a mist forming around my eyes, a warm, compressed feeling from my lids. That's when I realized I got out of the road just in time.

Driving down the streets I flipped off speeders by, wondering what sort of hurried people needed to drive like suicide bombers racing down a community college parking lot. Then I wondered why I wasn't doing the same.

I had a thing for her, Abby. Even if my friend's thing was the one penetrating her, I suppose I cared a little less as the day passed since that moment. But it still made me sickish, like an infant with the flu, wondering if the "*next moment*" would turn into the last moment.

Doggy-Style

BY THE TIME I GOT TO THE COFFEE BAR, that corporate drug dealing caffeine slinger of a store, the weed had settled in. Everything seemed to transverse in slow crashing waves. The world felt heavier.

I can't say it calmed my nerves any more than a sober feeling would have.

Walking inside I looked around at all the yuppies with their Gucci sunglasses still hanging from the tips of their noses, hiding that cocaine rush, or so I assumed. I watched as all the young people crushed candy on their phones or sent endless text messages like modern storytellers in unsaturated scenes. I could taste the air around me, a deep mustering of earthy herbs and bitter ailments. Colors were as bright as looking through a kaleidoscope.

Then suddenly sitting down I thought that I wasn't afraid. Until I felt that tap on my shoulder and a coldness rushed from the veins of my arm into the framework of my cranium. Those chemicals, the neurons playing bongo beats alongside my heart which stuttered and reset as if it were processing the components through outdated computer software. The components, of course, were the corrupted files now known as emotional responses.

"Hey." She spoke and smiled, as she did.

The colors of the world turned back and forth from greys and blacks back into illustrious rainbows of form. I couldn't tell whether I was really in love or if it was the fucking blend I smoked from earlier. "Did I scare ya?" She laughed.

"Yeah just, just a tad. So . . ." The words slushed out of me like rust from a drainage pipe. "what did you want to talk about?"

She stood very still for a minute before taking a seat. Suddenly I felt the urge to catch her, as if she were in freefall. But I knew it was the pot still coming on and out of me, so I snuck my hands underneath my thighs as fast as I thought I could. Then I waited and watched, mostly when she leaned over and I could see right into her shirt. Then I looked up to her cherry red lip gloss and watched the words float from the tip of her tongue.

"I promised . . ." She started, I snapped back in and was afraid that I was staring, and she had noticed and stopped her speech. But her eyes were barely open, somewhat somber, somewhat distressed. I never noticed the deep black of her hair until now as she twirled it along her thin fingers. "I promised myself almost two years ago that I wouldn't get back into this-this sort of thing. Because . . . I hurt a lot of people, including myself. I just - I want what's best, want to get by unscathed. Do you know what I mean?"

"Yeah, I think I know." And I meant those words this time. I actually (**ac·tu·al·ly** *1. as the truth or facts of a situation*) felt a connection between us, rather than that familiar embarrassment. This time the coin had flipped, she was in a position that sat heated along the dashboard of a '53 Corvette known as life. Living the dream or a fraction of it, for all it was worth. "I . . . I mean, we won't hurt you."

She looked even more moody, "I guess you really don't get it then." Out of nowhere she had a pair of menacing eyes staring back at me, another table upturned in the road that was conflict. "It doesn't matter what you, Frankie, or I want out of this. People are going to get hurt." She was stern, her volume increased and she gathered a few looks from across the room.

I sat there for a moment, giving her time to calm down on whatever heartbreak-blood rush she was in. Shit always seems to get so serious when you're coming down from an initial high. God-damn, "Listen, I've got scars myself. I got myself into this just as much as you have. Now we're both prisoners in the same cage or some shit. Look," I didn't want to break the deal, I wanted to keep it clean. "there's nothing you can do that will hurt either Frankie or I. And if you need some sorta' help downtheway, then ask for it. But now I get to promise you, nothin' bads-gonna' happen from this." I think I felt my balls drop by the time I hit the period of that last sentence.

Abby almost shivered, but she cracked a short-lived smile too and brought her hands into mine. This had been the first time in a long time that holding hands meant more than the prospects of sex. She said to me "That means a lot." Then she gave my hands a tight squeeze and let go. "You're a good listener, you know that? Not many men are. I figured you were like Frankie, just wanting to get down to business."

"Well, I am in that sort of business." There I went, letting my dick talk for me. It was one of many moments in my life that I immediately regretted, what I said milliseconds after. Self-inception at its very core.

"Don't ruin it." She got up and gave me a quick punch to the arm. The pain was quick and initial, so I knew the weed had run down. It mustn't be that big of a blow as I was surprised by the feeling of sobriety. Or perhaps it was all the adrenaline striking me like a hard spank, it acting as my dominator over the course of the remaining day. Whatever the case, I got up and followed closely behind, then next to her, and soon we were chatting away.

Abby and I had a good amount in common, and it was nice just to meet someone with similar interests. Soon I didn't think so much of her as just another girl with a hot body. She was still magnificent, but all at once she was also . . . just *human*.

We took our time together shooting the shit, kicking at rocks, jumping at ceilings and immersing ourselves in the absolute pleasures that were simple conversations. But the daylight was quickly fleeting, and our feet had eventually grown tired. After making fun of some fat guy in a Superman T-shirt we said our goodbyes, and took opposite steps back to our cars.

Mine still sat over by the coffee shop, with no idea as to where she had parked hers. In hindsight, Abby, although a tough girl, was very sweet and might have feared meeting up today. A girl's gotta' be careful, not just because of guys like me. Though guys like me were new to the business and, after some thought, ran the industry well.

But was I some sort of push-over? Turning the corner, I had hoped to run into some miracle. Fucking Jesus Christ himself taking a stroll down the lane and offering me a helpful tip as I walked on past him. Do you think Jesus, son of God himself, would ever make a good porn star? He slept with that prostitute, didn't he? I bet he works miracles in be-

"*Ah*!" was the first vowel I heard turning that corner.

I'd like to buy another please, as I caught my footing and yelled back "*Oh*!" Followed by a "*shit*" or "*fuck*" depending on the variable of trash talk my dirty mouth could conjure up at the time.

Then I heard something crash, the new iLife 16.2 or whatever crap the kids carried these days. And just like the latest and greatest phone, it shattered into pieces in the latest and greatest ways possible.

The screen had scattered into shards that resembled a ten-story plummet, the main body of the phone laid center to it all, some technological angel and its broken wings. Or Humpy-Dumpty after his fall.

"Oh shit, look at what you did asshole!" Some girl screamed, the high pitch nearly shattered my ear drums as I tried to hold the event together, rather than letting it unfold further.

"I-I'm sorry I . . . I was just walking and-"

"Well, why don't you like, watch where you're walking, douche?" She had that postmodern, contemporary attitude of being neutrally blunt.

Anger in twelve steps, emotions listed and chosen accordingly. She was one of those girls, like most these days, with some weird fucking color of hair, minimalistic tattoos around her left arm and over her chest, which I noticed was small. We're talking tattoos you could probably find over Google, damn birds with ribbons, anchors and hearts. Dumb fucking shit, in my own opinion.

"Well?" She began again, "You gonna' help me or what?

"Or what?" I got lost in my own observation of her.

"Or what!" She didn't like that one bit, grabbing me by the collar and spitting poorly worded sentences into my face. "You going to pay for that phone or you gonna' get sued pal." It was hard not to laugh at her.

"Listen, you ran into me." I spoke as I pushed her off and away from me.

She gave a pout and pointed towards me, her finger an inch away from my face. "Doesn't matter, b-t-w, my fucking phone is broken!"

I was getting tired of this fast, I just wanted to get home and sneak a beer, check Abby's video out, jerk one off and call it a night.

"Fine, you got a pen or somethin'?"

And like clockwork she pulled a sharpie out from the pocket of her short-shorts that must had ridden up her ass like a springtime bikini in the Caribbean. If it wasn't for the black tights growing down from the tops of her thighs I would have thought even less of her. I looked around for a piece of paper, but she just put her hand out and told me to "*Not be such a pussy.*"

I guess she was right, so I gave her my number, I thought I saw a smile peak out from the corner of my eye. But I looked back and she had adjusted her face back into the relatively apathetic look. She said, "*If I wasn't so damn cute, I would've called the cops instead.*"

I told her, "You wouldn't've called the cops without your phone (*dumbass*)." But that just made her giggle.

"Hey, even though you broke my phone, you're still pretty funny." She smiled.

I wasn't interested, but amused.

She picked up the phone doggy-style as if I was interviewing her instead of Abby this time. But she left the shattered pieces, then threatened me once more and said she wouldn't forget this. But the threat wasn't threatening, it was like listening to a kitten trying to bark, that shit's just not gonna' happen. She skipped away predominately; I was left there thinking to myself *what the Hell?* Then I looked back down and noticed something about the glass, it was pretty damn thin to be for any phone case, latest, greatest or not.

– 6 –

Let the Dick Talk

CURIOSITY KILLED THE CAT, but satisfaction brought it back. Nine lives for cats, they're either the luckiest or unluckiest creatures alive. And those two neighborhood girls, one of them ratted us out and we didn't see them ever again. My friend and I were grounded for a week each, with both our parents hearing about the event.

So what? A week in the life of a child is a fraction of a minute in the months, weeks, and days of drag we spend as adults. We only learn to appreciate what life gives when the hormones hit and it's all but too late.

Speaking about a minute in time, our curiosity only grew and soon it became something that neither of us could anticipate nor control. Almost like a sickness or rather an addiction, we began to play a different sets of games with each other.

The term "doctor" came with a new meaning, as we'd take turns "examining" one another. One of us would lay down while the other used various tools (small plastic tweezers or a magnifying glass) to extrapolate our private parts. It was thrilling to be used and even intimidating when the time came to use another. We were too young for erections, so it was all childish fun, I suppose.

One time we were hanging out in my best friend's basement, with music blasting and his bedroom mattress laying in the center of the room. The television was turned on and just flashed bright colors *and shapes, the kinds you find in Window's '95 screensavers on your monitor when it's asleep. Before we knew the word, it was something like a "rave".*

We were dancing, laughing, and having fun. There was no direction, no meaning or purpose for what we were doing. I was afraid at the time that we would wake my friend's mother, who was asleep in a bedroom directly above us. But he assured me we'd be fine.

Before long, things got out of control. It could have been some sugar high or just an adolescent rush of adrenaline fueling the system. But I took a seat on the couch, and my friend began to strip, piece by piece starting with his shirt all the way down until he reached his socks.

Bare naked again, and I was a spectator. Was this how the girl's felt, awkward and unknowing of what to do, say, or how to react? I wasn't sure if I should had looked away or kept watching him, a young boy dancing in the radiance of light by an abstraction of color within a television screen. The dark only lasted so long however, as it felt like seconds had gone by before the lights flickered on and his mother asked him what the Hell he was doing.

A few days passed on, the video had steadily grown since the last time I spoke to Abby at the coffee bar. The freaky girl with the weird multicolored hair never called, and I wondered if my phone number had been held hostage.

In the meantime, the three of us shot ideas back and forth like a game of table tennis. We hadn't filmed, and Frankie was getting anxious. The boy already had a few girls in his life as is. Something about a dumb male mutt must had been appealing to the ladies.

Then again, Frankie never found quality in the women he fucked. It was more about quantity, and even the girls he slept with were never around for all too long.

However, going back to it, the video had picked up an audience. It just wasn't what we were hoping for. Payments by these websites were a bit more difficult than expected. Overall, each video had gained around four to five thousand views. Multiply that by the number of porn sites and the variable amounts of credit we'd receive from each and we were looking at around $56.93 total. And with both Frankie and Abby there for the bad news, I felt as if I was giving a fiscal report in front of my fellow board members.

Stocks were down, I'm afraid.

"Well, sex is free, so let's just make another one!" Frankie proposed, though Abby sat with her legs crossed and elbows boringly placed above them in a stubborn manner.

"How 'bout not Jack?" she retorted, "If I'm getting speared, then it better be for a worthwhile reason. Last time I checked, boys, a lady can get laid any day she desires. Furthermore, you jerks still owe me."

"Abby, it's fine, calm down. Both of you." I was a circus clown juggling the frantic feelings between a child-like friend and a mother-like figure. It was strange to think about Abby as a mother.

She had the courage and independence for it, but getting wacked in a business ordeal such as this threw the notion off its stiletto heels. I guess there were milfs and cougars for a reason . . .

"We made money last time, *bitch*, so what of it?" Frankie's beer buzz must have started to wear down. He always got cranky without his tunnel vision blurring the lines between right and wrong, along with his moral sanity.

"Frankie, shut the fuck up dude." I replied, in defense of Abby.

But *bitch* must had been a word she had gotten used to long ago. I expected outrage, some sort of repetition of hate to boil and overflow out of this little sex-ed melting pot of ours. Yet she stayed calm and silent, just smiling at Frankie as though taunting him further. "Should we just do that pizza delivery skit then? Or perhaps the girl next door? We could get real edgy and do a brother, sister thing. Those videos aren't ever real anyhow."

"Frankie, you look nothing like you Abby and likewise. We need some real hard-hitting ideas here."

"Listen to you two," Jack was about to get off again, "everything's been done by now. Two cocks in one hole, shit and piss on a girl's breasts, casting couches and circle jerk gangbangs. There's nothing left for us, we'll just be recyclin' the same old shit that's 'lready out there." Then he got up, ripping my door open and going upstairs. Probably to help himself to another beer from my father's stock.

He did get me thinking though, watching Abby text on her phone, how all the old tricks had been taken away. It wasn't just our housing market, educational leverage, and social security that the Baby Boomers had taken from us.

It was classic rock, slick looking cars, and an ocean of porn. As I laid onto the bed I kept glancing back at Abby. It was much less looking to her for an answer, because none of us really had one. It was more that I wanted to see her hair glitter in the sunlight, and her chest compress in and out, allowing her breasts to contract. It was the bareness of her legs that I knew existed underneath her tightly wrapped jeans. It was the image of her mouth and the sounds it could make. Everything about her in that moment, just the two of us on top of my bed, made me believe that it was all a clever ruse. The ultimate tease . . .

"Oh shit!" I gasped as my body flew upward and aimed towards hers.

"Wha-what is it?" She sounded half frightened, and half excited by my sudden exasperation.

"Everything follows a trend. There was dubstep, selfies, planking. That stupid cinnamon chug or whatever. Anything on TikTok basically . . ."

Frankie walked in just as I was starting with a beer at hand. "You want us to plank naked? Planking sex?" He laughed and took a sip.

I got up on both feet, like Socrates, and the questions that begged a revelation. "No, you don't get it. Everything follows a *trend*; we just have to find that *trend,* right? Thankfully I already know it!"

The two sat and shuttered at the motions that my body must have been portraying. They edged it out of me, anxious. Desperate. Now was the time to strike, to blow them away with my obvious genius. At least I thought it was genius, or cleverness otherwise. "Webcam shows, webcam-fucking-shows guys!"

. . . There was no applause, only suspended silence.

"Guys, did you hear me?"

"Yeah, we heard you." Frankie spoke, chugging the last of his three-quarters full beer down.

". . . And?" I asked, liking the idea extremely well. "It's intimate, it's amateur, and it's as close as someone's gonna' get to being with that person. That parasocial shit online. I known it's been done . . . but with that person being the beautiful Miss Abigale I think that anything is possible." I tried flattery, and it seemed to work.

She gave a light laugh and winced her eyes at me. "Please, don't call me Abigale, you sound like my father." And I nodded in reply. "I like it, though I'm a bit afraid of the idea."

"I don't like it man, a million people watching us." Frankie burped out.

"We'd be the luckiest dogs alive if a million people were watching us. We'd be lucky to get a couple hundred . . . or a hundred at that. Besides, people are already watching you, that's what porn is dumbass." I snickered.

But he didn't quite enjoy my answer. "Don't be an ass-hat man, you know what I mean. It's fine if they're watching it pre-recorded. But live? I'd feel like I'd be on a stage. A God damn circus monkey.

"Frankie," Abby began, "let's give it a shot, all right? He's got a point and we could make money instantly through a cam service."

I smiled, at least I think I was smiling.

Suddenly I was in a state of perpetual happiness and I wasn't even high. "If we're gonna' do this however, we need some sort of gimmick. Ya' know? Something'll capture an audience's attention." I got the gears turning inside of my noggin. It didn't have to be elaborate or nothin', just . . . *something.* Then I had it, "Why don't we just stick to themes, you know? Fantasies. There's a whole array out there. If we could capture each one we'd have new material every week. Then," I was in a happy-panic, "we can take the footage we capture from the shows, edit 'em and re-upload them as videos of our own! Hit every niche and cranny of the porn market. We'll have so many tags to type up that we'll be as popular as a celebrity on Twitter."

"The easiest way is O-F. But I could come up with a fan page on Facebook, YouTube, TikTok and, hmm . . . maybe Instagram too?" Abby replied, seeming versatile.

"Don't forget Kick, the kids love that shit." Frankie finally replied with an ounce of optimism pouring over his metaphorical glass.

"If you do," I began in extensive excitement, "be sure to post when and what times the next shows will be. We'll have a calendar of events, we can invite people, strangers of course, to these online events. RSVP and some shit. Gain a fanbase, this is fucking solid."

So, it ended up there was no sex to be shot this day. On this day we shot photographs on our phones. We created bios, descriptions, and planned out film times. Friday was the best; we were all usually free right around 2:30pm or so. Shaking hands, we all knew we were in business. And the more girls we could bring in, the more events we could hold.

Fridays through Sunday's, from schoolgirls to young nuns, rush-hour entertainment and midnight specials. We'd take the likes of Stephen Colbert, Jimmy Kimmel, and Jimmy Kimmel, and boot them right off the air. Hell, we could take on Oprah-fucking-Winfred if she still meant a damn thing. Saturday Night Live would be a literal joke, and Joel Osteen would be praying to God above and the Devil below to take us off the online airwaves.

All those late-night television shows and Sunday morning prayer parades were the closest things to porn anyhow. You watch them hypnotically; hear everything you want to hear and see it all just the same. As a person you find some sort of sick pleasure in it. You might as well be stroking the old shaft or flicking the bean watching these so-called fundamentalists getting you off. Jerking that ego, molesting your perception, sodomizing your opinions, and sucking off the dollars, dimes, and pennies you'll push to get them to tell you that you're right, the world sucks, and there is a Heaven somewhere.

Too bad, because we had found our Heaven and it was right here in a small, dank bedroom with three college failures looking for a motive to do something more. But there wasn't another option, we were lacking a certain degree of skill, of trade, or perhaps the pieces of paper to prove it. However, there would always be the one trade that any man, woman, or person in-between could afford. And the price was low, a little flesh and flavor, some soft moans and a couple of squirms wrote the checks out in our names.

At least . . . that was the hope.

Thankfully Abby was a popular woman, or at the very least a woman in general. She had around 3,000 friends over various spaces of social media. Mostly men who wanted a glimpse, not into the real her but rather that real chest and sweet V-shape-sunken waistline below her flat belly that sat just above her jean line.

They weren't friends, they were strangers, and at least a handful were willing to pay. Social media was just a picture on a menu, a profile on a baseball card. You didn't need to know anyone to get your brain racing and genitals screaming over who you pretended they could be.

Abby was no different and was a willing contestant. Us men, whether we were behind the camera, center-frame, or watching over the screen, were just minor parts to a great machine that had been running 24/7 since the prehistories. Roman coitus on Spinitria's, Shunga sculptures with children present in the depictions of sexual interactions.

Since the beginning of time, culture and tradition, porn and sex, have had the industry's strive. They say we evolved from animals, but in my mind, I doubt we ever evolved at all. Not with sites like O-F, or the shit you see during 30-second ads on YouTube. Even the live streams on Twitch and TikTok can create controversy, if only for a week or less.

And that night, after the two of them had left, I jerked one off again to Abby's first video. I acted as if it were my first time, whether it was with her or whether it was back in eighth grade with Cindy Fredrick from Science class. I never thought that that day, back when I was still a young lad, could have changed my whole history with what I know now.

And what I know now is this: If you want money, work off instincts.

Yet nothing was more instinctual than the act of reproduction. Nothing could have ever been more natural and keener to the senses. Senses, I was wondering, that have changed over time. Still wondering, were they all still put together in my head?

- 7 -

Three, Two, One . . . Action!

WHAT'S THE FIRST DIRTY WORD you've ever heard? How 'bout the first one you've ever said? Did it redefine you, make a difference in your vocabulary? Did it piss off the feminists, slay literary enforcers where they stood, and demolish the absolutism of political correctness?

In all probability . . . No, it probably did none of those things.

But what it did for me in the seventh grade was give me a pre-pubescent stomach ulcer and my first boner (well, as a theory or metaphor). We were sitting at our lunch table, myself and the group. I'm not sure what we were, or if any of us were even aware of the labels, trends, clichés, and porcelain masks we'd wear to become a part of society. We were just a group of kids, young skaters, trading card players, and Saturday morning cartoon junkies; all sitting together sipping our cartons of milk and eating stale pizza slices as if we had been sent to some upscale prison.

Each of us were talking to several others at any given time. One guy at the table, some kid named Mathew, dared me to show him some tricks on his mini-skate deck. Needless to say, I got every question correct, "What's an ollie? Show me a kick-flip. How about a one-eighty?". The kid was a chump, even to this day I think back and wish I knew one word in particular: Fuck. As in "Fuck you", it would have been worth the detention. But instead, I overheard a different word that day: Blowjob.

Then the kid who said it caught me looking at him. He asked me, "Hey, you know what that is, right?"

Even I think he was afraid to say. But I just nodded my head in agreement, convincing them I was a part of their discussion. I listened closely, but the things they discussed sounded pretty gross at the time. A girl slobbering on my what? Her mouth around me, where? What was that about a tongue? . . .

The network was bound, working, and ready for the tremendous intake we anticipated. By all of this, I mean the modem in my parent's home upstairs was working and my laptop's internal system wasn't freezing.

The webcam was some cheap piece've crap that Frankie had always used two years back for online gaming and the like. The image of my room was a semi-blurred stretch of colors on a rough canvas. You could tell who we each were and could make out the details of our faces, no matter how bad the imaging actual was.

But it wasn't high-def and it sure as Hell wasn't professional. Then again, what was it that made porn a professional industry? Hopefully, ten years from now I could write it off in my resume, benefit from a 401k and have enough money saved within the first few years of it for an early retirement. That was, of course, if it worked out.

And there I go again, preaching the same damn prayers, hoping to catch God with his dick out so I could blackmail him into submission. Tell the world that God was nowhere near nine inches long and that the men of this Earth could finally stop giving a shit about the size of their member. About the sizes they saw photo-shopped onto magazine covers, exaggerated in film, exactified on stages, and seen engrossed along a 1920x1080 framed video.

And then, now speaking of the Devil, we were ready to film. I was stationed at the laptop, prepared to monitor the system, the webcam, and the people we'd draw in like fish of the sea. And boy, there were plenty of fish in this sea. Before even igniting the cam, we had a handful of guests, apparently drawn in by the title of our live recording: **Strip, Spread & Splooge! – 100subs2firstgoal.**

It was a telltale moment; storybook chapters written out in three words like offerings from wise men being presented to us in virtual fashion. Much like the image on screen when the webcam kicked on and the clarity went from a blur to a slightly lessened blur of Frankie shirtless and waxed, with Abby tied up in a set of black lingerie. I had to hide my stiffy underneath the laptop as I felt the hot air blow right above my balls from the hardware's fan. It was a struggle.

Then soon afterwards the comments came pouring inward:

Thorn321: sexy af!

bootyologist69: spread that pusy <3

scouba11: how big is he???

def_not_dave: fInally! mke me cumm!☺

It was hilarious and I was glad Abby couldn't read these. I knew she had thick skin, but even I felt as though I was being verbally violated. And I guess for a moment I saw how brave a girl like her must've been all along. But that moment quickly faded as I started to become jaded and watched as 1 Gifted "*donation*" rolled in.

That was it, it was becoming a thing. We were the Red Cross of Porn, taking charity that others could never write off on their taxes. Although I wouldn't be surprised if these types of people did.

"What're they saying?" Abby said while being felt up by Frankie.

"They're saying . . ." I wasn't even mad at Frankie anymore. All I saw was the light in her eyes and that same smile that had me murdered and buried six feet in the ground. "They're saying you're drop dead gorgeous." I smiled.

But she blushed and gave a gentle laugh, sharpening her eyes which pierced straight through my computer screen. "Honey, I've done this before, remember? I know very well what these *men* say." She spoke, then blowing me a kiss (or to the camera) before taking off her bra.

My fucking jaw dropped to the keyboard. We barely reached our first goal, yet she was teasing these men with a carrot on the ropes. She'd flash a nipple or two, give a quick lick against the top of her breast and then hide them in her palms. It was like something from the silver screen, something you'd imagine while looking through black and white polaroids stuck up in some old pervert's attic from the 70's. Then again -God damn- it had the same effect on us as it did on the previous us decades back.

Those of us from the past who luckily didn't jerk us out of their balls before inception, had crude ways of getting off. Now, everything was more real than real. Down to the pixels around a nipple, to the digital landscape of some college-drop-out's bedroom. But somehow people like us, just like those polaroid jerkers, found intimacy in what was shown.

Intimate, what was it that made something so intimate I wondered? So selfless and loving, enough to want to birth a child, raise a family, and so on. These were the questions I asked myself in between comments and connections.

drew08383 Gifted 25

digitalfury Gifted 10

Bejblover Gifted 2

It didn't take long to reach the 100 mark and Abby was living it up. Her tongue polished against skin, her eyes stared straight through the lens, her nipples were jagged razors, and her lips were a fucking bear trap waiting for Frankie's member to snap shut on.

And Frankie, as his hands caressed her and felt below her, was picking apart that chastity belt with two fingers digging deeper down. With his mouth suckling against her neck like some newborn without the concept of breastfeeding incepted.

Suddenly I found them both naked and teasing each other, though I felt as if they were teasing me. Yet, in that moment I sympathized with the viewers who all wished, prayed, and would "*kill*" to be in Frankie's position. Perhaps, so would I . . . and for an instant I thought I was cumming, but it was just my phone vibrating.

New text message:

Hey dnt wrry about the phone dad got me a new 1 Wht u doing 2night?

It was like reading Latin off a thousand-year-old wall from the Tower of Babel . . . underwater, with no diving gear and oxygen. Now I ain't no prick when it comes to grammar, punctuation, and all that crap.

But when it comes to the English language I expect to, at the very least, *somewhat* understand *what-the-fuck* a person is saying before I reply. But the sender was a mystery, and the recipient (myself) was a lost dog walking along the road and suddenly hit by a car traveling twenty miles over the limit.

No ticket issued, so I texted back:

Who is this?

– –

Between Two Hard Places

FOR SOME REASON A PAIN HIT MY STOMACH, something about intuition and instinct or another. That biologicalbullshit that we never recognize consciously, always conceive in publicity, are aware of during times of stress, and forget about the next day. The vodka remedy, the whiskey resistance, the tequila technique, the gin . . . nevermind, because gin is gross and for the UK to deal with.

We have enough problems here on the homeland, where women no longer cook dinner and fold the sheets; and men can barely make a living without a blow-on-the-job. Seventy-years of oppression and expectations, now shaping society into a dog-eat-dog world without either sex, or our own, ever owning up to the faults of our predecessors. I mean, our parents, who never taught us a damn thing worth believing.

As I shook the thoughts from my head, I turned back to face Abby, making out with Frankie. Hands grasping parts of the body otherwise uncensored and estranged in a rectangular frame. An elevation in blood flow sent straight into the genitalia. Perks in the nipples, the tips of one's fingers, and along each little hair of the body being spiked. Then there were their tongues, wrapped like two tight knots in conju- . . .

New text message:
This is myra the girl you ran into at the mall
dnt wrry I forgive you
lets get dinnr or something soon! ☺

I felt a crack along my cheeks, a weird smile taking me over. Then I recalled that colored hair, and Hot'Topic type of fashion sense you see in trending magazines and pop-star screamo bands and the picture eventually was assembled. I wasn't too sure whether or not this was a good idea or not, the idea being: whether I should reply to this girl's texts or if ignoring the signs would lead me on the right path.

But I had a dessert-dry dick, and the image of two friends mating right before my eyes saying otherwise. Speaking from my eyes, I forgot to keep mine on the camera as it focused on the wall, the other two dipping down into the seeping depths of my mattress. I zoomed back in, ignoring the angry comments from the few who had noticed my attentive absence. I was catching glimpses of Jack's fingers wetting Abby's lower lips with her own soaking . . . damn it all . . .

New text message:

Hey U there???

my parents aren't home we can get pizza

and may'bay have a lttl fun??? ;)

"*Fucking cunt . . .*" I accidentally murmured out loud.

"What was that?" Abby asked, probably surprised I even said a word. In fact, I was surprised at myself. I didn't think I said that word aloud.

With my phone in one hand and the webcam in another, now focused on an obscure area of Abby's ass, I refocused. "Nothing, it's nothing. Keep going." I waved on, but our small talk didn't distract Frankie one bit.

He had his locomotive entering her tunnel at full speed, whether or not I had the webcam sighted on either of the two. As they fucked, and boy did they, I could feel the heat rushing up beside my hand, as the other hand concentrated on texting Myra back:

"*I . . . can . . . in . . . a . . . but*"

– fucking spell check –

delete.

"*Bit . . . give me . . . ten min . . . utes.*"

"Hey Frankie, give her a little more, than finish up. I got other plans tonight." I said, as he gave me a grunt and I couldn't tell whether it was from the sex or from a rebuttal. But I figured he had gotten the hint.

Then as soon as I sent my reply, I received one back. It wasn't a set of discombobulated words, rather, it was a small jpeg picture. As it loaded in, I watched it like film reeling onto my screen. At first, I saw her face, then the edges of her collar. Soon her breasts loaded in, nice young and perky. Her belly button popped in, the razor cut outline of her hip bones piercing through, then a dip down and . . . Well friend, you won't need me to tell you the details.

A woman's body is a body after all. But a young woman's body is a slice of the apple that Eden had stolen from the tree.

So, I made a choice that I might later regret. At least I figured I might.

I waved to the webcam, locked it onto the screen of my laptop, made sure it was focused on the two and then I left. I didn't wait for a word from them, didn't make one last check to see if more "*donations*" had entered in. I had faith, like a pastor or a priest, and I was ready to split a bible in half from between its thick thighs. Luke seven, verse thirty-eight, or whatnot.

"Im done, where are you?"

I was halfway in my car, scrounging through my pockets for my keys. In a way, I had prayed that my parents wouldn't come in on the two. More so, I had hoped that they'd be ok on their own, especially Abigale. But if I was certain about anything, it was that Abby could handle herself.

By the time I had the engine roaring, my phone had chimed in an address, now appearing like some treasure sunken inside a lost city under the sea. I'm sure you know the one.

In an instance I was off, driving past the corridors and chasms of the urban dungeons. Watching the etchings of trees glow past my headlights, hearing the voices of nighttime whispers echoing from my open window, which put me at ease. I didn't bother with the radio; the noise wouldn't help.

My excitement ran down to the tips of my toes to the tip of my member. Then the slight jagged punch of my phone's vibration shook the flesh of my left leg, and I struggled for my phone, the ringtone playing '*Jack the Ripper*' in 16-bit form.

"Hello?" I said, driving down the road as rapidly as Clyde had ridden with Bonnie.

"Hey!" An excited voice charged through the static interference. "You're on the way, right? What kind of pizza do you like?"

It must've been Myra.

I thought for a moment, something clever, something sensual. Something you'd say in a movie or in the lines of a book. A book . . . "As long as you're around I could care less what's on the pizza."

It seemed to work; I heard her giggle as she inhaled. I heard the words before they were said, in lines of dialogue paved in soft velvet grays.

"Pepperoni it is." with a click of a kiss and the phone drawing blank static before I realized she had left me on the line alone.

That fucking tease, that fucking picture on my phone, I fucking left my friends to themselves and for what? A fucking-fuck.

Enough vulgarity and enough exposition, her house was on the horizon. If I was in a romantic song

I'd be singing "*I can feel you close*", but that just isn't so.

I was reading numbers to houses of addresses in a neighborhood I would have never of travelled through if it wasn't for the promise of pussy. I felt the clouds passing over the full moon, I felt my betrayal. I felt my erection pressuring the point between my jeans and my skin. I could feel the sweat underneath the fibers of my hair, the testosterone breathing, my scrotum letting loose and my mind imagining the best.

Number 3040.

Turning off the car and letting my jeans fall loose, I let my hand reach for my crotch. I gave myself a quick five'oh'two while letting myself get hard, watching the pizza boy deliver before I walked to the front door to face her.

As she answered, I whispered to her in the heat of the moment, "Let's fuck."

She had a blank face for a moment but just laughed at the end.

"Bae, I'm hungry, let's eat first, please?" She spoke.

As I begged, but it wasn't any use.

I guess she had a point, and I made one myself. She wasn't mad and I wasn't embarrassed. We ate a few slices each, watching shows on her phone. It was always a little violence then a little sex and then some story right before the episode ended and the screen faded to black.

I kept staring down her shirt and she kept staring into the plastic abyss of a 1080 by 1920-pixel planet. Then I rubbed her leg, and her hand left her phone while reaching out towards my cheek, bringing me in for a sloppy kiss.

"Let's not make this personal, kay?" She insisted, but I wasn't willing to answer.

I had recalled a pack of Viagra still stuffed in the crammed-up pocket of my jeans; I slipped in a hit and faced her again. I didn't have a word to say, didn't have a thought on my mind, not a blink in my eye nor a flick of my wrist as I brought her in.

Girls loved that sort of shit, that fake romance, the deadly devourer of souls. That Romeo's kiss in competition with Judas'. Bring on the cross, the poison, and the flowers at my grave. If I was to be laid down then I'd be laid in the crosshairs of someone's eyes, underneath the scars of their Walmart bought sheets. Bring me forth, from sickness unto health, from body into soul and I will conquer my mind as if my majesty had left his throne.

And I gasped as I felt her hand grasp my cock. I gasped as I felt the pills start to take effect, noticing my blood circulating in a unique way. Then I lost my breaths as I gave them to her, and I lost my senses much like my words . . .

– 9 –

Laid

LOCKER ROOMS. Do I dare say more?

Home to the swirly, a common ground for insecurity, and most importantly: ridicule. At least while you're young. According to our middle school instructor, we were each required to take a shower after P.E. I never did. I sometimes pretended like I had by splashing water over my face and over my hair. But usually, I would either wander elsewhere or hide out in a bathroom stall, as if it were a bunker of war.

I never really cared to compare or examine my member to anyone else's. It wasn't until my best friend convinced me, and I decided to bathe naked in the showers at our local recreational center's pool locker room. I was hesitant, of course. These actions were usually always driven by his insatiable ideas.

Showering, or at least mimicking what showering would be if I cared, that I noticed from the corner of my eye another man entering. I couldn't help but notice his length and his bushy top half. I only noticed because I wondered when we'd be the same way. Funny how a second-long glance could beg so many future questions.

Not soon after the older man had entered did a group of about four younger boys find us washing naked in the showers. They laughed at us, mocked us. It wasn't until we left the showers and got dressed that the four entered the showers bare-bottomed themselves. I got a loud laugh in on them as they quickly shifted to cover up their nakedness. But my friend was persistent in pulling me away. The time for child-like vengeance wasn't then.

The sun . . . it was a white light in a dimly lit room full of stuffed animals and poorly arranged candles, with posters of famous boy-band members half naked across the walls. I didn't see them in the nighttime, those shiny black bulb-eyes, those flickering fiery eyes, nor the saturated paper-plain eyes all staring at me.

And for a second, I stared back, wondering if all these qualities were what made a man a man. A hardened six-pack exterior that hides that soft, cuddly interior, symbolized by a burning desire for such. But for the next few minutes it didn't really matter at all what I was, inside, outside, or otherwise.

I just got laid.

Then came an uproar from the living room, large footsteps pandering around the place like an elephant lost inside a tin castle.

"Oh, fuck . . ." Myra began, jumping from beneath the sheets and clawing against her bedroom floor. She was like a street sweeper equipped with an eight cylinder and a turbo boost. At first, I didn't panic, until my pair of jeans bitch-smacked me in the face.

"Hey!" I yelled, before catching my own shit-stained underwear in my mouth. With a pair of socks and a t-shirt later, she came up to me, wrapped her hand tightly around my mouth and whispered to me.

"Shut the fuck up, okay? My mother got home early . . ." and my fucking eyes lit up like a Menorah in Auschwitz.

"Your mother?" I spoke as softly as I was frightened. "I thought you had roommates? I thought you said . . ."

"The only words out of either of our mouths last night were *oh*, *ah*, *mmm*, and some heavy breathing. Now would you shut up, get dressed, and get out before they come in here?" She said, frantically pulling the straps of her Victoria's Secret thong over her hips and into her ass crack like parchment mail.

"Get out, get out how?" I replied, panicking and accidentally zipping my jeans' teeth right across my testicles and gasping in pain.

She pointed to the window, throwing my shoes outside as I soon followed. Halfway ass-out, through the windowpane she grabbed at my hair and pulled me in for one last kiss before shoving me right out of the room. Tumbling into the bushes, out onto the dirt and grass of a freshly dewed lawn I looked about. Waving to some fat-ass in his morning wear from across the street, with his shocked face tantalizing, I leapt quickly into my car and drove off to the tunes of '*Jack the Ripper*'.

"I can't believe it!" I yelled in delight. My hands flung up from the steering wheel into the car's ceiling and back down in time to make a left turn. It finally happened, the years before had passed like turtles smudging through molasses in a whirlpool that kept on circling, creating a never-ending vortex of despair. Perhaps I was overreacting, both then and now.

The only thing that I knew for certain is that it felt good.

Not the sex, I mean the sex too. But the feeling afterwards always had a ten-times greater impact than the act itself. And the impact would be the same the second time, the third, and eventually it might wear down. Then I could move on.

With any luck onto someone who mattered more than just the typical fuck. Myra was that, the typical "*fuck*". Then I remembered a little notch inside of my brain and reached down inside of my pocket for my phone.

At a red light, I checked the screen, only to see I had 3 new voicemails and 27 new messages. As I opened the first message I read aloud in all capital lettering: "*WHERE THE FUCK DID YOU GO?*" all in caps. Then I remembered Jack and Abby alone in my bedroom, tucked away in my parent's basement, my room. I thought the worst might have happened, that my parents may had found them . . .

♫*And I know a place*
Where no one is likely to pass

Oh, you don't care if it's late
And you don't care if you're lost
And oh, you look so tired
But tonight, you presume too much
Too much, too much
And if it's the last
Thing I ever do
I'm gonna get you♪

I was there, at my parent's home. Abigale's car was gone, and so was Frankie's. I was already listening to the second voicemail as I crashed on through the door. My father glanced at me in his boxers with a newspaper and a black cup of joe at hand. He didn't look upset.

Rather, he looked very curious but said nothing as he walked on by. I thought to myself "*Oh shit, he knows.*" Based solely on the fact that he didn't say a word to me. The voicemail still going on, Frankie battering and bitching, Abigale telling him to calm down in the background.

I traded it for the third while running into my mother through the family room on the way down to my bedroom.

"Good morning, son." Was all she said.

I gave her a quick smile before running down the stairs to assess the aftermath. But as I did, I heard Abbie's voice hush me back to a place of peace.

"*We're heading home for the night. Hope everything is ok, sleep well. See you soon.*" I heard her speak before a moist popping sound reached the speaker and the phone hung up. There was a sigh of relief that could have blown all three pig's houses down in one go. But then, following a trail of empty beer cans I entered my room.

Frankie, the ass-wipe, had left his used condoms on my floor. Two of them to be exact, the sperm no longer white but instead an ugly opaque fluid locked in a bubble. I feared what my bed looked like. As I turned, I was surprised, it was cleaner than I usually would leave it. It appeared to have new sheets, and the comforter was tightly tucked in and around the edges.

At first, I thought my mother really had walked in on the two and, in a manner of decency, had made my bed for me. Another tool to be used towards reason for guilt later. But then I ascertained a more lighthearted outlook. Perhaps Abby had uncommon compassion for people *-for men-* like me. That she had made my bed, in a way feeling sorry for me.

After all, I assumed that she knew I "*liked*" her. Little did she know that her compassion had been betrayed . . .

Then a new message buzzed in my corner pocket, a tickle near my thigh. I was optimistic it would be her, revealing that the bed had been made by her own hands and that she was sorry on behalf of Frankie for leaving his '*specimen*' behind. Then again, I dreaded another message from Frankie. Only having read the twenty-seventh message from him in my queue I was worried that the other twenty-six and counting would continue to worsen by the word count.

To my disarray, it was Myra wishing me a happy day and wishing to see me again soon. If I were a Brittin or someone of European origin that sentence would sound something more like: *The little fish fancied another jolly fuck*. At least in my head that's what I interpreted.

God, what had happened to my naivety? Did I sacrifice it for my adulthood? Or was my childhood just the fermentation of ethanol-like hormones waiting to catch a match and alight?

And why did I care?

In that second of thought I came back to the realization that my teenage fling had found a man. Or boy. Whatever I was, it didn't matter. What mattered was the friction under the sheets. I was the polyurethane wrapped Christmas gift opened a night too early, and to be rewrapped for the next. The anarchist, crisis killing substitute for hate and all things wrong, as antidote made between free sex and a good morning text message.

It was quite horror-show.

I made a mental note, another small etching into the walls of my skull. A scratch against the bone. The numbers counting down in the concrete container of a prison. One more to add to the few. A few more and I might be happy.

If you haven't kept up with my collateral (*or clitoral*) references, just know that every man and woman does it. From one more one-night stand or a year-long relationship. Girl to girl and boy to boy, we all keep track. Each lover or fling, first base into the homerun.

Myra was now another irreplaceable stain marking the contents of my mind. Never to forget, never to forgive. But perhaps I'd use the memory for fun down the road or hours later in the day. Nonetheless, she'd always be a part of my list of love-makers, unfortunately.

Then my phone began to ring. Frankie was calling. If he was hung-over like I figured he was hungover, then he'd be one of two things: Pissed or chill.

"What's up man?" I tried to act cool, speaking softly with a clarity in my voice.

I heard him grunt and sniffle before I heard him reply with "Yo."

"Yo?" I replied, confused beyond a doubt.

"So, how was she?"

"Wha - was who?" I asked.

He laughed.

"Dude, there's only one reason why you'd leave like the way you did. *A girl.* So, how was she? Who is she? Is she hot? Was it that annoying girl?"

I forgot I had discussed Myra with him hours after my coincidental run-in with her. F-bombs blew apart any hope I had at hiding it.

"Yeah, it was the annoying girl."

He laughed again, "So, how was it? Stop teasing me man, Abby and I got ours. So how was yours?"

The bastard was relentless.

"It was good, she's a bit wild. Like's all of that biting and scratching and shit. Clean shaved though. Her tits are bigger than I remembered them . . ." But what had happened in my room while I was away? How much did we make, how long was the stream?

"Frankie, tell me about last night. What did I miss, man?"

There was a strange mixture between slugging anxiety and smoldering excitement that ended up just making me feel sick to my stomach.

"You missed it man . . ." He was alluding to something. He sounded happy about it, but the silence he left was leaving me shivering with antici-

Sixteen

. . .

-pation.

"Well, spit it out, damn it!" I half hoped my parents didn't hear me.

"Dude, we only streamed for like, half an hour more after you left. Hardly had to move the camera. We made over five hundred bucks." He started to laugh.

Then I started to laugh. Five hundred dollars for an hour of teasing, playing, sex, finish and cut the strip. Send the fucking reel to the theaters and let Hollywood do the rest. The file must be on my computer still. Bonus money if I were to upload it with our first.

"*Five hundred dollars*", I kept repeating the number in my head and probably aloud, but Frankie didn't seem to care. We've been trained to work forty-hour weeks, paychecks every other week for roughly around the same amount. But this, this was legalized prostitution gone virtual.

This was a whole new stock market, a pyramid scheme, the works. We weren't selling a product, much less any sort of memorable experience. It was there for the present moment, nothing more. It was a service we were willing to provide, even twenty-four-seven if permitted.

And whoever wasn't getting laid was paying for it.

"I'll call you later, bro." There wasn't time to waste.

Waking up my laptop, I pressed through the files of data to find the video. Just over an hour long, like Frankie said. I even took five minutes to shit, coming back to watch the last half I had missed. And for the first time in a long time, I didn't masturbate to it.

I guess I was saving my libido for tonight.

Anyways, I cut the feature into clips, organized them all artsy-like and shit. Then took to the internet in search of a wider fan-base. After the websites, there were our social media pages, profiles, and fillers for our new content. To keep people up to date.

We were even gaining followers, friend requests, and those tiny hearts and thumbs-up you see plastered for a day, then irrelevant the next. It was all becoming ours; like some phallic-shaped plant was growing. Like breadfruit on the branch. My bank account had more digits in it than I've seen in a while. But I knew Abby and Frankie for due as well.

Then I remembered, as my mother came downstairs with the laundry, I quickly shut my black book of a laptop. She dropped off a pile of clothes and to my dismay, my work shirt was placed on the top of the pile. She asked me if I had school today. I told her it was Saturday.

But I hadn't checked my schedule all week. It just didn't occur to me through my drunken hazes or blaze hazes or sexual hazes (*ok, we get it*) that I still had a job in between this crazy little phantasmagoria of a life.

"Work, I'm working today." I said, unknowingly lying or telling a convenient truth. And as it would turn out, my convenient truth was inconvenient to me. Three things that happened to me during the rest of this boring day:

One, I worked. My boss almost fired me but told me that we were so short staffed that he couldn't afford to. But one more incident and it was over for me. It didn't matter, I was making the big kahunas now. He could have fired me that afternoon and I couldn't have been any more than apathetic about it.

Two, when I got home at around six, I noticed that our video had already gained over three hundred and forty views since my time of uploading it that morning. Advertising had paid off. Social media was the spawn of all things wrong, where opinions ruled over actions, and amateur porn could be counted as a paid internship.

Three, Myra invited me to the mall. The same mall that our *incident* took place. She said we could take a walk, asked me to bring some beers that we could drink in the car. Then maybe, if I was a good boy, she'd do a bit more to me in the car. Public sex.

Nothing up till this point sounded so exciting.

"*See you in a few* ☺"

I texted her while leaving the house. Freshly sprayed, hair combed, nails clipped, condom tucked behind my phone in my left-hand pocket. Walking towards my car I felt like an astronaut about to board Apollo 11. The takeoff was smooth enough, with an intermediate stop at Myra's. Next was the *moon*, I mean *mall*.

This was one small step for man, one giant leap for mankind.

We finished a six-pack in record time. I was sure Myra could have put Frankie to shame, considering she drank four of the six beers I brought.

"Bring something stronger next time." She slurred, still an obvious lightweight. I shrugged her comment off, and we began our trek through the outdoor capitalistic hub of teenie-boppers, desperate housewives, and millennial-miscreants such as us.

First, she asked if I could buy her and I some drinks from the nearby cafe, which was a little less than an actual cafe and more so a place for the hip, happening, hilariously dull to-go and purchase a five-dollar drink.

At first, I didn't mind. I got myself a double-shot and she had ordered some six-dollar fat-free, almond milk with extra whip, minus one syrup splooge, make it cold kind of *goo-goo-frap-a-flying-fu-chino*. Stuff like that always bothered me.

How specific a thing must be, how perfect it must taste or look or smell. How reliant we are on the services of others to get the things we want, but never truly need. It made me pop an artery every time.

Then there was this clothing store. She had picked out a few different skirts and a frilly sort of blouse. Once again, I was the man with the wallet. At first, I declined, but then the blouse was traded in for a pair of lacey underwear and I gave into my primal instincts. I figured, *why not*? I'll be the first boy to see them in action and hopefully the only one, for some time.

Not that I was looking for a relationship. It was this weird contrast between wanting to keep something like a sexual partner exclusive, while not being committed to them yourself. Call me selfish, I guess.

It wasn't until the third and final strike that threw me a bit overboard. We were nearing the theater, and she said with absolute enthusiasm: "Can we please see the new-" something or another.

"You buying your own ticket?" I asked, a bit agitated and sexually frustrated.

"What?" she replied with the sort of innocence that a kicked puppy or a sad child would use to gather attention. But I wasn't having none of it.

"I've bought you clothes, I bought you drinks, I gave you beer. I don't even know if you're twenty-one yet!" I called out.

Noticing the faces looking in our direction, I decided to keep calm and keep my voice down before movng us over to a nearby fountain where the little kids usually rummaged while their mother's shopped. I sat us down and tried to reason with her a little.

"I'm not made of money, and I'm trying to be nice, but you're pushin' me girl."

All I heard was a giggle and all I saw was her smirk. Nothing could have pissed me off more than that. But she got up and pointed to the store across the way. "See that? That's where I first found you."

Then I recalled the day, the hot sun and awkwardness. The giggling brats passing by, the born-ready douchebags and the elder's nodding in disapproval. I didn't say a word, couldn't say one.

I was caught off guard.

"I think I remember the sign. Looking for amateurs, right? Well, here I am." She smiled.

If it wasn't for the booze still coursing, I could have seen the malicious roots growing in that sincere smile of hers.

"So, what?" I rebelled. "You want to be a part of our business, fine. I'll sign you up, we'll get you paid. But don't be playin' me, ya hear?"

Unfortunately, it was too late.

"Played? Boys are toys just waiting to be played with."

I could have punched her right then and there. Right in her God-damned throat, then slammed a knee into her nostrils till the blood started to flow and then maybe, just maybe, I'd let her off with a warning. But there were various complications to my wanted, emotional responses.

First and foremost, she was a girl. Second, we were in public. And third, I still wanted to fuck later. Fourth and finally, I started to realize how many lists had been made throughout this day. Perhaps it was a sign. Was I learning?

Apparently not, because her next few sentences put me up in awe, shocked in the bleachers to a one-man show. And I was not in the audience this time.

"Looking for amateurs . . ." I spoke softly, as if disappointed in myself.

"That's right, and you just fucked with the wrong girl. Wait, I take it back. You only fucked the wrong girl." There was that giggle again.

"I've been waiting for you for a while now, every day after school. I knew you'd be the right one." She was so caught up in her own success that I never had a second to think about what she was saying. "You know, you never did ask for my age. In that way, you men are all the same. You just want the action. Never the consequences afterwards, eh?"

Then suddenly she almost seemed upset.

As it hit me, I had no choice but to ask, "How . . . how old are you?"

The next line of dialogue would change every other view of my life that I had ascertained or substantiated until this point. It wasn't even a sentence, much less a word and more like some solitary statement. A defining anagram of complete complexity that would shake my once comfortable world to the marrow of my bones, right down to the nerves and sending signals into my brain.

Funny, I thought I always had things figured out until this point.

Then her lips flapped open like some fucking fish out of water and I prepared myself. I listened like no other. Listened better than I ever did to any one of my parents, teachers or closest friends.

Even Frankie would be ashamed.

"I'm Sixteen."

Theatre Theatrics

THE FIRST AND ONLY TIME I was put on suspension at my school, of any school, was in middle school. It was eighth grade. My class, whatever it was for, was in the computer lab learning the internet and how it works.

Some kids next to me, the popular ones, were looking up some . . . "explicit" subjects online. One of them, the boy, was looking up naked pictures of women. The girl, more specifically, was searching in terms like "penis" and "male genitals". It only occurred to me later, the differences between the male's overall common drive and the female's precise wonderment, was the emotions in-between. I had, by external peer-pressure, had chosen to look up some certain phrases myself.

"Needless to say" is a phrase used to communicate the inevitability of an event. In this case, we each got letters sent to our parents and were put in a room for a day, where we had to do scrap-homework for seven hours straight. Where no talking, speaking, or noise of any kind was aloud. Except on our half-an-hour lunch break.

I was provided with no lunch for that day.

To my surprise, at that time, I was approached by the "popular" two. I was the stand-out "nobody" during my whole three-year middle school experience. So, in terms, this was an incredible experience amongst the Seven Wonders of the World were.

We spoke with one another like equals.

I was flattered to even speak to a girl at the time.

They were surprised I was down there with them, in the basement level of some bargain middle school full of careless teachers and washed out administrative staff. It was one of the first and only times I actually felt accepted by other individuals, ever since leaving elementary school and looking forward to my high school "career".

Don't feel bad, I've dealt with it.

By the end of the day one of our favorite teachers, and most caring of our situations, brought us up into their empty classroom to speak. The three of us were blurry-eyed, looking up to her. She asked each one of us what we had "researched" that day.

The other boy went first. After explaining he had looked up nude pictures of girls, our teacher recommended that he learned to respect the female figure, not obsess over it.

When the girl spoke, our teacher proscribed a number of scientific books dedicated to the human physiology and an explanation of male anatomy.

Then, when it was my turn to speak she asked me, "What did you look up?"

And in embarrassment, I answered, "Butt-muncher." A term used to describe an ass-eating prick without having to use a cussword.

The word "butt" was of course what got me sent into their in-school suspension. A word that, as I explained to my parents a day before, was a stupid excuse to put a child in suspension.

I awaited her answer.

In all obviousness, I was an innocent proven guilty under a false and flawed court of law. And it must have been so obvious, that it hurt to hear about. Because at the end of the day . . . she barely bothered with me.

There we sat together, as a *couple* in the movie theater. I had bought the $8.00 popcorn, the $6.00 soda, the $4.00 candy box. Luckily, the candy was mostly reserved for me. Then there were the $7.50 nachos, and last, but not least, by any means, the $22.00 worth of two tickets to see a B-grade awful flick on the silver screen.

In total, $47.50 for a blackmailed date.

This doesn't even mention the $7.75 for the cafe drinks, the $12.50 for the six-pack, and the outrageous price of $35.63 for the clothes.

Once again, the new total being $103.38, almost a fifth of my three-way split check from streaming the past night. A hundred-dollar date with an under-age fuckbuddy and a stressful platter of unaccountable inactions. The words *'pedophile'* and *'statutory rape'* came to mind. I looked over to her in absolute joy. Then I looked at myself, with shaking legs and sweating palms.

It's nights like these a man, any man, could use a few drinks.

Yet, there we sat, our hands held together. I felt as though I had been handcuffed to her, and no it wasn't kinky. I became a prisoner in my own sexual explorations, a marked man amongst millions of others who had been black-listed likewise. For the first time in a while I was truly afraid.

Not nervous like I was holding that sign, or anxious like I was meeting up with Abby for the first time. I was purely afraid. Afraid to do anything else with her, but also afraid that if I didn't, she'd turn me in.

Some people think there's a black and white with no grey in between, like everything about the world is either/or. But this didn't seem like an "*Either do what she wants or get busted*" situation. It was a "*Get out ASAP!*" situation, in a sea of fifty shades (Once again, not very kinky).

There was a point in the film where the two main characters kissed. It was so fake it made my head spin. Just watching those two agape mouths smothering the other one of air. No tongue. Eyes shut. Wet sounds. Hands grabbing.

No wonder porn producers preferred a quick slap to the ass, better than a slap to the face like this was. And I mean it. If this was passion, then I must've been lacking it.

Very soon though I didn't have a choice. Like a chic, the cliché and needful thing that Myra was, she tightened her grip and tugged me closer.

"Kiss me, asshole." She said with a smile that could stump the curve of the moon. I didn't want to, didn't even have to. But I needed too . . .

                         . . .I spat from my mouth and kept on using the soap and water from the theater's restroom.

I was washing every crevasse of my mullers to the back of my throat. As if I wanted to deep-throat my damn fingers, as if I had an oral exam, as if someone would be scrubbing the roof of my mouth for a new job and I had something to hide. Though I suppose I was hiding.

Everything about me became about hiding. Myra texted me shortly after I had gotten into the restroom. The movie must've ended, and I was hoping to make a quick escape. But I guess I had been in this restroom for a good time. Though I almost gagged when I saw her message.

my house is fre 4 tonite
lets get outa hear ;)

This got me thinking, *How many nails does one coffin need*? In fact, it seemed as if my life was just made up of questions without answers.

But how would life be if it were made up of answers without questions? Probably pretty dull . . . and there I went again, questioning everything. Like how I was supposed to get out of fucking a ~~child~~, a ~~teenager~~, a ~~young adult~~. No matter how I said it, it never seemed right. If only I were born Islamic.

I think they're ok with that sort of thing.

Though, I thought fast.

Would I say I felt sick from all the coconut oil flavored butter that we spewed on our large bucket of corn? Nah, too easy to counter. She'd probably act all motherly, want to feel my sick stomach until I was good and hard again. "*Hmm . . .*" I thought aloud, crowds of faces roaming in and around me across the theater's bathroom.

Faces in the mirror as I stared at my own reflection. I could see children, I could see their fathers. I could see young men, just as I, with either that carefree look that I carried here, or that fretful disparage I currently held.

They would each come forth, stare, move their hands through the water, let the bubbles build and then disperse. Then, like blurs of lights in nighttime traffic, they would relieve themselves. It was like time was gliding past me, free of form and a constant I couldn't control. Maybe that made sense in some abstract way. As if to assume that any of us had control over the ending events in our lives.

Then it occurred to me, that I was taking up too much time standing around in front of a movie theater sink. Myra would be waiting, I assumed, impatiently outside of the restroom entry way, wondering what I was doing. Now I needed another excuse.

The turmoil was adding up.

Then my phone buzzed, I took a scarce look at the name. To my surprise, it was Frankie:

Dude getover here now!!!

I hav great news for us

That was it, my fat fucking drunkard angel from an iTalk 11. Who knew Frankie would get me out of this mess. It was my best chance, if not, my only chance to get away.

I strutted out of the restroom with some sort of confidence, or something that might have measured up equally. And there she was as planned, tapping her foot with a mean-looking reversed smirk cut along those still smug fucking cheeks. But I came in prepared, like America in Yemen, like America in Haiti, like America in Iraq.

Forget about the Bay of Pigs or Vietnam. I was the soldier walking out onto the beaches of Normandy with this shit.

"What took you so long?" She grumpily asked.

I readied my rifle which was my mouth, aimed down the sights into her eyes and fired:

"I was taking a shit, what?" That was it, the all-go-get-to way out of here.

Step one, of course. It's been proven time and time again that when a man says he needs to crap, then boy does he. You don't question it, whether it's the length of time or length of the turd. Just like a man would never question the length of time it takes a woman in the restroom.

The restroom, bathroom, outhouse, honeypot, or whatever else you'd like to call it, has always been sacred. Now, to initiate step two. . .

- 12 -

Boyfriend

THE DROPPING OF THE BOMB. "Frankie called while I was on the pooper, said it's an emergency. I kinda need'a get to his place a-s-a-p." And that was it.

I awaited her reaction, those sad little eyes and her quivering lips afterwards. Features I would much less miss, if not forget about all together when this was over.

But there were no quivering lips, no sad eyes. She gave something like a passing glance if '*passing*' meant '*to stay in place*'. Cool and calm she replied with her own returning artillery, "Sweet, take me with."

My eyes bulged forward, wide, white, and static. "What?" I asked, but she just grabbed me by the hand and tugged.

"There's no way out of this, so you might as well get used to me now." Then after a quick smooch on my cheek, to which I cringed and shook, I allowed her to lead the way. As we walked I texted Frankie back:

"Looks like Im bringn' company . . ."

The drive felt longer than what any App could calculate. I could blame the traffic in my mind, because there wasn't any out tonight. And there she went again, touching my hand like we were lovers. That night wasn't love. Although, I did love it at the time. The god-damn chemicals, it's all a biological trap.

"So . . . what does he want to talk about? I mean, it must be pretty important, right?" Myra spoke, twisting and twirling her hair in her hand. This small talk was murder, like a Charles Manson love song. At least he was a decent musician.

"No idea, just said to meet him at his place." I spoke without realizing she'd hear the next few words muttered from my mouth. "*As if it were your business . . .*"

"What was that?"

"Nothing," what a fucking night, "I said 'I'm just not sure about this visit.'" That was clever, I thought.

More importantly I needed to be careful. If I could get myself alone with Frankie, then maybe we could formulate a solution together. That isn't to say that Frankie's news isn't good or bad on its own. And if it were more bad news, then I might just consider webcamming my own suicide. Who knows, we might make more money that way. Might even make the papers.

No time to think though, just time to drive. Ignore the bitch, stop at every red light, and use a damn turn signal. Respecting the road but not its drivers, as I was cruising past any car that got in my way.

Minutes later, an eternity of minutes, it seemed, and we were there. Frankie was so excited that the bastard must've been waiting near the window. Before we even reached the first step of the three to his porch the fool was already at the door. He was clearly drunk, the usual.

But excited, jubilant, and surprisingly not at all mad at me. At least, that's what it seemed like. Though the pleasure strewn across his face melted a bit when he finally took notice of Myra, who I made sure to keep behind me like a stray dog to my back.

"Who'she? . . . Oh, she'sh the girl, isn't she?" He was liquid-slurred, shaken not stirred, and it was only nine at night.

"Shut up. Let's get inside." I replied, listening as Myra politely, and probably spitefully, introduced herself before following us in.

We walked down to the basement. Myra was attempting to make conversation with my best friend. All the while I was holding my bowls back as I endured listening to her whiny little voice pretending to be innocent.

Once at his computer I cleared a number of beer cans from across the desk and sat myself down. I was in no mood for anything much, whether it be good or bad news, good or evil, democratic or republican. Nevermind that last statement, I just wanted to get Frankie and I alone.

But the second I sat down my phone rang. I checked the number: Unknown Caller. Fuck. Frankie gave me a glance as he sat on his bed, Myra beside him. He gave me the old one-two-shoo into the hallway and I left to take the call.

I knew they'd be discussing unsavory subjects. A few that include sex, our sex life, her sexuality. Basically, anything regarding sex. I just prayed he wouldn't recruit her as another webcam model or the like. Then we'd be in even more trouble and Myra, that devil-girl, would have more ammunition than she'd know how to use against us.

"Hello?" I answered, not happy about the call. Whoever was on the other line probably heard the vile slue in my voice, the sound of madness in my mouth.

"Hi, I'm not sure if I have the right number. This is Kimmy."

Oh, God.

"Kimmy!" What absolute timing. If she was a nuclear war code, she'd be right on time to start the second Cold War. No, no, I had to think of this as a relief. I needed to talk softly, though I was sure the two were plenty fine and secure in Frankie's bedroom.

With my luck, he'd be fucking her by now and we'd both be black-mailed white males amongst a generation that sought closure for false rape accusations and problematic sex-inequalities. Of course, this all adds to the deduction of what's true and what's make-believe.

"How are you?" Are three words just as strong as '*I love you*' in any given sentence.

"I'm good, just thought I'd call. Although . . . I probably should have texted first." She gave out a laugh that was like medicine during these times of hopelessness. "So, whatcha' been up to since the last time I saw you?" She gave a small chirp at the end of her sentence. But it was such a natural sound that I couldn't help but adore it.

"You know . . ." I thought for a second. Do I be honest? Do I act polite? Do I insinuate that everything is fine and we can just go about life as though problems were systematic or morally constructed? Or do I just hang up the phone right now?

No, I couldn't, would never do that.

I recall one time in the first grade having a huge crush on Kimmy. Back then, I had told my mother about this '*crush*' I had. And at the time, it seemed unreal. Weren't girls and boys supposed to be afraid of one another, cooties and all that jazz? Anyhow, to summarize: My mother finally introduced me to her in front of her parents. We would get together afterwards from time to time, playdates and such. Eventually she became my first kiss. But that's a story for another day.

"You know . . ." *Did I just repeat myself?* "things have been better."

"Aw, what's going on? Sorry if I called at the wrong time. I've just been at my apartment alone and, well, needed someone to chat with. But if you're busy I understand . . ."

Oh shit. I didn't want the blame to go to her. And as I listened in the bedroom, I could hear those two numbskulls chattering about. But I knew I'd have to get back to them soon. Frankie, obviously, had important news for me.

"It's not you, it's me." Jesus Christ almighty, was I a bad replication of a former James Dean or what?

"Uh, ok." She said in a classic, unknowingly sympathetic sense.

"Sorry, sorry." I tried to mend the conversation. "I mean it though. There's just . . . just a lot of shit going on at the moment that I need to take care of. Thank you though, for calling and all. I really, *really-really-really* wish I could talk to you now. But maybe tomorrow will be a better day?" And God, judging by her reaction I would know whether tomorrow would be any better.

She took her time, the cutie knew how to tease. It was probably an unconscious response, *probably*. "All right, call me tomorrow. And if you don't, I won't ever call again." Her voice was playful, so I was safe for now.

Damn her for baiting me in this far though. "Oh-kay, you got me. Deal." I spoke, as we both gave into a bit of laughter before wishing each other a good night.

As I hung up the phone I realized, in the twilight of events, that I had upped the scales. Three different women in my life, all with their bits of trouble and all with their perks. What was a man to do, if not a boy or somewhere in between?

Back in Frankie's room the two were still scuffling about in meaningless conversation, but conversation at the least. Conversation was, of course, communication, nonetheless. And that was better than awkward silence.

Noticing me, Frankie's head began to shift with Myra's. Like watching two mannequins move in conjunction. Frightening in a way, fascinating in another. Then I watched Frankie get up from his bed and approach me like a modern Judas with a deep secret to tell.

"Come with me bud." He exclaimed. Myra intervened, but Frankie made it personal. Let's just say when Frankie gets serious, he's serious.

We walked out into the hallway, it felt like short-term deja'vu. "Dude, our video . . ." he left me in suspense, no matter how poor the quality of the suspense was.

"Yeah, so our video?" I questioned like a smart-ass.

"Shh, shh . . ." He trailed off, he must've had something worth keeping between us. "That video, it attracted someone. Somebody." The fucking fiend was talking in mistranslated code from some search engine gone berserk.

"What the fuck you talkin' bout?" I asked, noticing Myra leaning near the crack of the door. She was more of a whore than I anticipated.

But before I could slam the door shut on her stupid face Frankie pulled me closer and spoke, "A guy named Jack contacted me. I know, sounds'tupid righ? Bu-but trust me, this guy sounds legit."

Then who would have guessed it, another Jack with another brilliant idea. Though this time Frankie made him out to be a big deal. Something about watching our features, viewing our 'films' and whatnot. Being impressed, wanting to get together. A paid trip to Cali, no expense to us.

Mentions about Abby, more mentions about my camera angles. Said it was expert work, said it was artistic, embracing, stylistic. But most importantly it was *fucking sexy as Hell*. Frankie read the email through his phone, that this Other Jack was '*more than impressed*' and wanted to '*embrace our work within his own*', whatever the fuck that meant. He also mentioned that our video had gained over two thousand views in a little more than the two or so days it's been up.

All of which was good news. None of which was solving my problem.

"Frankie, this is great and all. But I have a problem."

Yet, the moment I constructed my careful words, it seemed as though fate had chosen a side against me. As if I were playing chess against a computer, destined to lose, favored if I won, Myra appeared from the confines of Frankie's dank bedroom. She began on some rant about loneliness and acceptance. Some real gen-alpha-type shit if you asked me. It wasn't until she mentioned being featured in one of our videos that my ears perked and my hearing became as sensitive as that of a dog awaiting orders from his master.

Sit. Bow. Play dead.

I wish I could.

"Maybe you'd like me in your next video." she shyly acted as she showed off some cleavage and bent her lips in that sexual fashion. A discount Vogue model if I'd ever seen one. She belonged on the front page of some Westword magazine or another indiscriminately ridiculous content coverage contagion of the sort. "I promise I'll behave, until you tell me not to." She winked.

I knew I had no other choice. "Frankie, we need to take a shit, together." I said and dragged the dumb-ass womanizer away. Once again, it was the ace of spades, the royal flush. How could she question it? So, I took us into the upstairs bathroom, stepped us into the shower and shut the curtain as if it'd help keep our conversation quiet. In case she'd be leaning against the door, like some CIA agent lurking into our collect calls and emails.

"So, uh, dude. You wanna ex'pla'ain yousel've yet?" He was getting worse by the minute.

"Myra, she's a fucking psycho man. She's fucking framed me. She said she was twenty. Maybe nineteen. Maybe she didn't say . . ." I thought about it for a minute. Frankie was getting agitated, bad news usually conflicts with the good. "What I mean to say is, man . . . she's fucking sixteen."

I waited for the reaction. I waited for the pedophilia comments, the KYS connections, the blush to embarrassment to abandonment. But it didn't come, all Frankie said was "Ae you kidding me dude?" I nodded my head to the truth. I never asked for an ID. I had hardly asked for a name. I was an idiot. It wasn't until the aftermath that I realized it. Too little, too late.

"I'm not kidding, dude." Was the appropriate response. The only response I had.

"Shit man, this could be serious. Like, seriously. Sixteen? You lucky bastard."

I almost threw a fist down, "Lucky bastard?" I questioned, "What'd you mean by that shit man?" I almost screamed but remembered that the harlot was probably stalking us from outside the door.

"Man, you kiddin'? Fuckin' a sixteen-year-old. Not to sound like a creep, but that's somethin' I wished for when I was sixteen. I see you're in some shit. But I - I'm also a bit jealous."

"Fuck you."

"Now I know why you'd left'd us that night."

"You already knew that . . ."

The jerk was leading me in circles. Anyway, anyhow, I needed to see this through. I thought and thought hard now. Frankie was no help, at least in his apparent state. Myra was like a virus shadowing our every move until the moment she could crawl back in and make me sick. What was I to do?

Then it occurred to me. This Jack character, maybe he could help. So, I asked, "Could you contact this Jack-guy, ask what his deal is? What he wants from us, what he's looking for. And maybe, if he could help me? I'm sure he's got some sort of insight, eh? He has to . . ." I droned away.

Frankie grinned, as if glad I was willing to contact some stranger from the internet for help. But as we began to converse, another intervention approached. And I could hear Myra's pitiful voice screech from behind the bathroom door.

"Someone's at the door!" She yelled, as if she needed to.

The doorbell did sound off. It cried in horror, as if to say it were in need, if it were desperate. A crying child in the crib or in the corner. We exited the bathroom and took to the front door together. I nearly felt as though I was with Frankie more than I was with Myra in terms of my relationship status. At the door, Myra behind the scenes, we opened it.

And there stood a young man, no younger than us if not a tad bit older. He wore a Jacket that had been torn, sewn, sunbathed and abused for years. Jeans ripped on the left knee. Beard short yet well maintained. His hair flowed like a fucking waterfall in the Sierra. Blonde, like a Nazi, blue-eyed and attentive. He stood with his hands held still against his waist, his face full of stoicism. And with one simple question we embarked on the end of our journey.

What I mean to say is, he broke our reality in half.

"Are you the two?" He asked, but we had no answer, just many more questions. There we stood like two nimrods in the middle of a spelling-bee or socio-political debate. He shook his head, then asked a different question, "Are you the two who have been fucking my girlfriend, Abigale? Are you the two from the webcam show?"

I wanted to play dead.

– 13 –

The First Time

THE LAST DAY OF EIGHTH GRADE was the first time I had ever played hooky. Though I had sat through half of the day in pure boredom. I watched as the boys snorted Powdered Sugar Sticks and sent dick-pics before it became fashionable. As for the girls, they were all frantic, frightened, and an A-cup away from becoming high school eye candy. Fruit isn't sweet until it's ripened after all . . .

Still a kid, playing hooky was something of a thrill. I felt like Pascal Payet taking flight. Hell, a middle school is one barbed wire fence and guard tower away from being a prison. Especially at that age. But the truth of the matter was, it wasn't my idea. Playing hooky, that is.

My best friend had found me, asked me to come along. He said his parents wouldn't get home until an hour after we should have been released and so we should just walked back to his place. Neither of our homes were very far off. Mine, being the furthest away, was only a fifteen-minute walk in total. His was probably five minutes less.

To get to either of our homes, we first had to cross through the neighboring cemetery and past our old elementary school. I had felt so much freedom along the way that I screamed in the streets every cuss word I knew. I recalled my friend using the word 'mother-fucker' once upon a time. I had no idea what it meant, he just told me it was the worst word you could say. I doubt he even knew what it meant at the time.

As I dropped F-bombs all along the urban pathways like a god-damn repeat of Pearl Harbor, we spotted something. It was a large pile of boxes stacked as high as we were tall, outside of some home along the driveway for trash pick-up. To this day there has never been a reason why we were so curious about it. But inside of the boxes we found piles upon piles of porno magazines. Everything from softcore to hardcore, anal to exhibitionist and so forth. More porn than a terabyte of data could hold. Right outside on a sunny day, waiting for us, and perhaps others to stumble across it.

So, debating quickly, we each grabbed two mags and stormed back to the cemetery. We didn't want to bring them back to my friend's place, nor did we want to get caught with them. So, we found a semi-shaded, mostly hidden statue surrounded by tall shrubbery. Looking through the magazines, our eyes had seen more than a child could imagine, whether it was imagining dragons or the anatomy of the human body. It was violation, fascination, the first needle in the arm. There was no touching between us. Only the giggles and laughs of middle school children about to grow into pre-teens. How fitting then, months before my thirteenth birthday, that I would become exposed to this.

To our center there was that statue. Some saint with an open bible, no words etched or written into the stone. It was a clean slate. We started ripping out images of women being penetrated and cummed on. Then, in a small pool of water nearby, we wet the pages and plastered the imagines onto the book. Paper mache porn read by a saint.

Perfect.

I woke up feeling like I had taken one too many shots of tequila the night before. Boy, I wish that were the case. Everything was a blur at first, literally. The rays of light from the window nearby looked like dissipating steam and the white walls were flat canvases lacking texture. With a figure by the bedside, I attempted to lift myself. But the pounding of my head knocked me back down into what I could only describe as the *greasy bed sheets of an unkempt room*. That's when I knew it wasn't my own bed I was lying in. Then the figure to my side started to make sense and gain shape as I focused on Frankie's crumpled over body.

"Frankie?" I muttered, a dried taste of copper along the partings of my lips.

He awoke and rose in his seat. "Hey buddy, how'ya feeling?"

"How am I feeling?" I wasn't sure if I thought it or spoke it. Clawing my way up I felt the shaking in my hands, which were scraped with tiny fragments of skin peeling back from my knuckles. "Wha - what the fuck happened last night?"

He laughed like a kicked dog, finding his own pain amusing. "You got your ass beat last night. Abby's apparent *boyfriend* stopped by."

"Boyfriend?" I spoke in hysteria, it hurt to even talk.

"Man, you really did lose it." He chuckled again, this time with a small heave. "Yeah man, don't know what got into you though. You seemed pretty pissed. The next thing me and Abby knew you had thrown a punch his way."

"Oh yeah? Then how was my ass beat?" I thought for a moment, trying desperately to remember.

"You missed. Fell onto the concrete face first. Then he started throwing kicks into you. If it wasn't for Abby running out from his car and stopping him, you might've been wakin' up in the hospital right 'bout now."

Son of a bitch.

You don't know real embarrassment until you pick a fight and knock yourself out cold in front of your best friend and potential love interest. Then it began to flood back, the anger I had felt. That volcanic rage that boils inside your stomach until you're ready to pop. I must have popped. Although, waking up now in my best friend's bed, I wasn't sure who I should've been madder at: Abigale or her boy.

"What's the pricks name? Where's he live? What the fuck man? What the fuck are we gonna' do about this? And where the fuck is Myra?"

"Slow the fuck down man, jeez. Myra went home right afterwards. She wasn't very impressed."

"I'm surprised that cunt ever is . . ."

That's when Frankie finally sensed something was truly wrong with me. It was only after those words that I saw an angry spark light up in him as well. Perhaps it was the aggressive nature of the male complex coming to fruition. Or maybe it was a lifelong friendship finally paying its dues. Whatever the case, we were on the same page now. Like a rock and a hard place ready to barricade whatever was to come. He snarled before he spoke, "What she do to you man?"

It almost felt shameful saying it. But I needed help. Everybody everywhere needs help eventually, even if they're too damn stubborn to ask for it. Even those fake-ass Caucasian cannibals with their buzzed heads and slacking extra-large jeans. Even the blonde and neon ex-cheerlead captains. Even the single mother on the corner of Federal Boulevard. Even me.

He listened in, kept me in check. Future's telling's, telling us nothing definite. It was an actual brainstorm. Lighting striking synapses and nerves. Neurological waves like thunder rolling in. A rain of thoughts flooding the room through strong winds of words. The atmosphere was beginning to change, the air thickening with the moisture of our mouths spitting out answers.

"First things first, we take care of the whole 'Abby boyfriend' deal." We agreed.

"She's not gonna take our calls man. That boy's prob'bly got her on lock down." Frankie said in a void.

I checked my phone, I had gotten a message from an unknown sender. It was Kimmy asking me what I was up to. Another cog in my life. Hopefully she was the gear that would keep this life of mine turning. "We might need to do this another time Frankie." I replied, but he didn't like that answer. And in my eyes, he could see a certain truth arise.

"Another girl huh? Dude, that's the reason why you're in this mess."

"Not just me Frankie, you were the guy fucking another guy's girl. We're both screwed if we don't figure this out."

"Then why, man? You a masochist?" He said. He might've been right.

"Remember Kimmy, from elementary school?"

It took him a second. Elementary school for us had already seemed like a faint dream from decades ago and gone. "Kim! Yeah, since when did you hang with Kim man?"

"Since now, I gotta' go." I replied as I rose up to text her back. I could see a quiver on his lips as he readied himself to speak. That's when I knew I needed a better explanation than '*she's a girl and I'm a boy, we practically were made to fit together*'. "She might have some insight man. Girl to guy. May be a better perspective than two guys trying to figure out a situation involving two girls and some Jackass."

He didn't like it but couldn't disagree. Letting me go I thanked him, made my way out to my car and drove. According to her she had just gotten out of class. School is where I should have been today. But it didn't matter, not to me. Life was more important in the moment, not the moments later. Youthful naivety disguised by arrogant early adulthood. There's always a reason for making mistakes.

You just have to make sure the mistake isn't too big to fix. This is where the crossroads lay. I didn't want to treat our first meet up in years as a business trip. Yet I needed help, and it's rare when a twenty-something young punk admits he needs help.

It wasn't a secret, not now, not then, that I've always had a crush on her. Ever since elementary school, having watched movies like Aladdin, I felt like she could be my Jasmine on that magic carpet ride. It seems as though Disney always lied when it came to the concept of true love, what it meant and what it was.

We were once playing "*family*" in class. I wanted to be the family cat. I crawled around on all fours, rubbed up against stuff. The only thing I didn't do was ask for more food, nap and not give a shit. And at one point I tried to crawl into her lap. The next thing I knew was she yelled and I was taken to the principal's office.

My mother met me there, they asked me what I thought I was doing. I just said I was the family cat. Apparently, I had touched her in the wrong places. As a kid, I never would have guessed. Now, I just see it was a stupid reason why my mother should be called into the principal's office. A woman of two jobs, the responsibility of taking her kid to school, picking him up later, grocery shopping, cooking. It's funny to think that women weren't still in slavery or slaves in general. The white picket fence lifestyle of yesterday was the oppression of today.

Maybe I'd tell that story today. We'd probably both laugh now.

When I got there, I avoided everyone's stares. I only cared about one pair of eyes, and it wasn't any of theirs. Then when I finally found her, the last thing I expected was a hug. It felt . . . nice, warm.

Comforting.

"How are you?" she asked, exuberantly.

'*I could be better*.' Was one option for a response, another being, '*I'm fucked*.' But instead, I chose the same old tune. "I'm good, you?"

"Good, I'm good. Biology was Hell but, that's nothing new." She laughed.

I couldn't help but agree.

We took a walk around the campus, just shooting the shit. I suppose you can't use that phrase when you're with a woman. Or would it be sexist not to? That was the reason why women were so complicated. We complicated them. The same could be said vice versa for sure, I'm sure.

We eventually strolled over to a nearby bench next to a juniper tree and just talked. It seemed like forever since I had the chance to simply talk.

With Frankie, it was problem solving, with Myra it was (*was*) flirtation, with Abby it was discovery. With Kim, it was reminiscing, the purest form of communication. No regrets, limited secrets, open and expressive. There wasn't talk like talking about the past, the present, and the future without it becoming complicated however.

"But you had your whole face in my crotch!" She expressed herself through joy and embarrassment.

"I didn't mean it, I was like, what . . . eight; nine maybe?" I laughed, giving that innocent shrug and watching her lips suck back into a repressive grin. She was getting a kick out of it and so was I. "Yeah, I thought it was weird being a kid. Then I got to middle school and thought it was weird, you know? With all the body hair and stuff." I couldn't help but chuckle at myself. "Then high school came and . . ."

"Yeah, still weird." She finished my sentence, I didn't mind. I almost appreciated it. Then she continued where I had left off, "Then college, well, also pretty weird huh?" She coyly commended.

She must had noticed a dying ember in me. I'll admit, with all this stress, it was hard to keep up with happiness. The strategic smile and laughter, the light-hearted devotion to the moment. It was becoming smoke and mirrors. But the smoke was dissipating and the mirrors cracking.

"What's wrong?" she asked, as if she had to.

This was the moment; this is where I would reveal the awful truth. Yet, staring at her, I didn't want to admit it. It was one thing to tell Frankie. But to a girl like her, a long-time crush. She was still so beautiful. Yes, it sounded like a cheesy pop song. But fuck it, those songs sell for millions, so I guess I had a catchy tune when it came to women.

There's more to beauty than just those pretty brown eyes, long dark hair tied back with the thin face and great sense of attire that showed off a pair of well-shaven legs. It was personality. One thing I never could find online, at least not genuinely.

"Please don't get mad or anything if I tell you this."

"Get mad? You're not a serial killer, are you?"

"No, no . . . no. But I sure feel like one." I was acting overtly dramatic. Start the reel, cue the applause. This was looking more like a B-grade sitcom than reality. I wondered for a second if that's how our viewers felt about our pornography. Was it just another Saturday night special?

"Well come'on, out with it. You know, you should never keep a lady waiting."

She was right, I shouldn't. I shouldn't have waited until any of this had happened, I should have shot it in the ass until it keeled over from blood loss or worse. I should have but didn't. "So, a week or so ago . . ." I didn't want it to sound recent, as if that would deter the seriousness of the situation. "I-I, I slept with a girl."

She waited, but I had froze. "Yeah, we all need to sleep with somebody, I suppose."

"You don't understand. Sorry, I'm sorry." I couldn't speak properly. "I slept with a girl who had . . . had lied about her age."

Then I waited and she thought about it. Sitting back and crossing her arms, she gave me a smug, contemplative stare. It looked like judgement, felt authoritative, but became neither as she replied. "I've done worse. You know, I once slept with six men in a cheap motel in Vegas." I was shocked, my eyes widened. "Yeah, I guess that's what happens when you carry a suitcase full of drugs around. We had, I think, two bags of grass, 75 pellets of mescaline, five sheets of high-powered blotter acid, a saltshaker half-full of cocaine, a whole galaxy of multi-colored uppers, downers, screamers, laughers . . . Also, a quart of tequila, a quart of rum, a case of beer, a pint of raw ether, and two dozen amyls."

Shit, and here I thought she was as innocent as they got. But it didn't seem right, especially after she gave me a good punch to the arm and laughed. "Hun, I'm just kidding. Fear and Loathing, you've never read that book?" I wasn't exactly fond of the joke and she obviously sensed that. "I'm sorry. Listen," she began again, "you're fine. Can I tell you about the first boy I ever slept with and . . . promise you won't tell anyone."

I nodded my head, but that wasn't good enough. She pushed me back playfully and said again "Promise?"

I promised, then she continued. "I was fifteen. I didn't know what love was. I just knew there were certain things that made a boy . . . happy." She air quoted. "I lost my virginity to my boyfriend of eighteen. Afterwards I was so ashamed that I knew I had to break it off with him. But he was afraid I would tell the cops or something. But there's something called Romeo and Juliet laws."

It was at this point I thought she was making shit up. "Really, Romeo and Juliet?"

"You're not listening to me." She said, and I refrained from speaking any more. "Romeo and Juliet laws, they pretty much terminate any assumptions made for statutory rape and the like. That's not to say that what you did was right, no offense." And I agreed. "But, as my parents had explained to me after I had told them, as long as we both consented to having sex, we would be fine. She did consent, right?"

"Yes. Yes, of course she did." I spoke in near-hysteria.

Next thing I knew I had a hand on my shoulder and a very pretty face looking into my ivory soul. "Then you'll be fine."

So, there it was, a possible solution. We got up, started to walk some more. There were more childhood stories to tell, secret crushes, and the pains of growing older. There was talk of past lovers, from sex to the first kiss, it all mattered just the same. Our lives weren't pixel perfect, but they were perfectly incomplete.

And that was the picture of the Mona Lisa in pristine paints on a fine silk canvas stretched across the sky. Romance was in recognizing our mistakes, finding our purpose and realizing that people, real, true, and profoundly unordinary people, were what made this world spin. Personally, I know I hate everybody, including myself. But this, I could never hate this.

At my car, again, she gave me another hug. But then something else came, something like heartbreak but happier. I felt a tense kiss reach my cheek and she told me "If she doesn't work out, give me a call. Please?"

Fairytale fiction. Was Disney right all along or was it just coincidence? Usually, I would take whatever I could get. But this, this I had to be careful with. More careful than fucking a sixteen-year-old or filming a boy's cheating girlfriend. This was a diamond in a glass castle. This, I thought, could mean something more.

"Yes, absolutely." I spoke.

My phone rang and I said my goodbyes.

I answered, it was Frankie on the other line. As he started to speak, I watched as she walked away. I waited, anticipated. There's one sure sign you know that a girl is truly into you. Then it happened, and she turned around to catch me watching her. One last smile and wink my way and I knew it. Never, does it matter, the action nor the context of the situation. If the girl turns around to meet your sight before leaving, you've made it. And then Frankie made it worse.

"They're here, both of them."

"What', who's there?" I asked, not paying attention.

"Abby and Michael, his name's fucking Michael, man. And they're asking for you. You almost done bro?"

"Yeah, yeah. I'm done. They at your place? I'll be right there." What a fucking roller coaster.

- **14** -

Pull Out

IT WAS LIKE A TRIP ON OPIATES, stimulates, and depressants. I couldn't anticipate which would take effect next. This time I drove slow, slower than usual. I wasn't excited, nor did it feel very inviting, although I had been invited. It was an invitation to my own walk down death row. If only the death penalty was eliminated. We wouldn't have this circumstance; we'd still be treated as humans. Not like cattle to the slaughter.

And what would he say? What would Abby say? Why now, if ever? I had half-hopes that it was over the second I knocked myself into the cement. I was clearly wrong. Perhaps every person required some form of recollection before moving forward. Maybe this boy - this *man*- was just like us.

I stopped by the liquor store on my way. Bought a pint of vodka, five bucks for the cheap, hang-over-guaranteed garbage. Grabbed an energy drink as well and chugged. First a sip from the bottle of vodka, next a large swallow from the can of B12, B6, bull sperm infused, cocaine leveled caffeine-based poison I desired. I might as well had been smoking crack.

And in my lifetime, as of now: I had drunk enough alcohol that I should have been on meth; drank enough caffeine to have snorted cocaine on the daily;

smoked so many cigarettes that, well, cigarettes seem to speak for themselves. I might as well have been cooped up in some piece-of-shit rental outside the edge of the city, where the politicians usually pushed the minorities and the homeless to. Some crack-house away from the popularity of sixteenth street mall, away from the nepo-babies and stay at home mommies.

Somewhere where they'd never find me. Piss-stained, wasted, away from the dramatic overtures of everyday life. Was it time then, to open my eyes to this apparent genocide.

Not in my lifetime.

Half-way till buzzed, my mind ready to clock out like a worker on overtime, a common occurrence in America, I felt as though nothing could stop me now. Life or death, that's how it felt. I either survived the oncoming onslaught, or I would beat myself back into the ground. Myra had been solved, for the most part. But this, Abigale, Frankie, this would change everything about our business. Reliability and the ethics involved.

Get paid to get laid. Looking for amateurs. We didn't have a clue.

One last chug, a deep, enveloping swallow. I was like the first prostitute to reach the likings of White Chapel. I wasn't sure what I was thinking, the mindset I had reached. All in all, I was a wolf. I was an actor, the world my stage. And my stage was a smaller stage, paid in debt to the world's stage. Classic Shakespeare, a never-ending tragedy.

Frankie answered the door; I entered as if entering my funeral. Why did it hurt so much? Was I betrayed? I wasn't even having sex with her. Yet, at times, my filming felt more intimate. There's a sacred belief in

105

some cultures that when taking a photograph, in my case taping an individual, you'll steal one's soul. Did I capture more than what was on the surface? Had I stolen Abigale's soul?

"Hey, yeah." Frankie spoke as we walked on through and into his bedroom.

"Bout time. You got some explain'in to do pal." Michael replied. At first, I thought his question was meant for Frankie. But then I heard him grunt and I looked over to see a glare perpetrating my sight. "This ain't the shithole I saw you filming in. Jacky or whatever, tells me it was in your bedroom."

"I . . . I was tol' to come here. Nowt my room." I squeezed out the words, the liquor being carried by surges of adrenaline, thereby amplifying my drunkenness.

Michael laughed, "Holy shit, you drive here drunk too pal?" and he continued to laugh some more.

"Quit it Mike . . ." Abby said, crossed arms and hidden in the darkest corner of the room.

Then all was quiet, as Michael turned to face her. "What?" he muttered to her, slowly making his way towards her. In a second, he had her by the wrists, she gave out a yelp and turned away with eyes shut. "You don't have the right babe, to tell me off like that!" He yelled, shaking her.

Frankie was the first to rise and run over. It was an immediate struggle, but eventually Michael backed off. "Yo, I don't wanna' see that here. And keep it the fuck down, my mother's right upstairs." He replied.

Michael, red-faced and furious, just stood in place venting. That's when I noticed Abby's hand move in Michael's palm and it closed shut around her. Then, looking at her face, I saw eyes full of tears. Not tears of sadness or even pain, but of sympathy. She was truly sorry to have put this no-life womanizer through so much. That's when I felt cracks beginning to form and run through my heart. That's when, liquored up or not, I couldn't take any more of this.

"So what?" I bellowed and grabbed at the room's attention. "What the H'ell do you wan, huh? Money, do you wan money? Are you gonna' black-ail us? Are you gonna' hurt me? And what abou' Frankie, huh?" I fumed in the blackest of smoke.

The cock-sucker grinned, "Frankie and I are squared away. The only thing I want now is from you. Take those videos down. Delete whatever you have on your phone, on your camera, the computer, the fucking works! And if I ever see my girl naked anywhere else except for my own bed, I'll fucking kill you."

It sounded like an empty threat. Except for the passion behind his words, the strain in his throat, the deep tone rolling through his demands. So perhaps he did mean it. Either way we -I mean me- didn't have much of a choice. This was an easy way out. I couldn't let it slip.

"Fine."

Letting go, Michael approached me with the same ferocity as he used with Abby. He spat in his hand, looked me clear in the eye and said, "Promise, brother's pact."

I looked down to his hand, curdling the bubbled saliva ball. Then I took mine, did the same and we shook. He awaited the word and I spoke as if it were a eulogy for a friend. "*Promise*." And with one lumbering shake we let go, wiped our hands on our jeans, and we escorted them to the front door.

I was second in line, Frankie of course leading, Michael right behind me, and Abby right behind him. I could feel her, her sorrow, her regrets. But she wasn't herself, she had become a shell of someone with spark. I never looked back at her during that short walk from Frankie's room to the front door. Yet, for all I knew eons had passed. I could only picture her naked. Not because I got a kick out of it or wanted a quick turn-on in the moment. It was like watching Eve make her final steps out from the Garden of Eden. The genesis of our own hubris, making its way down the red carpet of shame. It could have been worth those fabled fifteen minutes of fame, no commercial break.

Frankie and I waited on the porch. The two of them walked straight to what we assumed was Michael's next year's make-and-model truck. Must've been nice to be dating a guy for money. Michael himself looked back at us, with half a smirk and half of a snarl. But Abby, she didn't turn back. She hardly looked once at either of us throughout the whole event. She didn't wave or call out. And before she could climb into the passenger side I felt it, that damn volcano erupting again.

"You bitch! We trusted you!"

It must've caught her attention, because her eyes lit up like some wild animal in the night. Frankie put a panicked hand against my chest in case I were to run after her. In his defense, I did lean forward as I yelled. But it wasn't enough, I needed more. Too much steam and heat all pent up in me. It needed more of this cold-air release.

"We trust'd you! You trust'd us. Now you . . . you're just gonna' . . . Gonna' fucking walk away, eh?"

That's when I saw Michael approaching from around the bend of his truck. Frankie was whispering all kinds of things in my ears, trying to get me to stop. I didn't listen; I kept puckering out curses and cusses. Michael had almost reached me with a fistful of lead ready to piledrive me back into the cement.

That's when I saw his image disappear. Abby stood tall and silent, right in front of me. It very well could have been closer than a kiss. But the only thing I felt touch my lips was a wave of pain that shocked me as her palm collided with my cheek. The slap was loud, it echoed along the asphalt and streetlamps. It was the bang before the bullet reached. Then she just stared, her brow bent and lips partially cracked so that she was showing teeth underneath those red curved curtains.

"Do you know how much this hurts?" She barked out loud. I barely had a reaction, still stunned, I just glared back at her. "Stop thinking you're the only one this affects." She finished, whipping her hair into my face and stomping off towards the truck.

Michael still stood there, measuring me up. He walked up, Frankie was cautious, but Michael gave him a nod. A nod can mean many things, depending on the look one gives with it. In my case, Michael wanted a non-violent moment with me. Beside me now, like wind passing, he told me something I wouldn't soon forget.

"Man, you're not the first. And it breaks my heart I couldn't be her first, in more ways than one. But at the end of the day, we're all in a bit of pain. Heartbreak comes in one size, and it tends to fit all." He gave me the old shoulder shake with his hand and looked back to me for the last time that day. "Take care of yourself."

His hand released and he gave a salute. His truck drove off and we were left broken. I suppose the problem had been solved. I felt my phone vibrate but didn't want to look. I heard Frankie talk but didn't listen. What did we gain from this loss? What did we lose from this gain? Did it all equal out, was it all fair in love and war?

Was it love? I don't want to think so, so instead I didn't think. And without a thought I had no choice but to listen. That's when I heard Frankie ask me:

"Dude, are you crying?"

I passed two fingers underneath my sockets. Sure enough, there were warm salty streaks building prison bars along my face. The Indus River had been dammed up for so long that it was bound to break eventually.

– 15 –

Bed Sheets Optional

MY TRUE FIRST PORN SEARCH was at the petty age of twelve. It happened shortly after my suspension, was found out by my father, and at that moment I knew I would have to act more cleverly to conceal my insidious motives.

What I mean to say was, before this age, the only knowledge I had of the female body was a pair of breasts and a slit of skin where a penis would have been otherwise. So, in order to elaborate on my very first pornographic experience, besides the Playboy magazine's my father possessed, I need to identify my own curiosities. It begs one question when you are a young, mostly innocent, naïve soul looking for answers about the human body. And one question in need of an answer was this: How do girls pee?

So, as pathetic as it seems, one of my first expeditions into the world of pornography came from researching porn related to women pissing. Whether it was in the streets or in the bathroom, I became fascinated. I think it was a mixture between seeing how a woman handles her fluids in opposition to a man and the differences between our reproductive parts. As sick as it is, as it sounds, it was fascinating at the time. I'm fairly certain it didn't turn me on. I know of a few men who are turned on by the possibility of a woman urinating on them. I am not one of them by far, nor have I ever been.

Another story for another day perhaps.

All I remember is the hypnotism. I never touched myself at the time. I just saw the images and watched the videos. The women were so joyous. I figured out later that this was just a ruse. I noticed how they were never ashamed by the act. I also learned this was a lie in later times. Last, but not least, it seemed as though this was out of free will. Oh, how I would find out otherwise.

The saying goes that curiosity killed the cat. I'm starting to think, rather, that it had been philosophy. If there was anything that my student debt had paid for, it was philosophy. I had taken a couple of good classes. I never really passed them. But I always kept the books, because the books were always more interesting than the actual classes. And the books never grade you for knowing or not, what existed inside of them. If only people could play the part of books, never asking questions until they knew the full story.

Determinism was one base of belief I had learned to enjoy during my semesters. It stated that everything was planned, ready and willing to be carried out. It couldn't be fully determined but would occur regardless of whether we attempted to change it or not. The point being, we were all on our separate paths but there is little that can be changed about these paths. Everything, then, is determined from start to end. Einstein was a big believer in this. I guess true transcendence in the hands of God and the absence of free-will and the will to change was an after-thought from a pre-nuclear age. With that said, those people were destined to die. All one hundred and five thousand of them. Even Einstein needed a reason for an escape.

His was mine.

After Frankie's, I finally checked my phone. Moments later I was at Myra's. Myra sat next to me along her parent's coach. The room was dark, the television only ran static. The faint smell of vodka ran up my nostrils and made me feel ill. I only had partaken in a few good shots. But Myra had been drinking from the bottle since I arrived. She suggested we watch a movie, but the movie never came. This scene was as much of a scene from a movie in its own rights.

She sat there, stumble-fucking-drunk leaning hard against me. I was the crutch, her Jesus and savior for the night. Little did she know I was playing the Devil's advocate. As soon as the tears stopped, I would lurk out from the shadows and end this atrocity. No more black mail, no more satirizing sexual acts, I was over it.

That was until the words started pouring over the tears. Drama intensified with a single word placed into one solitary sentence.

"My stepfather rapes me." She squealed out from her quivering lips, taking another long sip from the bottle. My heart sank. "My mom, she really likes him . . . Bu-but, he rapes me. Rapes me all the time. The first time was in seventh grade. But sh-she loves him." And the quivers and tears turned into contractions and violent, sorrow-stricken compulsions. Uncontrollable movements like shivers caused by needles of heroine. Undefined sounds like wounded animals calling out to one another. The tears didn't match the eyes, so red, full of blood vessels grasping around the white sections of the cornea. It was almost as if life itself wanted to choke out the vision of this seemingly little girl. "And I . . . I-I, I just. I want her to b-be . . ." she swallowed, she gulped, ". . . happy. That's wh-why I can't t-t-ell her. That's why I do m-my best to not, not be at home."

"Then why are we here?" I asked, an arm around her in comfort. Funny thing when you act like you care. Funnier yet, when in some deep corner of your heart, you actually do but still fake it.

She wiped her dribbling nose against her sleeve and took a quick sip from that silvery bottle. "They're on vacation, up in the mountains. That's why I was surprised when she got home. I was afraid . . ."

"Yes?"

"I was afraid it was my stepdad . . . I didn't want you around for that . . ." The compulsions were replaced with conviction. The girl I saw before, who I was framed by and made out to be a predator

113

because of, now looked more like a woman than even Abby.

"Myra," I began. "I need this to stop. I'm . . . I'm so sorry about your stepdad. What he does to you." And it was honesty that sealed the deal, whether she was willing to take the deal or not. My bet was placed; there was no going back. Whatever came after was destined. "You can't keep me on a chain, always wired to you. You can't black-mail me, it-it." I almost broke down myself. Not because of what I was about to tell her, but because I knew the line didn't match up with the lie. "Black-mailing me into this relationship hurts just as bad as your stepdad probably hurts you."

I didn't mean it.

I wanted to take it back.

I knew it wasn't true. But I still said it.

The room went quiet, except for the static and sniffling beside me. Then she released herself from my arm. And we knew all along that something like this could never last. She was fucking me to forget all the fucking bullshit done to her by her stepfather. By the apathetic look in her eyes, I knew I wasn't the first. And who would be the next? Could I have fixed things instead? Could I really be the one to make a change in this poor girl's life or would I just pass as another waking daydream before sleep? No, neither nor none. I was the sleep. I was the embodiment of numbness, of her subconscious. Like all dreams, good or bad, you eventually wake up and let go. That's what I wanted, to be let go.

"I . . . I just wanted someone to love me." She said while one last tear fell.

And that damn tear fell. It fell like an atom bomb against my hand, unknowingly holding her by the thigh. The thing fell and hit. It was wet, it was warm, it probably tasted of the salt of the sea. That tear could've flood the south-east coast, rust the Titanic, and still have time to come back to me and burn a hole through my hand just like an acid drop.

Then there was her face, I couldn't look. Because I knew I'd want to kiss her lips and with meaning this time. I knew I'd want to apologize and make it better. But I didn't want things to be better for her. I wanted them to be better for me.

"I'm not the one." I told her before getting up and walking out the door.

What is a tragedy? A tragedy is when you laugh off the night in your crappy car, knowing you just broke another piece to a piece of a puzzle of a girl and still having to work in the morning. But instead of sleeping you drink it off a bit. But by the time the booze really tries to work its way through you, the drowsiness kicks in and kicks your ass to sleep. Then, all you dream about are the mistakes you made, laughing it off in a dream and knowing you have work in the morning.

I didn't go to work in the morning. In fact, I hardly cared about my shit job. Once again, the wish came about: "*Please, just fire my dumb ass.*" Maybe after being unemployed, I'd feel better or have an excuse to feel as miserable as I did. And why did I?

Young white male is depressed. The President just bombed another country, whose name we cannot pronounce. But up next, why marriages end in America and what you can do to prevent it.

The headlines ran through my head as I popped some pills of aspirin, laid back down in my bed and just stared up to the ceiling for a bit. There wasn't anything interesting going on. Not a spider crawling along the wall nor a message to be read from my phone. I just needed to blank everything out, wipe it from existence. Because with this god-damn hangover not a feat was possible, everything hurt and nothing was beautiful.

It wasn't about Abby or Myra, it was about them both. A combined force of destruction. Separate, they did minor short-term damage. But in the long term I feared they might bend my mind to the breaking point. Unless I eradicated them from existence now, there would be no hope later.

Or as little hope as there was now.

Then I began to think in abstracts. Was there anything more American than Kim Kardashian? Was the Chocolate Man a symbolic representation of the failure within man himself? How many licks did it take to get to the center of a tootsie pop, and was there anything more sensual than licks against tootsies before they popped?

And how was Kim . . .

"How was Kim?" I asked myself, rising from my bed like Nosferatu. I decided to call, thinking it wouldn't do any harm. She might even be happy to hear from me. It would be a miracle if at least one person was happy to hear from me.

So, the phone rang, and it rang, and it continued. Her voicemail reached me and I just hung up. If she were interested, she'd call me back. But almost instantly the phone rang back and I answered as if I was a cancer-patient awaiting my results. "Hey Kim, what's going on?" I answered as sweetly as I could.

"Kim? Dude, it's Frankie."

"Oh," what a major disappointment. I laid back down into my cotton-lined coffin. "What's up man?"

"I'm driving over, not much time to explain. Get a bag and start packing your shit man, my mother's probably calling your parents as we speak." He sounded serious and frantic.

"Pack my wha- what the fucks going-"

"I said no time man. My mother got curious, started snooping. She knows about Abby and the god damn webcam thing. I'm coming over, be there in five."

The phone went silent. For a minute I couldn't move, let alone breathe. "Just when things were . . ." I couldn't believe my luck, let alone the luck between us both. I thought we had a full-proof plan. I guess it was destined to happen. So, I broke from my paralysis and ran over to my closet and took down my travel bag from the top rack. It was a gift from my uncle, handmade and personalized with my initials on it. I never thought I would need it for this reason.

First came my laptop, my camera, pairs of socks and underwear, two pairs of jeans, five or so good shirts. I ran into my bathroom downstairs, grabbed all the essentials. Back into my room I threw a few CD's I owned into the bag, along with minor memorabilia and, wait. Why the fuck was I running away? I was never in the videos; I was never fucking some stranger.

Then I remembered, I was the one in charge of the sites, all the raw footage with me. This was true control. It existed but acted as an opposing force. So, I unplugged my small 20-inch television, threw a few movies I owned into my near-to overflowing bag. Simple stuff like Pulp Fiction and Antichrist to keep me sane at night. With that said, I threw the bag over my shoulders and my television in my arms.

That's when my parents' phone rang. I quickly answered it and hung it up, not checking the caller ID nor giving a shit. But before I could make it outside of my parent's home, I heard my mother's voice from down the hallway.

"Hey son," hear it goes, the last nail through the Mahogany square. My mother, of all people. I just didn't want to hear it.

"Yeah mom?" I asked, handle on the front doorknob, ready to make a run to my car if it came down to it. Was it cowardice that I feared my mother's love so much? A son's mother was worth a hundred wasted relationships and then some. But I needed to run, to hide and protect her and my father. Then again, no one really runs from anything. It's like a private trap that holds us like a prison. And sometimes we step into those traps deliberately. Was I a psycho for doing this? I heard Frankie's horn from outside, then my mother called me again.

"Could you pick up some half and half and a pound of chicken from the super-market today?"

I almost cried, but held it in.

"Yeah, I'll get to it now." I lied.

I wasn't going to the super-market. The fact that I was getting away with this was enough to bring me to my knees. It hurt more knowing she didn't know. Then I heard the phone ring once again and I left as I heard her answer it from the phone in her own room. Quietly shutting the front door, I leaped down the steps and to my car. Frankie calling me out, telling me to hurry up, that he had found a place to hide out for a while. That he had another girl set up for us. She would be with us by the nighttime. I didn't care, starting my car and following him by the bumper, I didn't even want to be awake.

Later that night I slept, as Frankie and some girl pounded in the bed next to mine, bedsheets were apparently optional. We stayed inside some cheap motel near my school, how ironic. He must have kept his phone on, recording, leaning against something to capture them. I could have done a better job in my sleep, and that's not a joke.

Honestly, I wasn't asleep, couldn't sleep. Between the wet sloshing points of penetration. Those horrid moans when, without exact context, sound more like a death rattle. I had calls all throughout the day after I had left. From my mother, from my father. Even Kim called me back.

But I couldn't answer. I was too busy unpacking, discussing things with Frankie. How they'd get better. What were our options. Thank Christ he didn't pay that girl. She was free revenue for us. In fact, I think she was from my English 122 class. It wasn't a surprise, everyone needed at least one good, regrettable night in their lives. Sleeping with Frankie must've been more than enough to satisfy that taste between the tight notches of her crooked teeth and lower lips. At one point, she had asked if I wanted to join in. I just kept on pretending to sleep, staying silent, staying quiet and kept to myself. Wrapped in shadows of the night.

– 16 –

Deep Throat Drinking

I NEVER MENTIONED MY ELEMENTARY SCHOOL FRIEND Jamie. Jamie was a tomboy, in fact many girls who were my friends back then were tomboys. Looking back, it made no difference, but I'm sure in retrospect it probably added up to something. Regardless, Jamie was taller than most boys in our first-grade class. She had long blonde hair that ran down past her chest, usually tied back in a ponytail. Most of the time she wore jeans and a long shirt to match her body length.

One time I was over at her parent's house. They had a trampoline in the backyard. We didn't have a trampoline until I was already in middle school. So, she was the talk of the class in that aspect, and I felt lucky enough to have been invited over. In fact, it was probably my mother's idea.

As a child, you never really had a chance to decide, decisions were made for you. When you grow older you start to wonder where the control got transferred. Hence God and Buddha and Ali and the like. It had to go somewhere, we just assume it's spiritual release.

Anyways, the trampoline. She and I spent around an hour just jumping, flipping and falling over and into one another. It was innocent. That was until we climbed off from the trampoline and out into the yard. I'm unclear as to this day what it was we were doing. Catching bugs, picking leaves from the grass, chasing each other with sticks. It didn't matter, because in the end I was the one who felt seemingly embarrassed and invaded. And it took a single knob on a tree for Jamie to say to me "Hey look, that's the tree's pee-pee." While shortly after speaking, she poured a bottle of water over the area and said to me "Look," with a finger pointed, "the tree is peeing." and giggled.

I guess I giggled too, but out of child-like courtesy. Inside I felt nervous, even anxious. I wasn't certain why I had felt this way. Was it because this girl knew about my body, what I hid underneath my child-sized shorts? Or was it because I wasn't sure what was hidden under hers? Either way, that was the last time *we ever had a playdate together. My parents never understood why.*

From what Frankie had told me, his mother got curious after the big Michael run-in days ago. She logged onto his computer, which was essentially hers, and researched which websites, files, and folders Frankie visited the most. She found the porn sites fairly normal but had noticed that Frankie's "Tax Folder" kept appearing as a main destination. It didn't take long for her to discover the rest.

She eventually contacted my parents after kicking Frankie to the curb. I was lucky enough to have not only two parents, but neither who were also alcoholics. Although it didn't make my situation much better, my father accepted my moving out of the house as the greatest apology I could have given them.

My mother, however unhappy with me, would sometimes transfer a bit of money into my dust riddled bank account from time to time. Enough to fill my car with gas or buy a bit of groceries for the week.

As for our living situation, Frankie's uncle who lived in town was an owner of a motel. A sleazy guy, sort of like his establishment, which was riddled with the likes of drug fiends and Walmart shoppers. This was the type of place you'd catch on the news where the anchor would pull out a black-light and reveal all the cum spots on the beds. It was also the type of motel that attracted nearby college kids over to it for a quick one-two, in and out before heading back to class. I know this because my school has its own share of whores, both men and women alike.

The motel was called the Essex Motel for fuck's sake. It has *SEX* in the name. And we got our room at a quarter of the price thanks to Frankie's '*hook-up*'.

Most nights I sleep in my car. His uncle assured us that we had been provided with the cleanest, least used room of the complex. I didn't give a horse's cock whether it had a five-star review to its name on Google Plus or a passing health inspection every other month. It was a shithole, and I was the shit that was clogging the pipes.

It had been three weeks since I left my parent's house. I miss them. It was strange for me, I suppose, that I would have missed being conformed to a household of free meals, no rent, and decent family values. Once more, it had only been three weeks in this setting and I was already sick of it.

And what had I missed during those twenty-one days of being away? I feared to think it over. There had been a few times during a boozin' session that I considered contacting Abby. Maybe start one of those three-way fantasies that all the young things and their mothers seemed to be into these days. Fight fire with fire. Or fight fire with Michael and convince her to come back for one more round of web shows. I suppose I was being too modest when I said I considered contacting her, because I eventually did.

Speaking of eventuality, with enough vodka eventually anything will happen. Take note that I did not exclaim that "*anything was possible*" with enough vodka. Only that the "*possibility of anything*" was more likely. Anyways, her number had changed and that ended my night in one last shot and a blackout.

Have you ever blacked out? It's not unusual to forget what happened the night before. Fortunately for me, I've been black-out drunk several times and have never forgotten the circumstances, nor causes or effects that took place during the night before. So, in conclusion, black-out amnesia is not a guarantee of ingesting too much alcohol. In fact, I wished it had occurred more often. When someone drinks to the extent of losing consciousness completely, it's because they want to forget something or someone. Not wake up the next morning remembering with a migraine and upset stomach accompanying it.

What a waste it was to waste away on purpose. At least if you wasted away without knowing, you could plead ignorance was the cause. But I was the cause of this.

I cannot say I didn't try to fight it. There's a certain stage in drinking where <u>one more drink</u> never sounds like it's too much. But it's always, always that <u>one more drink</u> that ends up being your last. You get the shakes, that plump booze-belly, thick head, and blurry sight. Fighting is a battle you will not win. By fighting, you stride to overcome it, move through it, wait until its end. You'll puke your guts out just to get rid of it. But all you can really do by the end is let it swallow you whole, just as you had swallowed it.

Yet this was life for the past three weeks. My job finally got tiresome enough to the point of me quitting. The price to see my manager's face light up in a secretive panic of sorts when a good employee resigns with a two-week notice is well worth the admission. But when a bad employee flat out quits, there isn't much surprise.

That was me and the dull look on my manager's face when he finally found a way to replace me with some other smuck-young-fucker thinking this crack-ass job was the start to a beautiful resume and perfect opportunities ahead. Oh, the naivety at seventeen. At least it was for me.

Either way, you pay for the ticket, take the ride regardless. That dull fucking stare into oblivion, well worth the minimal effort I gave when I was a registered employee and then after. I didn't want it, didn't particularly need it anymore. Frankie and I had two of our own ladies doing the dirty dancing for us and it seemed to pay off every few days or so.

Our show was still up, and I was filming every angle possible. Abby was missed by many of our original fans, all thirty-two of them. But since then, we had a solid fan base of one-hundred and fifty-four Likes on our Facebook page, seventy-seven Followers on our Twitter account, over two-hundred and counting on our Instagram, and an average of eighty to one-hundred-and-nine subscribers streaming our sex sessions. The videos I posted online later would vary between views; some got under fifty while others saw over nine-thousand views. This meant the pay was never consistent, but the rent here was never much. And the two ladies we found never minded doing the work. In fact, just checking the other day, our 'three-way two girls on one guy' video got over thirteen thousand views in a matter of a week, earning us a whopping forty-three dollars altogether.

The ladies, Michelle and Amber, were decent enough. Nothing you'd see on the front pages of Vogue or the Metropolitan Magazine, but decent. Make-up made up for poor looking girls and the potential for male mates. They worked for coffee in the morning and a couple of dinner dates on the weekend. But they mainly worked for the pleasure of their own notoriety online, gaining more followers, likes, comments, hearts, shares, tweets, and subscriber. More than what we were engaging with on our own media.

But that was fine by us, we kept the money and they kept what they believed was something worth more. The attention of admiration by strangers.

Speaking of money, the real money was in the web shows. They often played on different themes, thereby reaching as many audiences as possible, and potential fetish finders that we could. Mondays were usually Strip/Fingered/Fuck Poker. Tuesdays and Thursdays, we took off on account of everyone but Frankie having school. Wednesdays were also another night off for homework and my video work.

Fridays, we kicked off the weekend with a nice slice of Pay to Play, a tier-leveled game of cards where paying a minimum of $1.00 won you a card. There were four different levels for cards. There was the $1.00 card, $5.00, $10.00 and lastly a $50.00 card. If a member was to pay, say, $100.00, they would receive two $50.00 cards. Some cards were duds, others included a half-minute hand job, a ten-second ass-spread, all the way up to a straight five minutes of sex in any position that the member requested. Some cards could be combined. Others, such as one where a subscriber wanted to use an ass eating with a ball licking just wasn't practical.

But there were never refunds.

Saturdays, we just kept to the usual "*the more we raise the more you see and the more these two do*". Some Saturdays were three-ways. For some reason, I never got on in the action. They "*needed*" me for the choreography. I would have argued otherwise, if it wasn't for the first video on the first night that Frankie had recorded. That piece of garbage alienated half of our audience at first sight, so we never went back. I got my share of BJ's, HJ's, and groping, but I never hit home base. I even got a foot job from one of the ladies, but I couldn't erase the fact that a dirty foot was wrapping its stink all over my private parts.

Sunday was a fun day and no pun was intended. We usually flipped a coin on whether it was a role-play night or an oral orgy. By orgy, we just meant a whole lot of different oral positions and places across the body. We've been discussing making changes to the name, but it didn't really matter. Even when a subscriber was misled onto our show, they were still led there regardless. And no matter how mad they were about it at first, they usually calmed into that euphoric sense of arousal that charmed all our snake-like audience members.

Porn, in turn, was a free enterprise that did not discriminate. It was never racists, sexist, nor did it ever segregate its audience. Sure, you had your up-skirt Asians and your neo-Nazi deep-throaters. But none of them could ever be taken seriously. We all travelled to those lengths of the internet in search of the same thing, a release. Because of that reason, we were all sort of the same.

It sounded familiar, *have I already said it*?

The trouble with drinking all day isn't losing memories from the day before, just the memories of many days before. Our attention is already split and confused by all matters of GMO's we feed upon in Happy Meals and microwavable dinners as college students. Hell, even as kids.

If the world's population wasn't naturally radioactive by 2028 then there would be a God and he would have sent a miracle down. Otherwise, we were all royally fucked.

Perhaps that's why my drinking picked up, because I knew I didn't have control anymore. I wasn't the one holding the sign, it was destined for me, already in my design. And had the grand designer cared, he or she wouldn't have built a liquor store two blocks away from my school, which was three blocks away from my motel. You could say it was in the cards.

That's what I've been telling myself, anyhow.

I finally decided to get out of bed. Looking over, Frankie was already out the door. I could tell because the room was silent, the steam from the bathroom was still sipping out from the door crack, and his bed was just an amorphous pile of sheets. Straight away I walked over to the mini fridge. Inside were leftovers filled to the brim and a half-emptied bottle of Bailey's awaiting the near-to-nothing pot of joe that the senseless prick left behind.

Drinking also made me angry and when you're already upset about your current living situation, it appeared that everything was made to piss you off.

Here it was, the daily schedule outside of my porn-based schedule. In the morning, around eleven to noon, I would drink a few good mugs full of black coffee with liquor. By the time it was one 'o'clock I was ready to really start my day.

I began with a couple quick shots of whiskey to get my head feeling all big and my dick nice and long. Most days it was Fireball whiskey. The flavor helped it go down my throat without that awful, clenched feeling. Later in the day I might stop by the bar, buy a shot from their God-like array of glass shaped and colored bottles. It really was like a gallery, except you could literally drink in the art and feel it too. By the nighttime, around six or seven, I was ready to either indulge in as many beers as my gut could hold or just drink straight from a bottle of either tequila or vodka, depending on whoever ran out on a liquor run the day before. Then I'd wake up and start the whole process over.

Sometimes I'd take a day or two off to recover. This break mainly depended on the hangover. Today's hangover was relatively mild, so I figured an extra spurt of Bailey's wouldn't hurt. I got on my laptop, always plugged in next to me like a lover. Always waking up next to me, always knowing how to please me. But today seemed special, as I opened my email I saw a reply from our dear friend over in Cali.

thanks for the links, i see you guys have really been working at this. give me another call tonite and lets discuss future business, ok?
-Jack

– 17 –

Hooking Up

JACK HAD CONTACTED US while we were still with Abby. He was the man that excited Frankie beyond possible reason, more than any amount of pussy could have. I, myself, was intrigued. So, we began messaging him.

He would always ask to see our work, and we would always provide it for him. In the past month, we built a bond with a man who we knew very little about but felt like we could trust. He was apparently big over in Cali. At times, he'd joke and say he was too busy finding "*models*" on Craigslist to bother with a couple of amateurs. But he said he saw something in us. That something, he referred to, was ambition. It made him feel young, finding us, talking to us, seeing our work.

Said he was getting rusty. He needed some inspiration and our videos did it for him. And among the emails he had sent to me personally, it was my camera work that caught his eye the most.

Frankie, he was your typical Jack rabbit. But I was fearless, he said I wasn't afraid to really capture what people wanted to see, to feel. That this business is a real art form, if you make it one. I didn't believe it at the time. But with enough vodka . . .

My silent stare at the email was broken by the sudden vibration of my phone. It was a calendar event reminder; I had a date with Kim tonight. Besides the alcohol, she was the only other stimulant worth keeping around. We had grown to know one another, even if I was buzzed for at least a good portion of it. We would have moved closer as a couple, if it wasn't for my paranoia. I knew she was my age and I thought she wouldn't have alternative motives. But ever since Myra, I haven't trusted a girl in the same way.

I have yet to return from that moment.

7:00pm – 9:00pm
Santiago Kim Date

What was the time difference between Colorado and California? Another miracle of the internet, conversions. Whether it was a Euro to a Dollar, or San Francisco to Denver, it was a lifesaver all the same. Something that we could have known in our heads, if only they taught us conversions of time, money, and the like in high school. But all we learned was standardized testing and preparation for college.

With California an hour behind me, I figured a call at around ten tonight would be nine from across the rocky way. I'm sure that Jack had the day off or something, it was after all a Tuesday. A school day for me, though I never showed up. Not anymore, anyways.

Even if I did, I'd be too damn drunk to pay a spick of attention to anything other than who'd make our model count jump up to three. An increase in employees meant an increase in production, which in turn would drive our profits higher. College was much the same. More students meant more profit, as if an education had ever been the priority.

Then my thoughts halted, as Frankie entered the room. I hadn't even showered, let alone dressed myself. But he was used to it, I was sure.

He gave me the usual smile and entered the bathroom for a quick piss. I poured myself another coffee and Bailey's, then made my way to my bag. No clean clothes. I hadn't done laundry in a week, and it was showing. My t-shirt rags and beer-stained jeans from the nights of picking fights at bars or simply overdoing it were increasing in number.

Yes, I fought. As thin and out of shape as I was, it made me feel like a *man*. But what was a man but a pile of lies?

Exiting the motel room, Frankie asked me "Date tonight, righ'?"

"Yeah, Kim again."

"Hoping this'll be the night, man?" It seemed like a sarcastic comment rather than an honest question. Alcohol tends to fuck up rational thinking.

But I had learned to control my rage around him. I kept silent at first, until I was ready to give a word back. "Let's hope." I looked over and grinned, gave him a wave as I entered the bathroom, into the shower and continued my day.

The next four hours consisted of sobering myself up for later in the night, getting my laundry handled, and being as right-minded as I could. Kim was great, she was wonderful.

When I was in high school, I I never thought about a relationship as a pursuit towards sex. But now that I had experienced it, been a part of another person and been deprived of it, seemingly it stuck to my mind. A cycle of obsession.

They say that sex can become an addiction. What useless folly. We're programed for sex. Reproduction had its repercussions. But reproducing without reconciliation formed the foundations for obsession. I wanted her. I just wanted her to want me much the same. I didn't want to be alone in this.

Hours passed and I met her at Santiago's, a small family-owned Mexican restaurant off the Broadway. She was as cheerful and cunning as ever. Like a fox, she had a slyness to her. Her positive cynicism turned the world into a joke, tomorrow's worries into today's pleasures. We had a perfect chemistry about us.

"You know, America has just adopted every other culture's best of. Like, this Mexican food. Sure, you got your men and women straight across the border cooking it for us. But it's not real. A burrito here is still just a burrito. But a burrito across the border is a tradition." She'd speak; I'd listen closely.

"So, what's your point then?" I joked, persuading her to take her theory further.

"I'm just saying, what do we own? What is ours; what is truly American?"

I thought for a moment, though I didn't need to. Speaking with her was like swimming downstream with the current, rather than against it. "Guns, war, and religion." I replied. That seemed to make her happy in the most curious of ways.

"Religion, really? You're a dork."

"No, no. Hear me out, kay? Of course, we didn't . . . invent Christianity or nothin', but we did take it. Then, once we had it, we manipulated its believers, gave them the freedom to cherry pick from the bible, and made our very own American-Christianity. A customized God for any individual, much like a-a . . . a Facebook profile."

She sat back in her seat as we were served, bent into the table towards me and asked me, "Is that what you think?".

I told her, "That's what I know." And we had a little laugh.

We drank a couple of Coronas and made our way back to her place. It was nice, being anywhere besides that shithole Essex Motel. I had never brought her there. I simply told her my house was dealing with some problems. She didn't bother asking questions after that and was fine enough keeping sacred.

Her place was a decent sized apartment near the downtown area. Two bedrooms, one bathroom, eighteen hundred grand a month. That was the best she could do with two roommates, the best that anyone could do who was a part of this generation, unless they wanted to end up in my living situation. Her roommates were out for the night, so we had time to ourselves.

On the couch we made-out. It was an old hand-me-down from her parents. Most of the other furniture was bought from the bottom of the barrel from good-willed stores and online sales. The popcorn was microwaved, though it only sat on the coffee table across from us. On the small, 20-inch television played some foreign film she happened to favor. And in my pocket, I kept a latex, dollar thirty-three condom.

Besides the condom, this reminded me a lot about high school. In another sense, it was my only protection from being hurt again. Funny, protection from protection in penetration. Who was I becoming?

Destined, perhaps.

"Can we go to your room, by chance?" I asked. Usually, I'd require a few drinks before asking a girl to make her way into a secluded location with me. I was playing with fire, and I didn't plan on crying if I got burned. I had a fucking death wish.

"Yeah, that sounds really good."

She took me by the hand and led me into her room. It was the smaller of the two, considering her roommates were coupled and shared the same space. Regardless, for a seven-hundred square-foot space, the two-hundred square-foot room we preoccupied was worth more than a hundred acres of land tonight.

I laid her on the bed and hovered over her. All she had to say was "*Hello*". I replied with a deep, impactful kiss, picking up her tongue with mine and sucking on it until I heard her first moan. It didn't take long.

Working my hands along her breasts, I made my way down into her jeans. Oh, the heat. There was nothing else like it, that moisture, the smell. I kept my mouth on hers so she couldn't fight back. Then, in a shift, I removed her jeans. They were tight, so working them down past her ankles became a challenge at her calves, and then some.

But I managed, and she managed to remove my own. I'll admit, I was so excited that I helped her remove my own clothes. I got tired of wearing them anyways. Her top came off much easier, and her bra snapped off as if I were untying my shoelaces. Then, as we cuddled and squirmed naked with each other, touching parts, arranging pieces, a thought came to mind.

All in consideration of her pretty, brown eyes.

The curvature that wrapped the bones around her flesh along her collar. That deep, concussive indented V-shape into her crotch. When would I ever have this chance again? Forgetting the condom, forgetting the goal, forgetting myself completely, I swept up from the bed.

In the nude, I pulled out my phone, changed it to the camera setting with the '*flash-light*' feature and placed my phone on a counter near the edge of the bed. Yet, when I turned back to face her with the condom in hand, stolen from my pockets during the phone fiasco, she was in shock.

"Wha . . . really?" She asked.

I figured she didn't have to ask. "Yeah, is that all right? We got some great angles and honey, you look magnificent." I tried with flirtation, but it only seemed to enrage her more.

She had nothing to say. In the light of my phone, I saw her cover herself with the sheets. She started crying but was still staring with those doe-like eyes. It was a strange feeling, being judged for what I've been making a living from. Suddenly she erupted, our feelings for each other finally ended.

"Get out . . ." she wimpered.

"What? But . . . but I just. Nevermind, can we just?"

"Get out!"

Without another word, I left.

Dressing myself, I watched her keep quiet underneath the bed sheets like a child hiding from the boogieman. Passing through her apartment I felt envious of the hand-me-down and on-sale furniture.

Then exiting through the front door, I felt sad. But there was a cure for sadness, and it came in the form of anger.

So, I erupted, yelling towards the heavens. I didn't care who, if anyone, was listening to me. I just wanted to speak, wanted to scream myself. Did I do something wrong or did the world do something wrong to me? What the fuck did it matter.

"Fuck! God-damn! Why, why always me?" I screamed, yelled, cried, broke.

This was my personal responsibility as a man, and I had failed more than myself. I began cursing, down onto my knees and slamming my fists into the hard concrete. It hurt more, now that I was sober, but it mattered less because of it.

Running over to my car I gave it a hard kick, bending the frame around the front tire. That made me madder. So, I threw fists into the air. I bit myself. I cursed objects that knew nothing of human emotion. I wished to choke on every word I had ever said.

Then the fucking phone rang.

I answered in an inhospitable hatred, "What!"

"This is Jack, where the fuck was my phone call, bruh?"

Was it really that late? Ten after ten, according to my phone. "Shit man, I . . . I just got into something."

"Something or someone?" He asked hospitably, with dark undertones exaggerating the warmth in his voice. "Listen, if this is about a girl then give her up. I got plenty of those here in San Fran. What you need to do is this, concern yourself with this business transaction and nothing more."

"Wha-what, what are you getting at Jack?"

I could hear his laugh through the speaker of the phone, along with what sounded like a girl politely laughing with him. "Getting at? Bud, I want you to join my business over here in the Bay. From what you've told me, you're stuck in a real catty place. And from what Frankie has-"

"Frankie, is Frankie invited to?" I interrupted. The conversation fell silent and I could hear him whispering to his lady to leave the room. "I'm sorry Jack, I didn't mean to-"

"Enough man, is coo. From what Frankie's be'n telling me, he's got two ladies and a cush ass rep at this motel he's been workin' up. What I'm tryna say man is, Frankie's got no drive. Frankie ain't up for this horror show business ma' man. To be Jack, Frankie isn't comin' along with us. But you, you got the eye, the drive, the need to be somebody."

He paused, the jittered, glitch-like sound of smoke blowing into the speaker emanated. "I used to be jus' like you bruh. Not knowin' who I was, always wanting somethin' better. With me, you'll get your women, you'll get your dope, and a hella lot of dough bruh. You just gotta' trust what'm saying."

The way he spoke, the confidence covered in a smooth sensation to his voice could have convinced the Pope to take a hit. He had that Californian vibe. Myths say that the entrance to Hell is somewhere along Interstate 5 across the west coast. Others say Hell is in the Hollywood sign, its aura manipulating people into West Coast wreckage. But anyone in America knows that the east coast is where the real nihilists live.

Then there was the mid-west, between the manipulative and the uncaring. The calm collected little squares of land in the center of a nation on fire.

Did I really want to leave this life behind? Wasn't my comfort more than just another commodity? And what about Frankie, my best friend in the whole world. Where would he be once I was gone?

"So pal, what's the answer?"

There was no time to think.

If I asked for another day or two to go over my options, I was sure he'd find somebody else. That, or the trust between us would break. But what else was I willing to break to get this break? Frankie, perhaps Kim, my family, my schooling. Abigale. It was, after all, Frankie who had first been contacted by Jack. Would it be betrayal?

I had to speak, even if my voice shook. "I . . . yeah. Let's hook up."

"Coo, keep an eye on your email tonight. I'll get a flight set for tomorrow, pack yo' shit and be at the airport on time. I'll meet you when your flight comes in, give you da' tour and that shit. We good bruh?"

This was it, chapter two of my current life.

"*Coo . . .*"

– 18 –

Californian Cocaine

MY FIRST KISS was in an elementary school park while I was a freshman in high school. It was an odd contrast. Her and I were with several friends, just swinging on the swing set or climbing along the other areas of the playground. We had been dating for about two months then. It took me an unusual time to figure out when and where to accomplish these average feats of human sexuality.

I recall us just talking, we had gone to school at this exact same elementary school. We shared memories, had reminisced over our favorited teachers and discussed little things like other classmates whom we've all but lost touch with. I remember her falling off from the swing and was just laying in the gravel, laughing to herself.

I got off and mounted myself over her real gentle-like. She asked a question, something simple like a one-word analogy for "What's next?" I wasn't too certain myself. But I lowered myself down to her, pressed my lips onto hers and kept them there for what seemed like the night.

It was much less a kiss and more so two people's faces pressed together. After I got up, I stared down at her. Awkward. She just laughed and pushed me up. We held hands on the way back to her place that night. Should I have been embarrassed? No, not in the least bit. It was sensual, regardless.

Nobody reads books in America. If they do, then they should consider themselves lucky. At the airport, I brought one of my favorites with me. A short read by George Orwell titled 'Animal Farm'. If I had read it in school, I probably would have hated it. But on my own, it provided wonderment.

On my own, of course, was a weak analogy of its own. I was surrounded by people, all types of people. Families and friends. Businessmen and janitorial staff. Police passing the aisles from time to time. I was almost afraid I had been turned in, as if the contents of my laptop were just as dangerous to carry as a pound of grass or a tab of acid.

And suddenly I wished I had a tab or some shrooms. Had anyone been on a psychological high while 40,000 feet in the air? In a way, I think that would end up as a bad trip no matter what. As people walked, they walked as I did, quiet and content with the chaos around them.

The line through the gate was smooth enough. Though, every five minutes it seemed that DIA was patting down someone for inconspicuous terrorism.

Lucky me, it hadn't been me.

The train below the facility that ran between different concourses was always a trip. The first time I rode it was at the age of five. There was always this section going through where hundreds of pinwheels were placed into the walls. You'd watch them spin furiously as the train passed them. There were also abstract shapes that seemed to collide together with the speed of the train. We'd tell ghost stories about these sorts of things as kids.

As young adults, we'd discuss the conspiracies of this train. The Nazi runways, where the runways would form a swastika. Then there was the military bunker meant to protect the most privileged from whatever aftermath came from the Cold War. And there was the fucking monstrous blue bronco that would greet you on your way towards the airport. I say monstrous because not only did it buck up with glowing red eyes, but it also killed its creator in some freak accident. And let's not talk about what hides between its legs . . .

Stepping off onto concourse C, I made my way to the escalator. The escalators here ran higher than most middle-class houses stand. Then, into the concession-filled, souvenir cluttered lobby a song came on that I was familiar with:

> "♪ *When I look at the television*
> *I want to see me*
> *Starring right back at me*

We all want to be big stars
But we don't know why
And we don't know how♫ "

A classic, if I ever heard one. I was genuinely surprised. Usually in places with many people you'd hear the next big hit from some top ten list that nobody who works for somebody came up with, based-off the best sellers for that month and nothing more. It all came back to money. How much money did this song make, how much did the airport pay for the privilege to play it and how much are you willing to fork over for it? Most of the time it was those big studio produced songs that exemplified sex, written full of false love, and met a half-standard to appease anyone listening.

For all of the songs written about love and sex, there was never much honesty to them. Ville Valo was a lyricist who grew up running a sex-shop that his father in Finland. He ended up writing eight albums worth of lyrics to love songs. Songs so deep and meaningful yet would never be aired.

These pop-artists, they were no better than your pay-per-view porn. A business that I was about to rationalize. Love, I was certain I could fictionalize.

At the gate, Denver to San Francisco, I had ten minutes on my hands to waste. I figured, why not waste them on Frankie. Before getting here, I made a list. I promised myself I would change my phone number the very second I could.

Next, I decided to put my trust in no one. Not even Jack. God, their names were bothering me. Why did I have to meet a Jack while knowing Frankie all my life?

Lastly, I refused to fall for another girl again. I was to keep clean, stay away from that trap. Getting laid was one objective, but falling in love was an obsolete concept now.

So, the phone rang, as it always does.

"Yeh . . . Yo, what's up man? You . . . you didn't come home last night? Still on for Friday night's stream? I got some great ideas for the-"

"Frankie, stop." I could tell that the bastard had just woken up. In fact, it was earlier than my own wake-up call of noon. It was seven in the morning. I was surprised that I was awake. Four shots of espresso usually did the trick.

"Listen and really listen to me. I'm not coming home."

"Wha-" I heard him respond.

"Frankie!" I yelled, as a few people stared over me. I wasn't embarrassed, this was business. "I'm not coming back. I'm leaving for California. Jack struck up a deal with me and he . . . He didn't want you in the way, in our way. I'm hanging up now, have a good life, Frankie . . ."

I thought to myself how heartless I must've sounded. Not a peep came in from him, a miracle if I ever hadn't heard one through the phone. "Frankie, I'll miss you man. I mean it." Then I flashed my finger into a red stripe that ended the call. That was the most I was going to give back. Perhaps the drinking had made me bitter. But right now, as it were, I just didn't want to deal with it.

I didn't need to be justified; I was still another innocent bystander of an uncaring world. Did I believe Frankie would care that I was leaving? All I know is that he'd care for about a week. A laptop with a webcam cost as low as two-hundred bucks. He'd make it, make it work.

Just make it work, Frankie.

Time had never passed so slowly, besides the other ten times I've mentioned it. Time was a variable that went uncontrolled. Yet, my destiny was understood.

I texted Jack that I was boarding the plane and that my phone would be off for a good while. Without a text back, I boarded. Traveling down the white, narrow hall with small windows like scenes for a last view. I felt my phone ring. I left it alone. I checked my ticket and it read like coding in a system I couldn't manage. As soon as the stewardess greeted me, I asked:

"Excuse me but, where is my seat?"

She lifted my ticket from me and gave a weak smile, as though wondering how a punk like me landed in first class. *First class*! Jack really had the cash to back up his business. I thought right away, sitting myself down into what I would consider the Lazy-Boy version of an airplane seat, what more could await me?

Beside me was a man in a full-suit, bright red tie, reading the latest from Times. To my other and across the aisle, were more men and women dressed the same. Business formal fiends.

Some of them probably worked for mince, while a few were actual Wall-Street hounds and stock hunters looking for the next big kill. They'd watch our investments, our retirement plans and welfare checks, and wait until one piece of the puzzle fell. And as soon as it did, like vultures, they'd swoop up the carcass and eat everything right down to the bones.

Even with the leanest meats. Hell, people buy bones online. Consider the skeleton of the entire market, the motherload for vultures like them. The sooner they pick apart the skin and muscle, string out the intestines and pluck away the heart, the sooner they can watch all of us collapse. And in the end, it was always their gain.

It's these continuous thoughts that kept me away from everyone. Everyone, including myself, and thoughts about what I was leaving behind. But in the end, I was editing my hometown. New beginnings were the latest versions of American freedom.

"Hey, how's it going?" A man said while placing his luggage in the upper compartment. For once in quite some time I finally could say I felt embarrassed, looking down at my single duffle bag. Funny, how my whole life could fit in a compact bag, zipped, and tied down between my feet.

"Hey bud." I responded, not wanting to be rude.

The man beside me was interesting enough, more so than any other person packed and cased in their one-piece formal suit. He wore a flannel blazer decorated in faded black, bright yellow and pale orange squares. His undershirt was some strange Hawaiian shirt embedded in differing shades of blue hibiscuses. Plain brown dress shoes that were crowned by the hair of his ankles, a pair of kakis that were a size too short. He had a long brown beard that looked mangled and long brown hair pulled back into one of those unbearable man-buns.

Regardless, he looked the part of an interesting character. More reasons for a guy like me to avoid him.

"I can't stand flying, gives me the bumps, you know? Goose bumps, of course. Being thousands of feet over land, could send any man into a septic coma if you ask me." He spoke again; I could see his hands watering as they gripped hard against both chair arms.

"Excuse me?" I replied, confused. "Septic coma? I think you're using the wrong word, man."

"No, no, no young man. I know what I said." He leaned in and whispered to me. "When you shit yourself so bad that it sends you into a coma . . ." He smiled and leaned back into his seat awaiting take-off.

I stared back into space, not knowing what to make of his comment.

If there's one thing I could tell you about flying, it's that driving causes 250,000% more accidents per year when compared to flight-based accidents. That isn't to say that it is still quite frightening to fly. But the worst part is the takeoff.

When the plane starts driving along the runway, it builds up this insatiable suspense. You know what's about to happen and there's nothing you can do to stop it. Then, there's the actual take off.

Imagine the world's longest, highest, and fastest roller coaster. Except, instead of feeling the inertia of the climb, all you feel is the fall. Of course, the plane isn't falling, but at the rate at which it climbs, it's probably the closest any of us normal people feel to being launched into space. Your head gets pressed back by sheer force, your body's organs seem as though they're being sucked into your spine, and the air tastes thinner. Only for a minute.

Even after the takeoff, the man beside me was tensed and clenched to his seat, while the other to the window was casually reading. After a while of silence and some music however, the man began to realize that the worst had ended. The stewardess came by with drink orders, on the house, with a mid-flight meal later. I asked if I could just live here for a while.

She laughed lightly before asking for my ID.

Then the man beside me leaned in once more, this time with an outstretched hand. "Justin Ables, pleasure to have survived that with you."

I reached out and shook his hand, my fingers nearly slipping between the sweat of his palm. "Nice to meet you, Justin." I said, waiting for him to look away before wiping my hand against my jeans.

"Say, where you head'n anyhow mate?"

I took a second before answering to shut down my iPod, knowing this might last a while. "Cali, the San Fran area."

"Ah, I see. Play in a band? Starting your own casting couch?" He laughed.

"In fact, I . . ." but before I could start, he answered for me."

"No, of course not, you're gonna' be a big Hollywood actor, eh?"

"Actually, Justin, I am starting a . . . well, you know. Porn business." I whispered the last sentence, not wanting John Doe beside us overhearing.

Then, Justin sat back and gave me a long, unusual stare. I asked him "*what*", when I meant to ask "*what of it*?" But he came in closer, again. "And that's what you want, right?"

"Of course it is, what a dumb question." My politeness had run out.

He smirked, "Okay, okay partner, no need to get upset."

But I had every reason to, as if a two-hour flight was long enough, this chump was extending the time by ten-fold. "So, what, you're going on some mission to help starving kids in Africa or something?" I battered and spat, returning to my music.

Yet, before the second headphone entered my ear, I heard him say "India, actually . . . You know, I use to be in the same business, kid."

My ears perked up, removing my headphones, I was excited and willing to listen. "*You were*?" I thought, "Where can I find your work?"

"You can't, well, at least not easily. I'm sure someone out there has copies of it. But . . . I put that in the past."

"Then how can I tell that you're not lying?" I asked, the stewardess soon returning with my drink. A classic Jager bomb, only without the shot glass in the cup. The Times New Roman reader by the window had some latte sort of drink, and Justin just sat with his cup of water.

He took the water down in one huge gulp, then showed me his arm. As the sleeve rolled up, it reminded me of a typewriter pounding lines of dialogue so quickly that no human could ever keep up with the reading. Line after line, imprinted on his skin. The arms of a Jewish holocaust survivor might have been impressed.

"This isn't your usual depressed mid-life crisis." He smiled a low smile. I don't think his eyes ever left me during our conversation.

"Ok," somewhat taken back by this man's honesty, "Got any tips then?"

Then, his smile grew larger than I'd ever seen. In two words, he put me on a plane ride straight into the jagged Rocky Mountains below.

"Get out." He said, then erupted in laughter, gathering the attention of others in first class. When a lifetime of waiting ends, is it considered an intentional death sentence? Perhaps I wasn't in the right mindset for such thinking, or listening for that matter.

Off the plane I hurried out with my luggage. Justin, unfortunately, was able to keep up with me, calling after me past rows of others making their way back onto land. I knew I couldn't ignore him.

"Yes, Justin? I really have places to be. This isn't your stop anyways."

"I know, but I got at least another hour before my next take off. Maybe you'd like to catch some grub somewhere quiet? I know this pretty decent tasting Indian place near gate twenty-three."

God, was he persistent.

"Not really hungry, thanks."

That's when I felt his hand reach my arm. I turned violently and gave him a look that begged more questions than I had to ask. But he must've noticed my distress, because his hand subsided and his body language became relieved. I could tell he didn't want to provoke me further.

"Hey, just in case . . . well, if things don't turn out how you want them."

"I said I'm fine." I replied. But his hand held out a business card that I was resilient in acquiring.

"Please, even if it goes straight into the garbage." He smiled. I hated that smile of his, it was something pure and honest.

When growing up around fake faces and masked individuals, this sort of courtesy was unusually mistaken for alternative intentions. Even then, I took it, stuck it in my pocket all crumpled and sorts, and turned my back to him. I had an appointment to make and I couldn't be late. I was ready to taste that Californian cocaine.

But the memory of his tattooed arm persisted. Like a stain along a blanket of courage. I couldn't help, on my way to the airport lobby, think about that damn tattoo and what it said. As if it were written just for me:

"A Better Man Was Once A Bad Man
But A Bad Man Can Be Good Again"

– 19 –

Joyride

EVER WONDER IF WHERE YOU ARE, whether in the present, past, or wherever you're going, consisted of someone getting off? In a way, it was natural for people to feel pleasure in otherwise unusual places. But if we were just cavemen again, would the location make a difference? It was dominance over distastefulness long ago.

As a growing boy, any destination was another desperate attempt to feel good, if only for a moment. Gas station restrooms on long family trips, hotel rooms in other states, swimming pool locker rooms, and even college stairwells. Not always alone, but usually alone. Sometimes it wasn't always me.

I'd turn the corner in my high school and find one-week long couples groping each other down some empty hallway or between bookcases in the library. The parking lot was especially scandal prone.

I recall a close friend of mine being taken to the principal's office one day. We all asked why, eventually, but it was those of us closest to him that were told the whole story. He had missed a class and there were serious enactments for doing so. His story was, he had been getting head from a girl during a car drive and he wasn't about ready to stop until she was finished. So, he drove her around in circles for a good while until they both decided to park and conclude *their actions entirely. The cost being an hour and a half's worth of Spanish education.*

Funny thing was this girl, Mariah, had been a good friend of mine since the start of high school. She was a sweet girl, a headstrong Latina-fighting type with a soft side for boys like me. Boys with swoopy hair dangling in our faces, tight jeans that everyone predicted would cut circulation off from the parts of us that mattered most.

Just a week before this incident she had been holding hands and cuddling with me in one of the main hallways. In the next moment, I had to decide who to stick with, her or my other close friend. Sexual division came in more forms than just whose genitalia matched whose gender identity. It was a device that could end friendships and alter viewpoints of people

I heard stories about cheerleaders sleeping with an entire team of football players. But when it came to a little oral fixation from one friend, who you thought you knew, sometimes you took it personally.

I saw him waving from his red convertible Lambo. Red leather suit-Jacket much the same color, wide Oliver sunglasses with pure silver rims with lenses that matched and a shirt tattered with images of 80's porno-magazine covers. Right away he felt like my split personality, everything I was hoping for in Cali. I wanted to call him Durden . . . but he was Jack.

And it was Jack's slick tongue and tempting wave of hand that had me transfigured. I threw myself towards the back door of the Lambo and attempted to open it. It was locked.

He laughed and told me to just hop over the door. Needless to say, I looked like an untrained lapdog confused by the hoop I was supposed to jump through. If there was a judge, I doubt I'd score more than a three on my first attempt. But that, he didn't laugh at. It was the mistake of acting like a righteous, proper Coloradan kid from the suburbs, that got him into that giggle.

"Finally, eh?" He smiled, wide grin. Teeth like diamonds if I'd ever seen them. His mouth could've bought out Shane Co. and their disgusting radio broadcasts on the daily. No wonder women could fall for him; he had 32 reasons. Buried in his gums were any woman's best friend.

"So, what's the plan for the night?" I asked, as we sped off, wind blowing where there was none. In fact, in the sports ridden, hatched down ceiling of his custom Lambo, we were able to make the wind blow in gusts.

"Really pal, straight to business, huh? Not wantin' ta' sit down, get a bite, get laid?"

My ears perked, "Oh?".

That made him laugh, so hard that at the red light the passengers next to us looked over. He gave them the finger and cruised right through the intersection, a car honking behind us. I'll admit, he seemed careless, but I trusted him like I hadn't ever put my trust into someone before.

Maybe it was because he was all I had here. I could barely rely on myself, after all. "Let's get some'tin to eat, eh? Burgers sound chill? In and Out seems appropriate enough. Then you can meet the ladies, we'll see you off to your room and business starts tomorrow. Coo?"

It must've been the translations in his three state-away accents. "Coo" I said, I tried. Seemed satisfying enough, and he didn't laugh, just smiled. The engine roared, the speedometer read eighty. He reached for the glovebox and pulled out a pipe.

"Wanna hit? Don't be a square man. I know all you mountain folks love the green stuff. We ain't much different here. Fuck, it should'a been me that moved out there." He burst, pulling a lighter from his pocket. "Well? Give't a light, square." He teased.

At this point, what choice did I have? I took the token from his hand, while watching him puff out his own cloud, adding to the atmosphere. But with every puff came ten enormous huffs, coughs, and convergences from my lungs.

After a single inhale, I felt my chest attempting to reject the insurgency of smoke and plasticity of THC invading my veins, crawling into the neurons of my brain. It hurt, the first cough. Then it hurt every cough afterwards, seemingly growing worse.

But during mid suffocation, I fell into midflight as the chemicals rewired my brain. A feeling of heaviness along my shoulders, but lightness under my feet. And with the hood down and a cool breeze blowing from miles across to where the coast lay, I felt as though I was a seagull finding shelter from migration in flight. I didn't have to worry.

Jack had the wheel.

Jack was in control.

Jack was in control . . .

"Yo, pal, pass that shit back." He stuck his words to my chest like a fucking dartboard in a Hell's Angels' bar. I thought, as I passed the smoking stack back to him, halfway through a red light, wow . . . So, this is bat country.

"Fucking bat country." I spoke, letting an invisible paralyzing mist of sorts take me over.

"Bat country?" He said, took a puff and laughed then replied, "Yeah, can't stop here. Too weird to live . . ."

"Too weird to die . . ." I laughed, I giggled, I felt free with glory.

I made it. My passion was taking flight. I was a new man and beside another man, we were driving towards destiny. Whatthefuck did I care about family and friends? I had a camera, I had memories to learn from, and I had Jack. I was au courant, ultramodern, original. All my hopes and dreams had finally met their crossroads.

Although I was alone . . .

"No, I'm not alone." And as I said it, I didn't realize it came from my mouth aloud.

"Alone? You ain't alone bro. We'll freeze this country under high waters. We got the talent and now, you one of them."

So, we hit the nearest burger stand. Something notable across every other end of the midwestern beltline. Something significant to those who have never tried it. A burger so good that it was recognized across state borders, across a thousand miles of American soil.

In reality, it was just another fast-food joint. With the same sad slack, sack, and shit kids working the register, and hopeless teenage slave-runners working over oceans of boiling grease and dripping sweat into the chasms of deep-fried fries and madcow patties broiled over stacks of crusted oils atop a plaque of scratched sheet meats. The same single-serving, with or without cheese, tomato, lettuce and onion-based service industry questionnaire. Add mustard, add mayo, add ketchup, upgrade meal size, increase price range, college-affordable, non-deductible, every-day-deal menu item with no coupon needed, that you see every day.

But it was food, deep fried and coated in grease, smothered in sauce, and as addicting as a needle full of heroine. After our order, we hung out around the parking lot, eating our burgers and smoking our dope. Nothing new or out of the ordinary in any context.

Reagan wanted reform, and what he got was a kick in the ass and a swastika across his forehead. What we got were cheap-ass hamburgers and fries, in supply to the growing nature of the lower middle class. I was one of them.

But not for much longer.

We ate our "*cheap-ass*" burgers and fries, then continued towards what Jack mentioned as "*The House*". It was the center of operations, it was the motion in control, it was the hard drive and backup, it was the pentagon of whores, milfs, teens, amateurs, sluts, blowjobs, penetrations, and creampies. It was everything that could turn you on with no off switch in sight. It was the high that kept on giving. It was the product of 28% of all popular and trending porn videos on the top ten sites in every country of any internet connection.

It was futuresex.

It was centered along Wealthy St., the Golden Brick rd., and whatever other analogies I could come up with. Two stories, five bedrooms, three bathrooms with a kitchen the size of a studio-sized apartment. The front side had more windows than a greenhouse, and everything was the color white. Pillars lined the forefront, as we walked on through the brick laid encasing into a front yard that was worthy of a country club.

Inside was lit by a chandelier so bright that a child of the third-world would've got down on their knees to pray to it, as if some Sun-God lived here. The entrance was a lobby, with a staircase that reminded me of "*Tony*" and his Colt AR-15. "*Hola a mi pequeño amigo.*"

Walking on through, the backyard was fit for an elephant, with a pool in the middle, garden off to the right, tool shed to the left. Tall green bushes guarded the bright red brick walls that ran higher than the horizon. Except for a glass doorway that led onto a porch built on the hill that the house sat. On that small porch were two chairs that looked over a small white picket fence, which overlooked the city far below.

"This is where we conduct business." Jack spoke, as I became mesmerized by the city lights. "This is w'ere we bring the new girls, and new boys. This is w'ere we talk script, w'ere we shoot shit, negotiate, make lingo, and fire any ass'ole not willin' to work."

"Ever film up here?" I said in amazement.

Jack burst into laughing. "If we ever filmed up here, than all of America would know where we 'ere and that's not what we want coo' cat."

"I think I get'cha." But I wasn't really listening, just responding.

Look at that fucking city, a million shining lights comparing with the stars. Colors confound to each stripe of the rainbow. At this height, I felt like I could fly. Then Jack nudged me, pointed with his palm aimed into the empty seat nearest me and I sat.

After he sat down, he opened a small chest that sat between us along the white entanglement of wiring forming shape within the circle around it. That French bistro set by Ethan Allan. Inside the chest was some of that Californian Cocaine. At least half a kilogram of that snow white, dressed in a satin bag stitched with Chinese oriental silk. He removed a glass pane with soft velvet rubber corners to keep it hung a centimeter above any surface. Then, with a small silver teaspoon he laid some against the glass, cut it with a razor sent straight out from its thin cardboard coat, cut it and then formed four lines. Handing me a golden rod, he asked me, "So, how dedicated are ya'?"

I took a long minute to focus, on him, on me, on the future. Then I decided to screw the fucking future. What comes is what lays ahead.

Nowadays, I just wanted it all.

"Very . . ." I replied with the strongest grin I've ever initiated. Then, in the heat of the night I stuck my face down to the first line. Took the gold stuck up my nose, inhaled a little bit of air, exhaled carefully to not blow the blow away, then snorted. I went down the whole line in less than a second, leaving a little behind.

Right away I pulled back, wiped my nostrils, twisted my head forth and forego. I pressed my pointer finger against the entrance and pulled out, looking at the insignia of blood stained on my fingerprint like ink ready to reach the form of paper that would have me sentenced for a half decade or longer.

Instead, I licked the discharge and gave Jack a look, as he presented his palm once more to three more lines like Great Kings waiting for their baby Lord to ascend and swallow the hate of the world. All for a paradise, but paradise was here.

Jack moved his own finger over my leftovers, pressed, lifted, and rubbed what was left along his gum line. I learned from this, as I snorted, shook, and consumed what was left. It tasted stale, tingled underneath my lip. Then I offered him the remaining two lines, not wanting to seem rude.

But as he replied, I got the idea. "They're yours pal, consider this a welcome gift. Just hold off on the next two for a bit. Don't need'a in some coma before day one begins."

I heard him, I listened intently.

My perception became skewed, everything seemed louder, livelier, like 400 grams of caffeine had just been inserted into my system.

"So, what's the deal Jack?" I asked, it must have sounded aggressive. But my focus led me to the table and I wanted to pick it up and smash it to the floor. Wanting to take it in my arms and throw it, along with its designer and all the inspiration they ever had, take it and watch it tumble down onto Hollywood Boulevard where all the rich actors, comedians, musicians, and others would see it. Then we'd see a new song written, a future joke told, an act commissioned or a memorial erected.

"Pay attention, kid." He said, drawing my attention back to what mattered.

He saw the confirmation in my eyes as they reached for his own pupils and we met in agreeance.

"Usually I have a role for a cameraman, an editor, and a' script writer. But you seem'a capable enough. So how'bout this? I'll give you a likewise pay for all three positions. Two thousand a shoot shoul'be enough, righ'?"

I was in shock and would most likely suffer from PTSD after this night. "Two thousand a sh-shoot?"

"Yea, don't even needa' publish it. We gots'a guy for that biz. We gots' everything we need here. I own three different studios, so we work with our own girls and get paid by other actors and actresses, as well as them directors for their own gigs. We got everything down to clockwork here, kid. We write, we produce, we finalize, we sell. We'll be published, and updated on social media. We got ourselves some hundred fake accounts that relay our videos across all corners of the internet. We have DVD's, Bluerays, MP3's, podcasts, conventions, and downloadable content.

All in 'are possession. There ain't nothing we don't have, that I don't own. And I'd like you apart of it."

"I'm honored." As I spat my words, I recovered. I took that golden rod and sniffed. Halfway down the line I began to feel that burst again.

Next thing I knew I was in a limo, finishing my line. Girls all around me, giggling, with Jack in the back just laughing, drinking, smiling, two arms around two girls. Two more surrounded me. I wasn't sure what was going on, I just finished another line along the breasts of some chick, and I didn't even know her name. I looked up and she smiled, pressed her lips to mine and I lapped my tongue with hers. After that, I drew in air and yelled over to Jack, "Where are we?"

He smiled, one hand groping a breast, the other in-between the legs of another girl. Like Sesame Street, we had women of every color sitting next to us. His fingers were moving on each, they moaned and wiped their hands against his chest, his crotch, his thighs. They gave him kisses along his neck, his arms, his hands, but he never replied with his lips unless he had something to say to me.

I asked again, "Where are we Jack?"

This time he seemed to hear me, and spoke from across the limo, "On a joyride." And he blew me a cocaine kiss.

Too Real To Be

IN HIGH SCHOOL, we sent notes to each other between desks. It took too much time to text a message, especially when we didn't have each other's numbers. We could draw pictures, use our own emoji's, say anything we wanted, and still be able to take it home with us. Tucked somewhere between our biology notes and algebra homework.

This girl, Christie, had an ethnicity that was somewhere between Philippine and Spanish. She had a medium complexion with squinted eyes that were not brown but blue. Dark hair flowed past her shoulders half-way down her back. She was a cheerleader. She had the same music taste as I. We exchanged times and dates to concerts we'd like to meet up at. We never did, but our messages remained within that Spanish class.

Another girl by the name of Laura wrote me a letter the day before Christmas during Winter break. She had been happy enough to had made out with me alongside her friend on the night before but wanted to remain friends. There were intersections of color, swirling lines, and neat quotes that referred to a secret language that only we understood. All written in crayons, hilarious.

Then there was Dee. Dee was short for Deana. She was Latina, quite popular with the half-time gangsters that fought outside of the Taco Bell which sat a quarter mile away from our school. She was short, obnoxious, but loveable enough. One day, she handed me a letter to read during my final class in English Composition. It read something like:

I believe I can trust you never to tell anybody else this but . . . I think I might be pregnant. I'm dropping out of high school. The guy I'm dating is abusive. Sometimes I cut my own vagina. It feels better than sex. I enjoy the pain more than the pleasure. I don't know what's wrong with me. I'm not ready to be a mother. I hope the child dies inside of me.

Waking up, I felt unusually hot. Rising from a pile of pillows with sheets draped across the room, I saw from my side the balcony doors had been left open. I couldn't tell whether the heat was storming in from the balcony or escaping through the vestige.

Then, as I attempted to stand, I felt a pressure holding my right arm near to the floor. It was a girl, one from last night in the limo. She was the oriental one, Philopena perhaps, with hair that flocked well below her shoulders. Hair strands so straight and sharp that you could cut an apple down the middle and tongue the seeds from its' core.

I tugged a tad harder and finally my force gave way. She let me go, but in doing so sent my hand flying up until I had smacked myself in the face, giving out a small yelp. My one, small F-bomb was enough to wake her in a panic. She pushed herself from me and threw her arms up in some sort of defensive manner.

"Please . . ." She half-yelled, half choked. Then, when the silence between us grew more apparent, she dropped her arms and looked to me. Those brown eyes were a landslide falling straight over me. "Oh, sorry. Bad dreams, I guess. But . . ." she spoke and slithered herself onto my lap, one hand holding her own weight against my leg while the other fastened fingers up to my lips. She traced my outlines with the delicacy of a mother. "So," she began again, using her tracing finger to instead wipe the sands out from the corners of my eyes, "how was your first night?"

"Ugh, uh, I . . . can't remember much, actually . . ." Cat had my tongue. I feared she was the cat. God knows what that tongue would be used for later today.

"Hey, there he is! I see where Kyra ran off to last night, no surprise really." Jack spoke, bursting into the room.

Kyra, in response, immediately stood up, pressing all her weight against my leg. Even for a petite young lady like her, that shit still hurt. That's something these romance novels, songs, and films never catch onto. How painful everything really gets, love or not. It only takes so long before an arm wrapped around a lover goes numb. It's only a matter of time until two people want to kiss and they end up swinging their heads into another. Even fingers grow tired of holding onto another's hand.

We got boy bands writing songs about never letting go and holding on forever. That type of lovey-dove-bullshit sounds strenuous and tempered, as if these band have never held a hand for longer than an hour, around a shoulder for a day, a kiss longer than a minute. These things we fantasize, they become immensely unfortunate after some time, like anything, the feeling fades. A fault of the nerves under our skin. Even sex can last for too long.

"*Fuck*?" I thought out loud, by accident, Jack staring at me as Kyra pushed him out from the entry way.

"You're a real dick, you know that, Jack." She said, her mouth moving an inch over his collar. As described before, Kyra wasn't very tall. But when enraged, she looked like a fire-spitting dragon. After she pressed on and out of the room, Jack came closer to me.

"Fuck what? Kyra? She gets wit' every new boy we hire on night one. Don't expect the same courtesy after today."

"Oh man . . . Is she, safe?" I asked.

Jack gave me a stern look, followed by a hard slap across the head.

"Ow!" I yelled, "What the fuck was that for?"

"I don' hire no street roaches nor pole whores man. What we got here is quality, is safe, is the best shit on the market. An' you were lucky enough to getta' taste, bro."

"I thought you said she sleeps with every guy on night one . . ."

"Enough man, we had our fun. Time to get to work, we gotta' busy schedule. At noon, we've gotta' girl on girl with toys, unscripted. Then at two-forty-five we're taking Rebecca to the other side of town for'a public car fuckin', different studio handl'n that affair. Then at four . . ."

"Jack, what. I mean is . . . holy shit man." I was astounded in absolute awe. "We used to make a few videos a week, not a few videos a day."

Jack gave me a look much like that of a disappointed father, then his voice picked up in volume, as if to say I was the beta scrap and he was the alpha, *so pay the fuck attention.* "This ain't your KinderCare crap from Colorado. We work non-stop, five days a week, take the weeken' off for relief, then get right back to it. You coo with that kid?" He spoke and I nodded my head. "Kay then, let's show you the equip and get started, we ain't much time left, already ten after."

"Ten after? Ten after what?" I got up, my head started swirling. I must've had more than just a few lines last night.

Jack smiled and gave a quick laugh, "Ten." He replied and left the room.

I didn't even know where my clothes were buried, then I looked down and noticed I was bare nude. I would have felt embarrassed if it wasn't for the migraine, joint pain, and dried blood clotting my nose.

During our drive we were accompanied by two ladies in the backseat. I asked if they were lesbians and they laughed, kicking their feet into the back of my seat. They told me "Don't be silly, we do this for the easy cash. Licking pussy hurts less than taking it in the ass."

Then, Jack jokingly reminded one of the girls that she had a scheduled anal shoot later in the week. She didn't seem so happy after that. In the meantime, Jack explained to me a few notable things:

One, although we shoot anywhere between ten to twenty videos, capture up to fifteen different galleries, and stream on a nightly basis each week, that the number of women one would see online in the porn industry is very small. But that fraction of a fraction of the world's population could fill a small country, nonetheless.

Yet, they still came in few and far between, the ones that were willing to do this *gig* that get the benefits of it. That wasn't to say that women or men are hard to find for these videos. But finding good ones that have character, composure, and the talent to make their audiences howl was another story.

He said to me, "If a girl doesn't cry after her second shoot, then she's a keeper."

Secondly, these women were expendable. Most never lasted more than four to six months before their audience grew tired of seeing them. For a cameraman like me though, I was indispensable. "A pussy can be easily replaced." He'd say, "But a good cameraman and editor is harder to find."

And third was the pay. Jack "*owned*" up to twelve different "*actresses*" and four different "*actors*". Each had a specialty, each was either a different race, gender, or age. And each got paid based on the products they provided.

Gallery shots ran low, only around five hundred for twenty pictures or so. Your regular man on woman videos ran anywhere between eight hundred to three-thousand dollars, depending on factors such as length, content, settings, and even stories. Man on man and woman on woman typically sold for less.

As stated, Jack owned three studios of his own, one in Sacramento, another in San Jose, and one down south in Los Angeles. The one in Los Angeles operated as a modeling studio for upcoming child models when it wasn't being scheduled for softcore, hardcore, and everything in between.

Sick, isn't it? Jack'd rent out his studios to others managing a different industry and use them for his own work later. Everyone who worked directly for Jack stayed in his mansion and paid five percent of everything they made for rent. Another ten percent for a manager's fee, and another ten percent for food, drinks, drugs, and so on. Basically, a quarter of everything I was about to make was going back into Jack's hands.

But I felt fine with it.

He still guaranteed a six-hundred-dollar paycheck per video, four hundred per gallery. What had I said before?

Why buy into a debt society, working nine-to-five service jobs, going to thousand-dollar classes four times a week minimum, competing with the paper quality of your degree to another mother-fucker who may be six-grand deeper in the grave than you? When you both end up with at least one foot in the coffin, one hand holding the nails. What did it matter? Drop out, get laid, and get paid, that's my moto.

"We're here. Cindy, Dona, we ready?" Jack asked with his head leaning, lighting a cigarette while facing me. His eyes were content and he lifted the corner of his mouth to reveal a smile that only I could see.

The girls nodded, he must've seen it in the corner of his eye because he gave me a wink with the other and turned to exit the vehicle. If you've never been in one, a Hummer is usually too tall for its own good. But not for Jack, who stepped down without worry. I made the leap and moved to the door to let Dona out, helping her down a step at a time. "Hurry up over there!" Jack yelled from over the roof.

"Ah, screw you, Jack!" Dona yelled back, down to the asphalt and pulling me to the side. "Don't take him too seriously, he's a good boss . . . mostly." She whispered, then pushed me away, looked over the hood and pulled me back in. I felt her ruby lips brush up against my earlobe and she said to me "Hey, make sure you get my good side, love." Then she gave me a kiss and pushed me into the door.

Giggling, she walked over to Jack and Cindy, Jack still asking where the Hell my dumbass was. So, I grabbed the camera, a Sony NXCAM 4K Camcorder.

It cost as much as four times the worth of my first car and shot video worthy of a triple-B budget film.

"Fuckin', get a move-on!" Jack yelled once more.

We were inside the Los Angeles studio, as the child modeling team was leaving the vicinity. They all shook hands with Jack, unknowing as to what was about to commence. In fact, all given, they'd probably be watching it the moment they got home. Funny thing about business, it boils down to a few important sectors:

Advertisements – *Before any video, 15 seconds or so of an ad, usually featuring Ron Jeremy or the like, would play before starting the program.*

Subscriptions – *Those who pay get the opportunity to skip these ads, to be notified of upcoming releases and get special previews of upcoming content.*

Sponsors – *Any great porn video requires a great penis enlargement pill or vaginal sensitivity medication. One or two secrets to perfect sex and so on.*

Merchandise – *Specialized and customized dildos, flesh lights, and blow-up dolls. T-shirts featuring porn-site logos. Bumper stickers for your car. Bluerays for your in-home surround-sound 60-inch television and the like.*

These factors combined created a perfect business, regardless of ethics. If it sold, then it produced assets, developing profits to conduct a wide range of entertainment to keep an audience attentive. Simple and short answer, you watch, you buy, we gain, and we keep producing.

In the porn industry, it wasn't hard. Not nearly as hard as the young men we made, produced, subdued, seduced. The women and their clits too. It didn't matter the race, the gender, the sexuality, the sex, the status, the position of a person in their life. That was the solution to profitability, as well as the decline of individual security. It didn't matter who, what, or where you were. Porn was and has always been malleable, ever since Marilyn Monroe stripped for the Playboy, ever since Eugene Pirou and Albert Kirchner produced the first ever erotic bathroom strip-tease. A Le Coucher de la Mariee.

Ever since the invention of motion pictures we've recorded our bodies naked, and vunerable. Ever since, we've recorded our mouths opened wide, breathing heavily, our bodies pulsating. Black and white to color film to 4K to 3D to virtual reality; anything but the real thing kept us wanting.

Nothing was different about this shoot. The ladies weren't attracted to one another, but in a matter of some smiles, some kisses, hand gropes, and licks across the chest, anything became possible. Funny how money could manipulate anything, right down to the sexuality and identity of an individual, even for thirty minutes or more.

A day at a time, it didn't matter. As long as the job was done, there wouldn't be another one like it for a week. And in that week, one could do anyone, be anyone, even themselves. If they loved passionate anal sex with the French kissing and ass grabbing, hard pounding, man on woman rather than woman on woman empowerment that they still controlled, they could have it. But in this one-thousand-eight-hundred seconds of screen time, they still had to pretend.

It was a gyre of hypocrisy. Yet there I was, capturing every angle, making sure to show what was rarely seen from any person's point of view. The downward point, the backyard scene, the penetration, deprivation, elimination of personal perception. It all became an elimination of process, destroying what we saw and turning it into what we wished we could see. Two mouths breathing into one another, two parts rubbing erotically from one side, an orgasm in a fish-eye lens, a subsiding climax brought to you in black and white. Then color coming back, just as the girls came again, and again, and again . . .

The next shoot involved some made-up scenario between a cab driver and a "*local tourist*" convinced to fuck in the backseat for a free fare. Jack handed me a bag of white powder as refined as the sugars produced by the third world people who slaved away for coffee companies like Starbucks and Imperial Sugar. I snorted two lines and was ready for whatever came next.

At first, I was placed inside the vehicle, strategically positioned so that the camera would not catch me. But soon, as the undressing began and the penetration started, I was moved outside. Through the windows, like a protentional voyeur, I captured intimacy that had no substance. On the inside along the leather seats, I zoomed in on the penis entering and exiting the vaginal walls. Closing in, opening again, just like my shots. In the end it was simply reproduction. Everyone did it, everyone wanted it. Nothing new nor different, nor wrong about what I was doing.

Right?

Right.

So, another sniff of that Cali-Coke and a blunt of Jack's best, I was ready for another shoot. This time we had a script. A popular one at that.

Babysitter caught masturbating by an older sibling. The two began to screw on the couch, on his parent's bed, then in the shower. Father comes home early, now it's a two-on-one. The actress got paid extra for an anal creampie, while the other man, supposedly the son, got to cum on her face. Good enough, the check was written and we were on our way.

During the car ride I recall her asking if we had any wipes hidden away. She should've asked for a butt-plug. But Jack came prepared. I became Jack's mental image.

I wanted to be the help, the support for these women, simply because I wanted to control them just the same. I knew I'd never be in the same scenes as them and their men, women, and everyone who identified as something else. But I at least wanted the excuse. A reason for coming inside of them, cumming outside on them. Being inside, like a mother's womb, like a warm, comfortable tomb. Like history rewriting itself. I wanted to be there; I wanted to be . . .

One last act for the evening. We picked up Kyra and headed to our studio up North in Sacramento. A simple gallery shoot. The set was supposed to be ready by the time we arrived. Yet, even with all the money in the world, things sometimes never go as planned. The set team was behind schedule and we were left waiting. In the meantime, we smoked some drags, snorted a couple more lines, and shot the shit together.

"Liking it so far? Bet'cha never seen as much pussy as this before." Jack exclaimed, aware that nothing could compare to the absolute absurdity and complexity that was capturing naked bodies interacting on digital film.

"Hah ah . . ." I excluded, letting the feeling of energy and anger enter me through the white, extracted substance. It was pure. I became pure.

If God was cleanliness than I was the Devil in disguise. Dirtiness embodied, selfish and concise. I wanted it all for me, nobody else. I'd finally fuck the world, every person who ever screwed me over. My family, my friends, they meant little to me now. "If only some ov' those pussies would fuck me back, I might be a fraction happier."

Jack sneered, as if he'd heard it all before. "They ain't on camera cat, so it's all up to you. On their off time, they might be willing. But some ov' em', after a whole day of fucking, might be sore and dissatisfied. Be careful who you choose and ask kiddo."

Then the set was complete. Some home and garden décor with a brother and sister scenario. Whoever wrote these scripts was simplistic. But thinking about the average community of individuals who listened to Lil Wayne, Beyoncé, Eminem and Drake, it didn't surprise me much that this stupid shit ever took off into the hundreds-of-thousands of views into the millions and more.

Simplicity was the greatest secret, left in the open for all to see. Idiots, morons, degenerates, and even geniuses flocked to what made them feel good. That was me, the good now existing in the world. At least I felt good, huffing, puffing, inhaling and exhaling flavors and faults. I was the disease, but also the cure. I was the purpose behind the flesh. I made what could be seen and turned it into fantasy.

At eight P.M., we travelled to another studio that we did not own. It wasn't customary, but it was business. Like politics, you must keep a good standing in the world to mask and make it seem as though you had the right intentions all along. Nobody knew, nor suspected, we had sponsors from fast food chains, independent video stores, and sex shops across Hollywood Boulevard and beyond.

Sinners and saints, we all felt the same compulsions, impulses and oh . . . it was so natural. This time we had a priest, with a young male joining us. Of course, he was eighteen and older, but the acts he performed and the things he said were beyond any fictional thirty-year-old boy. All in a day's work, I thought, as we ended the night and travelled back to the mansion.

Once again, Kyra came to visit me. I asked her how I was the other night.

She responded with, "Well . . . you were pretty out of it. Could hardly keep it up. But you were so passionate, so sweet. You wanted to hold me, cuddle with me, talk to me. It was all too sweet; I couldn't help but give you all I was."

I told her I was confused.

She told me to shut up.

In the morning, I found her wrapped around my arms again. Only this time the bed had been made, with the sheets entangled around us, pillows still lying beneath our heads. Something else much more organized. Jack entered, awoke us, it was half-past Nine. More shoots, more scenes, more scripts. Kyra exited, this time with a kiss on my lips, and a slap to Jack's chest.

"Love, kiddo. It doesn't exist in this world of ours."

I shooed him off, showered, got dressed, brushed my teeth, combed my hair. I entered the living room to grab some grub and then we left. Three girls this time, in the backseat of our Hummer H2 SUT. Today we only had two video shoots: Man on woman scripted scenario, poolside water boy, sun-tanning single. The other was unscripted, full-on penetration with a nut-on the back at the end. Not a special day, quite boring in fact.

On the way, I thought about the trends. Watching the fads permeate. It was hip to care, and to hate it. From hairy to shaved, fat to fit, public to voyeur to amateur to teen to old to anal to creampie to outdoors to indoors to threesomes and foursomes to orgies and gangbangs to singles to mothers to brothers and sisters to daughters and fathers to friends and strangers. Sets and stages back to amateurs at every angle. It was all inside of our power, and we gave it all to give it all back, for a price.

And you're right, I get it.

You're perfect on screens in pixel format. Let's assume we're right and not wrong. Let me make amends. But don't give us your sad, sad trip. It all makes sense that you're the perfect person. Let's live this imaginary life.

Ever think that feminism, equality, and the support for such things has led to the thought process that everyone is beautiful? And, in assuming so, we can make a profit from any sort of individual.

In fact, it would be wrong to exclude the midgets, the immigrants, the retards, the transgendered, the disabled and so on. Everyone was perfect, *is* perfect, as long as they make *us* a profit. And if they cried, just give them some medicine. And if they say no, convince them otherwise.

With Benjamins and cocaine, weed and molly, dancing each weekend and smoking dope in between sessions. Let's not focus on the pain of showing ourselves to thousands through a webcam. A broadcast centered around our holes and holy parts. Let's focus on that money, that buys us that Cadillac, that supports our spending, that earns us that Gucci belt, that wins us that vacation down south to the Carabine.

Why don't we focus on the future rather than the present and the past? What else could matter more, retirement and longevity? Tomorrow is another day; we've been taught to learn from the now and apply to the next. Not the next month, year, or decade, but to what our future says is our duty. Dental, vision, healthcare, outside provisions, making a living.

Whatever your parents told you to do was probably correct. They just probably never told you how to hold on to an accomplished task. Only how to reach it.

If you look at our second video of the day, it explains it all. Want retirement? Want dental, physicals, vision and those meager provisions? Take an eight inch up the ass and it won't matter. You'll be halfway to a proper savings account in no time. College loans become pennies to the dollar. Full time positions are just jokes. In this business, you just give up your body, your sanity, and a likelihood that you'll never leave. Then, within a few years, you'll be made a King or Queen.

These were some of the first lessons I learned as the day rolled into night. I would stare, focus and crop an area of footage that wasn't appealing. Make sure the white balance was in check, that the audio wasn't too low. If I wasn't filming genitals into other genitals, then I was filming fake kisses, a passion for fashion's sake. It was all derogatory.

It was all meant for one thing.

Then, when Kyra walked back into my room, I knew for certain it was all for the same thing. Pleasure, away from the pain. Purpose, derived from insanity. Addiction, made clear by the see-through glass bottle of liquor we drank. It was all as if it were mandatory.

I was all but explicit and exploited by it. My life had changed, but I wasn't sure who had changed it. Frankie and Abigale, Jack and Kyra, or the business itself? Or I, compelled towards it. The dreams I had that night, of a simple life, became wholesomely unrealistic.

– 21 –

Lamborghini Blues

A FRESHMAN IN HIGH SCHOOL, I HELD MY FIRST HAND in the dark seclusion of a movie theater. It took about an hour and a half of a two-hour show before I got the guts to do so. I remember being so eager, always looking down at her hand.

I'm not sure if I even watched a moment of the movie past the first act. What mattered more was resting to the side of me, along the armrest, and creeping closer in. I recall it being very sweaty . . . That relationship lasted about a week.

At the beginning of Sophomore year I had an old friend from elementary school turned to girlfriend, respectably. It started as an awkward guessing game of who liked who. Like picking petals, which I probably did numerous times. I turned a whole field of daisies into a dirtied parking lot just to know if she felt the same. Three months this time. Want to know how it ended? Refer to Chapter 18 and add a month onto that night, and you'll catch the cold drift of that winter.

Then finally, as my sophomore year came to an end, I found myself with a girl whom, in all teenage consciousness, I never thought would be the one. Not, of course, "the one", but "one" of the "ones". What I'm trying to say is that I fell in love for the first time in my life, truly.

It started in marketing class, me being a sucker for Asian girls, introduced myself right away. She didn't seem very interested at the time. In all honesty, I can't recall how it worked out exactly. I just know one day I was invited to her house. We watched The Pursuit of Happiness featuring Will Smith and his son before the daddy issues began. Then, when summer break came around, we found ourselves hanging out on every day possible, riding bikes to and from our houses. I spent more hours with that girl than I ever have doing actual homework.

A cool summer day came about, and we ended up in each other's arms in a school playground. Funny, just along the other side of the school yard would be thirteen-year old's taught by eighteen-year old's teaching ten-year old boys and girls how to smoke fags. And above us, there would be a kite sailing by. We just lay in the grass silently for an hour or so, until the sun started setting and she asked me a question.

"Hey, are we . . . just friends?"

I wasn't sure what to say, or how to respond. Obviously, we both wanted something more. But I didn't want to be rude, didn't want to seem too forward or aggressive. I just . . . just wanted to lie back down in the shade. Instead, I made an average teenage mistake, average blasphemy for an average idiot like me.

"Yeah, we're just friends." I replied.

We didn't hold hands nor kiss in the playground for the rest of that day.

I felt sick. "Fucking headache, damn . . . God damn, hey!" I yelled. "Keep the fucking music turned down . . ." as I was holding on to the aching in my skull.

Kyra awoke beside me in another one of her panics, something I had grown use to for the months that I had been in business with Jack. She reached around and laid an arm over my abdomen. "Hun, there isn't any music playing."

"Wha . . . Bullshit, then where is that sound coming from? Why is it so damn loud?" I didn't mean to sound so distressed, so worried, so upset. But this headache, like taking a bowling ball to the forehead, something I had experienced on a date, straight to the skull. The blunt force of just sitting up kicked my ass right back down into the sheets.

"You must'a taken a little too much last night." I heard her say, although her voice was muffled and nearly mute.

"You're one to talk." I replied, as I felt a pillow smack me in the face and I watched her storm out the door. "You're just mad 'cuz I'm right!" I yelled, soon finding that it was my own loud voice echoing in my head, like some dumbass mut barking in a corridor of empty thoughts.

"Fuck, it better be Sunday."

Eventually I got out of the bedroom, crawled down the stairs and saw Jack still shirtless in a pair of sweats. A real indication it was still the weekend. So, I calmed down and grabbed some cold pizza from the night before. Jack said his usual *"Mornin'"* followed by a dry snort. I sat down, head still pounding, Kyra nowhere in sight. You could see the living room clearly from the bar area of the kitchen. A couple of the other ladies were watching some MTV Reality garbage on the household's sixty-inch television.

"Can't wait till them birds leave, then'll it be game time with ma' sweet Playstation. Wanna' join, little World War two shootin'?" Jack asked. I wasn't the only other guy working in this dig, but he treated me better than the others, like a mentor of sorts most days.

But in my current state, there wasn't a chance that I could stand stereo surround sound gunfire and flashing with bright 4K lights. "It's Sunday today, right?" I asked, ignoring the question in hopes that he wouldn't ask a second time.

He laughed before telling the two other ladies to keep the volume down. "Pal, it's Saturday, where you been?"

"Saturday? I thought yesterday was Friday?" I said, drifting off into a complete comatose of exhaustion and nausea again.

"Nah bruh', that was the day before, today's still Saturday. Hitting the coke a bit too hard, eh?" He knew, I knew it too. "At least you ain't at Kyra's level yet. That girl's gonna drive me up the wall soon. She was a week late with rent last month."

I woke up from the coma; my face had planted itself into a pillow of pepperoni and cheese. Wiping myself up before Jack could see, I replied "Really? How's that possible?"

"Kid," He'd begin with that stern tone of his, like stone rubbing against stone "she ain't the first. Won't be the last. Some girls' round here, they need a lil' somethin' more than booze and powder to keep themselves feeling clean."

That period at the end of his sentence solidified the issue. The less we asked, the more the issues resolved themselves, one way or another. "I think I'm going for a drive today, Jack."

"Suit yourself." He replied, taking himself into the next room and laying straight across six legs of three beautiful women who all cried out in annoyance.

"*Jack!*"

It took a moment, a minute, maybe two, maybe ten. I had little expectations for myself, hardly being able to count the days, let alone count the time I spent huddling over the toilet puking. Combing my hair with a bit of cold water splashed up onto my face. Spraying myself down with a manly perfume. I didn't have time for a shower, it would feel better at night anyways.

I was in a heat-stroke from the coastal breeze, so humid and warm like a fruit rotting on the sidewalk of some hundred-degree street corner of Tijuana, Mexico. Jeans on, one leg at a time. Button up shirt, royal purple. I took a swig of mouthwash through my now burning gums beneath my teeth and spat. Making my way to the garage I spotted her, my real lady. Angry red, sharp as a dagger Lambo, Aventador 12-15 model with the works: Side diffusers, rear wing, wide fender, reinforced for safety.

The second that garage door was raised to the top, I sped out as if a green light just signaled. Who was I racing? I was racing myself.

I sped down those winding roads to the main streets, so fast that the sound of my rear wing cutting through the light breeze sounded like a jet streak painting through the sky. At the first red light, I laid out a line, snorted. Green light again, I rode off. Traffic along the freeway was a still-frame. Other cars around me might as well have been obstacles never moving as I crisscrossed my way through the lines of people. I became the asshole driver I always hated. Now, everyone hated me and I adored it. I was the road; I was the fire.

Walk with me.

Windows down, stereo blasting, destination nowhere.

As I flew, I wondered many thoughts. Where did Kyra run off to? *As if I really cared*. What was our next shoot supposed to be? *Didn't matter in the moment*. Had I edited our last video, scheduled it for today at noon? *I guess I'd find out as soon as Jack called*.

And the most important question of all, where was I eating? Where any Californian would go: Out-N-In Burger. It wasn't perfect, in fact, I preferred Lucky Devil's. But Out-N-In really spoke to me on a level that only a porn-producer and editor could feel. I wasn't a tourist; I was the fucking crowning achievement to this city. From Denver to Cali, I was reborn.

I had become a cannibal of sorts. Every video shoot, every girl, every angle. Between the butt-tocks to the breasts and between the legs, I ate it all up. I was addicted to the scenes and sweats, the ten-grand a week on average or more. Sometimes, however, an eight-dollar burger with fries and a drink was enough to quench the hunger of an undertaker, taking in all the sex and burying it into the internet's archives. Smelling pussy, smelling cum, it sometimes rubbed off on you like the smell of a butcher in a meat factory. It was never flattering, but you grew used to it and it was the cheesy, moist, that beefy smell of a burger that reminded me at times that I was still like everyone.

Although, I only felt human sometimes.

But I wasn't really, was I? Why do I always ask the obvious, of course I wasn't human. Strap a camera to my forehead and put me in the bedroom of every virgin, whore, prostitute, mother, daughter, father, uncle, brother, friend, stranger. With me in that bedroom I'll be capturing you like the discovery channel's hiding in the bushes nearby. I was looking for professionals. Professional teens, professional amateurs, professional porn-stars and up-in-cummings alike.

I wasn't much of a poet back then, guess I never found that muse. I was as straight as a crooked arrow that landed somewhere near the bright side of the barn. But if I had to, I'd write something like:

Cocaine high got me flyin' like
Doves in the sky, doves of a wedding party
Became my party, birthday party
Jumping into my birthday suit but
Still singing my Lamborghini blues.

There it goes again, some sick carousel of questions. What was it, exactly?

I had the money, had the car, had the girls, had the career. Yet, sinking my teeth into my perfectly cooked, medium-rare burger, lightly salted fries, and fizzing soda, I still felt empty. Not completely, it was like a pit in my stomach.

No, higher.

In my heart?

Perhaps, or perhaps, it was up in my head.

All in my head like some mental illness had inflicted me. Could I use a Ritalin, some Adderall or a sample of some Dexedrine? Maybe I was misdiagnosed. Perhaps I needed an Abilify, Risperdal, or Effexor. But maybe another burger would do. You're never quite full when you're a drug fiend. There was the answer, right in front of me. I had all the medication I ever needed. Enough to kill a full-grown white-back male gorilla, and then one more.

I thought about my favorite idols on the way back to the place I called "*home*". Each and every artist, musician, and other that had inspired me, that I knew would never give a fuck about me. They would never know me and, in any situation, most likely wouldn't want to. Who was I but a Grinderman? I wasn't the inserted, the penetrative, or the penetrated. I was the reason for sixty-four million eyes watching porn a day. At least I had a reason.

It wasn't even a minute before Jack called me, when I pulled back into the garage. I pulled in, noticed my gas gauge was near empty. I'd have to fill it up on my next outing. In a way, I was hoping Jack was gone. I liked him. But somehow, I always knew when something was up. That straight face, squinted eyes, combed back hair and bawled-up fists. He was serious about something.

"Wha's up Jack?"

"Close the damn garage door next time." He started, walking over to me and holding me by the shoulders as I barely gained my balance after exiting my car. "Listen, need a man with me tonight. We got some business down in Escondido."

"Escondido, you're serious? There ain't nothing out there but rural houses that all look alike. Plain, boring, typical." I responded, but Jack just tightened his grip.

"This's serious mate, I got a job to do tonigh' and I need someone I can trust beside me. Can I trust ya'?" He asked.

All these questions, I should've bought one more burger and fries. "Yeah . . . Yeah Jack, you can count on me."

"Good . . . good." As he wiped the sweat from his brow. Something was happening, a something that I didn't like not-knowing about.

"What camera should I bring?"

He looked at me as if I were a child. "We won't be film'n nothin'. This thing's serious." He spoke, pouted, blinked once, and walked towards the door before adding, "Nine'o'clock, we leave at nine bruh'." Then he left the garage, disappearing for a while.

I stood there like the last tree breathing air in a suffocated planet. I guess that's a bit of an exaggeration. But when the coke cuts off and the booze leaves the blood stream, then it ain't far from truth. I knew what I needed to do.

Get to my stash in the drawer next to my bed, maybe get one off with Kyra before nine came around. Although, looking at my phone and reading the clock from the double-vision blur of neon numbers in, I knew I didn't have much time.

She was in the room, the usual. She must've just returned from a shoot; I could tell because of the lipstick smeared and legs tightly crossed in pain. Must had been a large cock or a long day's work to get her to double over from under the waistline like that.

As I entered, I heard her yell something along the lines of "*What the fuck?*", "*Where you been?*", "*I've been so worried.*" and "*I need a hit.*". Kyra had become somewhat of an oblivious addict at this point.

It wasn't subtle nor was it hidden from anyone. I could tell by Jack's tone, whenever he spoke about Kyra in any way, that her opiate attraction had turned vile. Before it acted as a medication, something a doctor would prescribe with side-effects and all (*chance of death, chance of stroke, possibilities of internal bleeding, depression, anxiety and the realization of our inevitable end*), but now it had become a crutch. Couldn't blame the girl, walking into the room with her half-heartedly tearing over the sheets. When someone chooses to mate with strangers, one does not choose where their soul wanders off in the process.

"Take a hit with me, please?" She sounded so sweet, so pitiful.

"I'd rather take you on." I replied, for once not as interested in the drug of choice and rather the drug that gives until you die. That vaginal-drag called ecstasy, except it was all-natural. Though she didn't seem too amused by my smart mouth this time around.

"You know, I just asked if you wanted a hit. And maybe you'll still get one, right to the fucking cheek." She snarled.

"Hey bitch," I didn't mean it as much as I said it, "I'm not in the mood, kay? What's got you so worked up anyhow? You hungover? You relapsing?"

I saw the pillow fly by my face. "Fuck you, fuck you, fuck you!" She was really at it as I watched her throwing fists into the mattress.

For a woman, she seemed like she could lay a good wallop onto a guy, and for a minute I genuinely felt terrified by what may come flying my way next. The alarm clock, the lamp, a five-fingered felony. They'd probably still arrest me under suspicion.

She dropped back onto the bed and shed a tear that was quickly scooped up and smothered against the sheets. "I've had a rough day, kay? Had to get my asshole bleached, nails done, haircut, eyebrows plucked, and a load of other things before I'm able to start shooting again."

I had become Jack's sense of apathy.

"Well, don't take it out on me." I spoke, sitting beside her, helping her with her sleeve. "Let me handle that." I said, laying her head onto the now pillow-less bed. I took the needle, like murder between my fingers. I plugged her in the vein and watched as she sucked it dry like a baby sucks a tit. Her eyes closed and she was gone.

And injecting myself, so was I, until . . .

"Cindy!" I called, coming down the stairs. When Kyra got this way, I always found an alternative girl. They never liked it, always wanted to be treated like more than a plaything. The second I joked I could grab the camera for them was the moment they just gave up and gave out.

"Wake up prick." Was what I heard next.

Did I black out? I didn't think I was that drunk, nor high or anything else. Was it the sex or just exhaustion? Fuck, did I even have sex? The days had been blurring for weeks now. It appears they're becoming hours, even minutes.

"Hey, woah . . . Jack, hey. Wha . . . what time is it?" I asked while half asleep.

"Time to get your dumb ass moving." He said, exiting to stage left.

I got up, nothing but underwear on. To stage right lied Cindy. I knew I must've gotten something for my time, looking across the flowery lacing wrapping around her buttocks, that string-wide thong tucked up between her cheeks as she laid lazily on her belly in bed. I had never seen her so beautiful, not between

183

takes nor scenes on camera, or in audio files of moans, screams, and panicked breathes. Cindy, sleeping nearly naked peacefully in her bedroom was more serene than anything I had filmed yet.

That just meant I needed to perform better.

Downstairs, I was at the car. Jack rushed me to get in, so I slammed the door and didn't mind the seatbelt. I just said "*Go!*" and we were off.

He gave me some sh'pil about a schedule, being on time and whatnot. It was only a quarter past after all. Although, judging by his stern, affirmed facial expression that lacked any emotion beyond contemplative corrective absence, I was certain that whatever we were about to do was a serious affair.

More than any ten to thirty-minute video. Even more than a twenty-one plus photographic gallery. This wasn't about a girl he had contacted through Craigslist to do a one-off. When he threw me a pack of fags, I knew he wasn't joking around.

That's when we stopped at some forgotten Hollywood production studio and he handed me a ten millimeter, Glock 20 fitted with a generation four extension, custom leather grip, red-dot sight attached to the barrel and a custom skin-slide, I had more of a feeling of what tonight meant.

"Stay in the car coo' cat, I'll only be a minute." he said before stepping out into the darkness of some blank studio.

And there I held the gun, high on snow and ready to pull that trigger at any single mother-fucker willing to take a bullet for their life. Funny, I recall something about this being a federal handgun. Looks like gorilla-warfare is still well alive and sold at a chain-retailer near you.

The gun got boring fast. It was terrifying, having such an object at hand that could end a life instantly. But after that promised minute, it became twenty, and the gun grew less exciting in my hand. Instead, I just started smoking, laying my arms out of the window, my chin holding up my head from my arms as I lazily dragged in and blew out large puffs into what seemed like a cold night in Cali.

By the half-an-hour mark I had smoked about half the pack, covering the asphalt against the car's wheel in ashes. I went back to the gun and practiced my aim at random items along the area: a strutting antenna atop a building, a broken window to another studio, something that moved that I could have sworn was a racoon.

Then I argued with myself whether or not the Glock's safety was still pressed on or off. I didn't want to find out the easy way. Then again, finding out the hard way could cost me my life. I simply put it back down and went back to smoking my cigarettes.

As my legs were starting to fall asleep, that's when I stepped out and leaned up against the car door and lit one more. Forty-five minutes now, I know because I had been counting each minute since Jack had left.

My phone illuminated from the depths of my pocket every sixty-seconds without fail. I thought I had been anxious, remembering my shaking legs as Jack had first left the car, with me chittering about in boredom, a different type of anxiety. The stars above were pretty and also pretty useless. Couldn't do nothing but see them, not touch them, taste them, feel them. I was sort of like the stars.

"Hey!" Jack called from a distance, quickly closing the gap between us.

"Hey man, what took you so long? You said just a min-"

He held me by my collar and nearly pressed his forehead into mine as he spoke firmly "Yeah," his spit kissing my lips, "I also told you to stay in the car. Didn't I!"

I wasn't sure what was going on. It all seemed so sudden and so unnatural. I think I felt a shiver down my spine, a quake in my stepping. Or perhaps it was just a twinge. Then I spoke as softly as I ever have. "I-I, Jack . . . I'm s-sorry man. I'm sorry I . . . I'll stay inside next time . . ."

He must have seen my fear, smelled the sweat building on me and seen the steam fall away with the breeze. Jack was staring at a ghost or at least a man pale enough to be called one. Letting me go, he grabbed the pack from my pocket and lit a drag for himself. He gave me a pat against my cheek and said, "I get it." Inhaled, exhaled, and resumed.

"I'll be a bit more hoppin' next time."

I shook my head in agreement.

Ready to leave, I was making my way back to my seat. That's when I felt his hand pull me aside, pressing against my chest. He held me there in a coma or a mass paralysis brought on by shock. Then, taking another Camel out from its pack, he gently placed the cigarette between my lips, flickered the lighter, and patted me on the back as soon as the smoke rose.

"Don't take it personally kid, jus' business."

Not wanting to do anything but sleep, I agreed. "You're right, you're right Jack."

"I always am." He grinned; he smiled.

- 22 -

A Scenic View

AT AROUND ELEVEN TO MIDNIGHT I'd patiently
wait until my parents fell asleep. I'd pretend to be
watching television until I was sure that they were both
knocked out cold. Then, I'd shut off the lights, walk
down the squeaky hallway to my room, close the door
without entering and make my way back to the living
room.

Then, into the backyard. My bicycle was in the
shed behind my father's four car garage. That's really
where the journey began.

All throughout the summer I would do this, break
curfew and head into the woods. Not really the woods,
but a public park, nonetheless. At times I'd see
strangers drinking, trading drugs at a park bench, or
couples making "love" in the playground.

From there I took to the trails, passing
neighborhoods and wild coyotes, foxes, and others of
the like, with their glowing eyes contemplating my
journey in the full-lit moon. After about half an hour of
riding past blacked-out homes and rough dirt roads, I'd
be at her house and in her backyard, my bike hidden
in the bushes nearby.

On the weekends she liked to "sleep" in her
clubhouse, one that her father built when she was a
kid. It was also her idea to have me "sleep" in her
clubhouse during these weekends, though her parents
never knew.

This was where I learned to make out, touch
tongues, suck on hers, her sucking on mine. I should
have gotten the hint by then. Even when we stripped

187

down, nothing except for our underwear on, I still hadn't the slightest clue. Neither did she, or perhaps she did, but was waiting for me. Unfortunately, that time never came.

Was my first love meant to be my first love making? We were an inch of fabric away from being bare skinned. She was probably wet without thinking twice, I was probably hard without considering it once.

So, what happened, where could the difference had been made? I was a minute away from sex, every week for six consecutive months. So, what held me back?

After that night Jack and I had many more of these "*trips*". I figured it was a drug deal. Once every two weeks, every Saturday night at warehouse 88 on the outskirts of Beverly Hills. With how many drugs Kyra was on, I was surprised he didn't need a pickup every weekend.

But that was none of my business, and I never asked any questions. I just sat quietly in the car, smoking cigs, drinking a forty, doing whatever passed the time.

Even with the state of things, society surely labeling me a villain, there was still worse people. Like your alcoholic, occasional drug-user with a 2.50-megapixel sensor, wide angel, 1080p view on whatever naked body chose to reveal itself that day. I thought that our audience was more likely to kill someone in a DUI than I was filming the content that they'd enjoyed watching. Even with the drugs on the side.

I made money and I loved it.

My school bills were paid months ago. It was the end of the summer and I cared nothing for the conventional, convincingly condescending and confirmative caricature I use to find comfort in. Your four-oh-one-kays, saving for retirement. To Hell with it all, I was living a life stuck in elevation. Fuck cloud nine, I was ten times higher always.

Societal villain or not, I was still the most American man those purple mountain majesties and the amber waves of grain had seen floating over their beautiful halcyon skies. I got more puss, made more money, smoked more dope, drove a shiner car, bought only the best, and couldn't be compared to no other. I was the pimp ghost riding in that rap video you watched on MTV2. I was the Wall Street Journal's #1 article on success, and Forbes most favorable millionaire.

A millionaire. I wasn't there yet, not by a long shot. But if these few tens of thousands got me where I needed to be, then what would a million do for me? I had everything but my own house in this neon city.

Then it occurred to me, those poor bastards who went bankrupt after winning the lottery. Hundreds of millions of dollars handed out was still a hundred-million dollars taken back. The poor man's game was to win, only to watch it all crash back down as if it were nineteen-twenty-nine.

I went up into my room and found Kyra as usual. I knew she had a gig today, because she complained all last night (or the night before) about it. Something about a public threesome, near to the highway. A couple of perverts were supposed to "*act*" like complete strangers as she "*acted*" her way through giving out her body.

It looked like she wasn't going to make it this time. Lying on the floor, she was naked and her body coated in a thick sweat. I wasn't worried, the heat around this joint was stupendous at times, without today being an exception. Laying down on the bed I let things be. Then, time disintegrated with matter dissolving into thoughts again.

Suddenly, I had appeared in a generation of great wars. I was a soldier with a rifle and no mercy towards my enemy. But had I known that my enemy, the same blood that had traveled an ocean, traversed the same lands and settled, was a part of my own, I might have bit the bullet first. That German blood running in me, my father, my grandfather, and other ancestors. Then, stomping across a barren wasteland of dead earth and smoke pillars in the distance, dead trees scorched, and hills lined with bullet casings I watched.

Approaching the edge of the enemy, near the streamline, the crossroads of the battlefield, I stopped and stood tall. And in front of me was a window, turned into a mirror, and I saw myself starring back from enemy lines.

My reflection changed as the white picket fences rose amongst the dead. Bright yellow paint jobs along perfectly aligned boards of wood built a home suited for a family of five. Father married to a mother of three children or more.

The grass was green, real estate and car loans were cheap, milk ran like water, and food abundant like the oil that lubricated our Chevrolet Bel Air. And my wife lubricated me, when I wanted, when I asked, and when I didn't.

I sat at a desk most days, filing, filling in forms and building up a retirement fund that was also supported by the war I fought in. No education required. And in the forms, files, tax exemptions, and union appeals I helped write, I saw my children's names and wondered about their futures.

Then I saw it, my siblings playing on a beach. Sandcastles we would one day rule, seashells we collected like free currency, waves incoming as if it were a warning. But we never did mind them. Times were changing with the drugs, with the music, with our rights. Everything seemed significant and the fights were easily won. After a critical economic crisis, two world wars, a lost war in Vietnam and then some, letting women vote was the least of our worries.

We gained what our parents gave, learned from a sculpted educational system not based on income and profitability, gained jobs that kept the greater ideals before consumerism took command. We'd say it was hard work, smoking our dope, standing hand in hand with a flower between our teeth, breaking a wall, holding a sign. Little would we realize that the words written on our picket signs came from the same wood as the picket fences of our parents. And little did we know that the same picket fences that our children would hold would be the same rotting wood we had already expended in our lifetime. Like a sign that read "Looking 4 Amateurs".

Then I saw him, for the first time in my life. Out of his mother's womb, bloodied, with a smidge of hair atop his nearly bald head. His eyes opened and I saw that beautiful hazel shade turn from blue to green as his pupils widened. He saw me too. Then, from below, I watched the umbilical cord get cut, some blood poured out in a sudden rush. And, , I watched his eyes close again, every time he fell asleep. Yet, as I waited, I watched as your lids slowly opened and I saw my own eyes looking back at me in their reflection . . .

I felt a pinch. Looking over, it was my own hand wishing me awake. How long had I slept this time? It was Friday morning, looking at the alarm clock that read: 11:47. But it was still dark. "Fuck . . ." I mumbled, Kyra was no longer on the floor, but I could see an imprint from where she lay. "Is it Friday or not?" I wondered, then panicked.

Much like an anxiety attack, I rushed through the door. I found Jack, making out with one of the ladies, Monica, judging by her darker skin, along the cushions of the couch while watching ESPN Central all in one go. I spoke, short of breath, "Jack, what day is it?"

He stopped, pushed Monica away and looked at me. "I thought you were going to bed cat?"

"I-I . . . what day is it?" I had myself on repeat.

"Bruh, it's Thursday night, about a minute away from Friday and we gotta' busy fuck'in schedule tomorrow start'n at ten. You gonna' be coo' by then or wha?" He sounded serious.

I became Jack's obedient mutt. "Ye-yeah . . . Just, nightmares and all. Must'a woken up, how much did I drink?"

Jack looked at me in his own dazed confusion. "Drink, you hadn't been drink'n at all. You came in and crashed, went straight to bed with Kyra around eight." He told me, but thought out loud, "Or maybe . . ." He started the sentence as if it were a prelude to a threat.

As he walked towards me, I put my hands in the air. "Jack, I don't want no trouble man." I begged, as I felt his hand snatch my wrist and bring my arm to below his level.

He scanned my arm, near the veins and vessels. Next, he checked the other, same routine. Then he stared me in the eyes and told me, "Man, you look'in clean. Just old wounds, nothing recen'." Letting me go, he patted me on the shoulder and apologized. "Tha's my bad bruh, just . . . you know. Gotta' make sure you ain't takin' nothin' after Kyra."

"Kyra?" I sounded stupid, very well knowing how much she had been shooting up. Opiates, heroine, coke when she could, alcohol when acting "*on the stage*". "She isn't handling things well these days, Jack." I pleaded. Though, my answer left me unsure, whether it should have been said at all.

Jack laughed, then carried on, told Monica to beat it, then faced me once more. "Do you know where Kyra is at the moment?" He asked.

I didn't even answer. Perhaps I gave a half-nod but was transfixed in the moment.

He laughed again and pulled me with him into the backyard. Outside the air was cool, calming, and collected. The dew in the morning would fall like crystal beads off blades of grass and if I were lucky, I'd fall from my bed in a gentle haze after this night. We stopped before proceeding any further out, towards the glass door to the porch. That fabled, scenic outlook. "Buddy, Kyra's waitin' for us."

Again, I couldn't move. "What do you mean she's waitin' for us?" Was I so pathetic? Had the answer not yet called itself out to me, was I too blind or too stupid to see it? Or, perhaps, I just wanted to turn away.

"Yo, cat. I know you'an Kyra have gots'ome history together now. So, les' jus' leave it like that, histor-ee."

"Then, why am I here?"

"You're my witness." He replied, before taking my hand like I was some bride and dragged me nearer, carrying my footsteps. I made my own pace now, walking forward, I felt as though I would be the one stepping off the edge soon. For a time in my life, I wanted this walk towards the glass door to last an eternity or more.

I wasn't ready, I didn't want to see her go, didn't want to see what Jack had in store for her. But as soon as it began, the door opened, as though the walk did not exist. Like it was all a memory fast-forwarded.

"Ready, kiddo?"

I was Jack's left hand.

I didn't speak, but he shook me and smiled. Not looking, I could still see that devilish grin from the corner of my eye. He let me through first, following closely behind. He already had two chairs across from her.

There she was, wrapped in a blanket, shivering and pale. But the moment our eyes met she smiled and attempted to stand. I moved in, not to hold her, but to quickly catch her as she fell back down into her seat. Sitting her down, I looked and saw she had been through much today, her voice was sparse and raspy. Her hair was made up of lines consisting of unintentional dreads produced by the puddle of sweat that was her earlier bemoan. Jack called me over and I knew I had to leave her there. Hovering over her, she placed a hand over mine. It was so warm and sensual. I hadn't felt this human for some months now.

"Kiddo . . ." Jack sternly reacted and retracted me from her, placing me into the seat beside him. He lit up a cigarette and even did the courtesy of lighting her one too. He handed me the pack without ever leaving eye contact with Kyra. It was then in Jack's movements and motions that I felt something coming like the pull-back of the tide before the tsunami struck.

"Kyra, how did your hospital visit go today? Doctor say everythin' was in order?" I had never heard Jack speak so eloquently before, much like a charismatic politician, like Adolf Hitler if he had the humility of Gandhi.

"Hospital, what were you . . ." But before Jack could glance back, I knew not to speak further.

Instead of punishment, Jack insisted that I know the truth. "Kyra, why don't you let your plaything in on what happened this afternoon while he was asleep, less than ten feet away from you."

"He's not my plaything . . ." She mumbled, but Jack pressed a glare and gave her no choice but to explain to me that: She had nearly overdosed a minute before I entered the room. Instead, she was put into a state of shock that her body could not withstand. Thankfully, it was nothing too serious, obviously, since she was back here so soon. But if Jack hadn't come up to find her for their shoot that day, it might have been a whole lot worse.

With that she looked at me and wept. She probably could tell that I was sourly disappointed in her. But who was I fooling? If it wasn't Kyra on trial, then I'd be just as guilty all the same.

"I'm sorry, I . . . I know I need help. I-" She was a pitiful wreck, like a small dog hit by a semi-truck and splattered across the highway for nobody to find. I could see some resemblance of genuine honesty in her gaze, but it wasn't enough. Not behind the pressed curtains shading the entry wounds into her veins, I knew they were they.

I knew well enough. Tears, broken speeches, choked breaths and a dismal ray of some kind of hope fluttering behind her eyelids. Not even a Disney film could fix the mess she was in.

"Stop, Kyra, this has been going on for far too long." Jack replied, cold-hearted like a stone sitting in a winter freeze. "What was it you said earlier cat? She isn't handling things well?"

"Is . . . is that true?" She asked me, staring as though Jack wasn't even present.

"I . . . I-" I had no words. I wanted to defend her, wanted to get this shit-show over with. But somehow I knew, the show must go on.

"You don't have to answer her." Jack replied, standing up and cutting a median between us. "Kyra, look down there. See that?" He pointed below, from the pretty little scenic view.

I followed him and her. Below were more lines of multi-million-dollar houses, oasis's of one-thousand-foot square pools and palm trees lining driveways. Then his finger moved half an inch higher and we followed along.

There was the red bricked wall gating in the "*community*" of counterfeit sunspots and new moons that made up the supposed stardom around this town. His finger kept creeping, slowly lifting the fog of war beyond us.

And beyond the wall was a higher-middle-class neighborhood from across a barren field of green grass. In that higher-middle-class establishment the grass was not as green but was plastered similarly to the dank dirt that hid those housewives and married businessmen's sins in secrets. From there were convenience stores, grocers, barista-bastards, and cash register vassals.

No grass, just concrete.

Then, from that point forward were the middle-class, lower-class, and homeless populations. They were particularly placed sets of people, if they could even be looked upon as human. The somehow wretched, yet most moralized and religious. The God-fearing working class, the street urchins of a modern era, the downdraught, the sickened. Kids without reasonable educations, purposefully, so that they'd never compared to the privately taught wealth of the future. Minimum waged social warriors with hearts of gold and pockets of dirt, never meant to amount to anything more than the debts that they owed from the start.

That's where Jack's finger pointed. It's where Jack's finger stopped. "That is where you're heading, tonight. Back to where I found you, where you came. That worm-infested little fuck-hole of nothing and nobodies." His finger fell down and over onto her. I couldn't see it, but I knew she must've been frightened. "And if I see you respond to another ad, whether it's mine or an associates' of mine or any motherfucker in between, I'm coming. Whether it's over Craigslist, Facebook, Instagram, I'll be coming."

Then he turned to me and spoke, "Coo cat, if you ever meet up with this girl again, I won't just be coming . . . I'll already be here."

Those were the words that shook me, not with fright but of some winter storm approaching. Shivers fled up and down my spine like lightning storms bursting through the clouds. I felt my hands shake, so I cuffed them.

I was ice cold.

I wanted to speak, I was tired of not speaking, so I forced out what I could in the most plain and unaltered fashion. I was a child speaking his first words again. "Jack, I understand. You . . . you can trust me."

He smiled; it looked crooked in the bare moonlight. "I know I can, I kno'." His voice changed again, some

Devil with three faces. The father, the abuser, and the wiseman.

As I was, God-fearing, I should have simply joined Kyra down in those streets.

– 23 –

Online Celebrity

RELATIONSHIPS WOULD COME AND GO. I once dated some blonde bimbo, near-to high school dropout, spoiled by her mother's money and her daddy's alimony. She was all right, I suppose, lacked any sort of true personality and never had much to say, which dragged the days that I was with her on and on and onwards.

Her room was reminiscent of a spilled dumpster, her bed was never made and coated in thick hairs from her cat. The only thing more disgusting than her lifestyle was, by no measure of surprise, her vaginal cavity, which was strongly guarded by a husky layer of pubic hair and reeked of decaying fish. The "smells like fish" stereotype regarding a woman's vagina had, in the history of the universe, never held truer.

A week later I broke things off with her. Some say it was due to the daunting smell that still lingers on my fingers to this day. I just thought she had no substance and if I was going to get serious with a girl then she might as well be more exciting than an American Girl™.

So, in months passing, I found myself a little Asian girl. Daughter to a psychologist mother and architect father, not nearly as exciting as it sounds. She was typical but at least she had a layer somewhere below the surface. The surface, however, was the jagged, crusty exterior of an otherwise sociopathic masochist. Still a step up from the last, in my mind. Her problems mainly stemmed from being an adopted child, suffering from anxiety and depression. She was constantly stealing and lying from everyone she knew.

Though, I still made her my first. That's when I discovered that sex could get kind of boring, at least with your first. I can't begin to imagine how high-school sweet-hearts, one and only lovers, married folks and Catholics, keep their sex lives so interesting. After our breakup and a few years later, I discovered how this rather dull girl ended up getting her kicks in bed. She liked to be choked.

A violent act that I believed was only sexualized through porn. I would have gladly of given her that, if only I knew.

Kyra was a passing thought when I drank too much or when I had a long sit on the toilet the next morning. Otherwise, the weeks passed with the same old routines. Shoot a scene, head home, find a house girl, drinks or drugs, then call it a night. Wake up, repeat. At this point, nothing could phase me, I've seen it all.

From every sized dick to every shaped pussy, shaved or dirty, dark or light, black to white, gay to straight. You get the gist. Whether we were in public, a studio, or some cheap hotel room, sometimes we'd add another *lover*, and somedays we'd add a little violence.

Whatever to spice up the production, but I wasn't there for the script. That much got tiring enough, half the time we didn't have to use one. If anything, I was almost certain that our "scripts" were half-written by AI, if not completely written by AI. Funny, to think about a computer writing a sex scene.

Half our days were much like throwing a dart at a spinning board marked by differing genres of porn. Whatever it landed on was what we did. Unless we were providing our girls to another studio, website, or producer, then it was their game, not ours.

Nonetheless, things began to drool on around this joint. Perhaps I just got bored easily, I'm sure they have a medication for that. Seems like they have a medication for everything these days. Not saying that they all work, of course. Those penis enlargement pills never do, trust me.

But one time I tried some Viagra we had stashed away in the cupboard and I couldn't lose that erection for half the day. I should have contacted my doctor like the commercial specified. One thing those pills only mentioned were the side-effects involved. Headache, upset stomach, muscle pain (mainly in my groin) you name it, I had it the next day.

"Anyhow, no more dick-talk. I get enough of that during every shoot, and I mean every fucking shoot. Man or woman, gay or straight. Shit, here we go again with the lists . . ."

"Talking to yourself again?" Cindy asked, she was lounging on the couch watching some obscure viral video shit. Shortly after asking, she turned her back and laughed at some video shorts. She must have been short some number of braincells today to be even close to capable of laughing at those.

"Sorry, guess I was." I trailed off again, now intrigued by what she was watching. Not because it was remotely funny or very clever, but because millions of others had or were watching it at this very moment. It stunned me, surprised me in awe. My mouth felt adjacent and wide. This was what click-bait news sites were calling the "*New Media*", stupid fuckers pulling faked pranks and high school kids acting, well, like high school kids; stupid.

"Really, is this all that's on?"

"Fuck off, this shit's the dope'st."

At that point, I gave up conversing. To think that I slept with Cindy more than three times would be like believing I owned a sex doll I kept in front of the television screen. Scratch that, I suppose that's what she amounted to. Video after video involving some loud mouthed 30-something year old gamer gabbing on about nothing; semi-politically corrective feministic trans-advocates preaching about societal inequality amongst a fabulized minority; with stupid videos featuring stupid people doing stupid things and saying stupid stuff.

That's when I knew that ideocracy was more than a shitty C-Grade flick about an up-in-coming reality. Mike Judge wasn't entirely wrong, we were heading towards a more ape-like state of social affairs. And Jacklin J. Schaffner played his part in the bigger picture fifty years prior to now.

Damn dirty apes.

Content creators were worse than priests when asking for donations. They've sold out more times than there were advertisement companies to provide sponsorships. Created a persona as fake as the cheapest plastic mask on clearance at your nearest Spirit Halloween.

They weren't funny, but you were expected to laugh. Somehow, in a futuristic sense, we had advanced from laugh tracks and neon signs that spelled out LAUGH, to just knowing when we were supposed to. The moment would hit, when we knew something should be funny, that moment of climax, and we'd pretend. But we wouldn't cum, reach that point of ecstasy. But we believed in it, wanting it to be true, so much that we made believe in it.

And that single-second laugh, always similar to a one-hit drag from a cigarette. A momentary high without the imperforate bliss of a fully smoked joint. Never satisfied, but always craving another drag, another hit. Soap operas and daytime television had it right to begin with.

Now we've moved further along the spiral, though it's hard to say whether we're moving further outward or into that abyss and furthermore if it even mattered. Or maybe, it was just my inner dialogues going feral.

What am I saying?

This type of thinking could do me in. I needed an ol' fashioned spicy Bloody Mary to hold me up. "Hey Cindy, I'm makin' myself a Mary, want one?" Figured I'd show some courtesy. She was a woman after all, no matter how dirty she got. I remember one time filming her, she had one guy in her vag, another in her mouth, and a third inside her-

"But . . ." she paused, waiting for the catchline by her favorite internet celebrity. "Uh, but don't make it too spicy, kay? Thanks babe, love ya!"

She always did that, said some dumb catchphrase like "Thanks babe, love ya." Followed by a wink and a blown kiss. Maybe courtesy should have been killed years ago, if we only knew what counterfeit lives we'd lead later.

Pouring in the tequila, combining it with the mix and some tomato juice, diluting hers while adding some ground pepper and extra mix to mine, I got to thinking. "Hey, think I could be an online celeb?"

She just laughed, walking over she grabbed her drink, took a sip, then kissed my lips and told me "Not a chance."

I wanted to slap that drink right out from her hand.

Later, after other discretionary actions, I'd go to jail on charges of assault. Maybe even attempted murder. I wanted to spit in her face and tell her off.

Intangible whore, fucking slut, cum dumpster, fuck machine. I wanted to fuck her hard, take ten Viagra's and penetrate her until there was nothing but a gaping hole that wouldn't snap shut. Much like her mouth, always open, talking about as much as she'd suck dick on my camera. I wanted to prove her wrong.

So, I chugged my Mary, that spice biting my tongue, that liquor hibernating in my liver for the next ten minutes before hitting. By the time it hit, it had been thirty minutes and I was at the nearest technology store, you know the one, Greatest bang for the buck and what not. Unbeatable prices, expert service, whatever other bullshit a company could claim. I was at their computer section, non-specific, looking for a USB based microphone that could connect to my laptop, audio editing software, and some of Warhol's showbiz for takes.

The cashier was some miserable 20-something nobody with a slightly above paying minimum wage and obvious student debt sewn to his shoulders like badges of dishonor. He reminded me more of my past self, a year or so ago, than I cared to recall. His language almost sounded scripted,

"Hello. How are you. Did you find everything all right." It wasn't a question, it was consistency. "How's your day been going." He'd semi-ask, attempting to pretend to be interested. All the while I remained stoic.

I couldn't tell if he thought I was crazy, suicidal, or apathetic. It became a fun game to play. "Sorry, I'm new here." He broke the silence. I wasn't even sure what he was apologizing for. "Your total is three-hundred and forty-one dollars and sixty-eight cents, sir." He sounded nervous and I would have been too. If it wasn't a plasma television, any amount spent over one hundred would've scared me shitless. But these days, hundreds were dollar bills.

Then it hit me, "Did you just call me *sir*?"

By that question, he seemed confused.

I looked to his name tag, "*Tyler*".

I said, "Tyler, how old do I fucking look that you feel the need to call me *sir*?" I was in control. Between the tequila and implanted ego growing with the leftover Viagra flowing through my cocaine infused bloodstream, I swept him up like dust on the counter. I put a George Washington on the counter and asked him, "Is this enough for you to wave my bill and quit your job?"

He looked at me, then came distress as he said again, "That'll be three-hundred and-"

But I already heard the sh'pill, "Yeah, yeah, three-hundred and forty-one fucking dollars and something-somethin' cents." Then I laid two more hundo's on the counter and asked again, "How about now? Pocket it, take it, it's for you."

He kept silent, I could tell he was unsure. He told me to wait a second and headed to the backroom. Next thing I knew a manager was with him, like a slave dog, a bitch mutt, but still his abiding master.

"Sir, I'm not sure what's going on here. But you're forty-one dollars and sixty-eight cents short of your bill."

Now I was pissed, I felt betrayed. "Listen pal, fuck this enabler." I pointed to his manager, who looked about ready to call security soon. "This stupid fuck only got his job because he's wasted the past better half of a decade sucking dicks and doing nothing but being whipped in the back by the corporate office. You - you still have a chance man, beyond that student debt and kiss-ass attitude. Do what I do, invest in what's popular, that will never die out. Porn baby, it's all the rage." Then I threw down eight more Washington's.

He looked long and hard, this time contemplating. His manager was not as amused as I had hoped. Wasn't a wonder, men like him were hopeless, raped by higher-ups, seduced by salary jobs and cross-country positions.

Their dreams never amounted to anything more than a possible twenty dollars an hour to keep their heads above the rising tide. They were the reason for a lack of revolution, a lack of devotion to their countrymen.

Their God was the guy at the top, the lonely king at the center of all fraudulent audits, lesser accountings, and bailouts. Enron in the eyes of the believer, the walking shadow, strutting upon the stage, a poor player, an idiot full of sound and fury; amounting to nothing.

"Take it, this is yours." I spoke, as if settling a debt, as if comforting the love of a lost one. As if I were Enron, in the name and face, accepting settlements rather than admitting to the truth. I was a forty-billion-dollar lawsuit waiting to fail. At least I wasn't Deloitte or Price Waterhouse. It was good to be American after all.

"I'm gonna' have to ask you to leave sir." The manager told me. I didn't even bother reading his name tag, as if he mattered.

His life was made up, given up and replaced with anything that was considered sustainable. If this man ever found happiness, it would be by a 9mm bullet through the skull in an empty apartment room on the bottom floor where the mice scurried and the spiders formed their webs.

I gave in, I had my fun.

"That should be enough to cover the costs, take whatever is left." I told the guy, walking out into the world I faked, but the world I knew.

In a way, I figured Tyler would have to hand the money over to his superior. He would have to record it as an additional capital asset. But I knew better than most that he'd just pocket it for himself, people that weren't in higher positions such as his boss' were usually more desperate than the average, bottom-up worker. Blue collar my ass, we've all become shit-shovellers.

I walked out of that store without a care. No matter who the money goes to, it's just Lydia's marketplace in repeat again. Precious minerals or Great Seals, doesn't matter, neither can produce an electric current nor build a monument. It's all just bullshit and they can have it, take it, keep it.

– 24 –

Online Antichrist

I NO LONGER WANTED IT, IN FACT I've been attempting to rid myself of it ever since I've obtained it. They might think I'm crazy, but I'm not crazy. Crazy is the desire to obtain more than what you're worth and what you're worth should be no more than the next person in line. But this is capitalism, and I'm cheating at every step of the way. Whether it be in porn or the social media industry. If it had been either, then I would have been in Tyler's position.

But here I am, hundreds in my pocket and nothing more to do than throw them about the place. To people less fortunate, to people that would have been like me, people like me. In an instance, I wanted to turn back, go through those self-opening doors, flip-off the guy whose job it is to greet the customer at the door, walk back up to the manager and throw a punch to his smug fucked up, acne induced, pity-prone face, and watch him fall to the floor. Have the cops called, flee from the scene, make it out alive, eventually get caught and have my hands cuffed under penalty of law. That would give me a reason to get out of this shit show. But it was the shit show I had always wanted to see, so why was I complaining. Maybe I was going crazy?

Back in my Lambo and then back at the house, I ran in a kindergarten frenzy. At my laptop I set up my camera, plugged in the microphone and had the audio software ready to record. Then I sat there for an hour and wondered to myself, what the Hell was I supposed to be recording?

What I had seen was a small glimpse into the world of digital, social media-based, online entertainment. I was sure I was more than entertaining enough for the populous majority. That overcrowded congestion of roaches.

Had my mind become that perpetrated by the thought of degrading everyone around me?

It didn't matter if I got my million views, hundred-thousand subscribers, one thousand Patreon users. sending me money and ad revenue. Pumping out dollar bills per every thousand views, retweets, and likes. The more attention I gained the more invincible I would become. And with it, riches produced by the poor man.

There were only a handful of millionaires that could make a definitive living off social media. If I were to make half of what they made, I would become an even more finite autocrat.

So, I thought for more than a minute, perhaps I'd start a blog. But what would the subjects be, could they simply be subjective? Nah, they'd *have* to be *subjective*, wouldn't *they*? If people were to relate, then what would they relate to?

Alcoholism, substance abuse, pornographic video recording and editing as a main goal and career set within a personal lifestyle? How was I supposed to relate to people when I related to less than one percent of this country's population?

Nevermind that passing thought.

I could probably manage to play video games for a living. Move my fingers across a joystick, press buttons, click triggers, and most importantly create a personality. From watching others, I've learned that the greatest personalities have been crafted through loud, obnoxious reactions to common and coherent things; being generally annoying when it comes to the average attention span; developing a highlight based on a none-sight; relating to the weak and making it strong; pretending to be fake while right is usually wrong.

Now we're talking in riddles and rhymes, though, that's what the average person likes. 40 perfect kills, no deaths; a speed run in under an hour; three or more jump scares within a thirty-minute time frame. The longer the length, the more time spent by users watching it, the more ad revenue it made.

So, *let me bullshit you. Let me relate to your past, to your concourse of relatability, to the general foregoing fads and this year's trendy hot topics. Whether its 80's fashion, 90's topics, or the 2000's previous politics that lead us to the point of a war-raving fake feminist or a retard leading in his bankruptcy, this is where we are. Let me talk, just speak my mind and save the consequences for tomorrow.*

Allow me to be your online antichrist.

But I couldn't even get that far, no tomorrow in sight. No matter how many recordings I did, I would always be revising a script. I would attempt to keep it safe, like a newscaster or a mass media website. I would always tend to keep things to the sleight of hand, future friendly, and co-current with the popular topic of the day.

I bought a few games over my laptop and I sucked at them, always remarking on my poor ability to advance through a dungeon or playthrough on the very first level. Then, after an aggravating amount of anger I switched back to a blog. Discussing my personal life, showing off my car, examining my household, discussing how I was '*feeling*' at the current moment.

And after uploading a few various videos I had no views. No one seemed to care what a six-figure pornographic camera man had or did.

It hurt my head.

I needed an Advil, but I feared that would interfere with the half-wasted bottle of Jager I had beside me. It was fucking hot inside, perhaps because I had been working up a sweat making these videos. Don't believe me? Ask yourselves this, how come talk show hosts such as David Letterman, Ellen DeGeneres, Dr. Phil, and John Stewart make figures in the millions per season? It ain't because they're real, they've been acting like they're supposed to be interesting for an hour.

I've been at it for six hours and haven't seen a single view more than my own. It punctured the ego, my pride pouring out onto the hardwood flooring, leaking through the boards and dribbling down like a pathetic rain into the first floor. Now I was too drunk to make anything worthwhile.

I needed a distraction, a muse even. But a muse was a rarity in a household full of golden sluts and their filthy film members. So, I'd see if Mariah was around. She was the new girl, had only been around for a few weeks now, she seemed susceptible enough. Besides, a tramp is second best to a slut.

"Mariah!" I called down the stairs, steadily gripping onto the railing for balance. "Hey, Mariah . . . you here?" I tripped over my own feet along the last step, barely catching myself on the end of the rail, in time for Mariah to catch my stumble.

"Yes?" She spoke in a sassy mid-teenager fashion. She was always a character, ever since she moved in. Not that she was special or nothing, but she had a unique style that must had separated her from all of the other fish.

Today it was dyed pink tips, a hot pink top overlaying a lace bra, and some sort of thrifty, leopard-skin skirt. She was barefoot, neon pink toenails. The girl had a thing for pink.

"Doin' anything?" I asked, hoping the question sounded as tangible as it did in my mind when I spoke it.

I noticed her scowl and give a deep pout. "You too, huh?" She huffed, beginning to turn away.

But I couldn't let that happen. Grabbing her by the wrist I pulled her back around. Near inches away, I could taste the cherries from her cheap Walmart brand perfume, smell the moisture from her mouth begin to dissipate. "You're not seriously busy or nothin' eh?" sarcastically, I murmured in her ear.

She gave a violent tug, broke free before pushing me away. I started to stumble again, almost affording a one-way ticket to a fall on my ass.

"Hey, what's the big deal! You do this shit for a livin' don'cha?" I wasn't stupid for thinking it, right? I already had her uploaded onto four different galleries and two big-budget online flicks. I used my most precious resources on this girl, my time. My time filming, syncing, editing, uploading. This was the least she could do for me in return.

But she left me very little room to speak when I heard her scream. It was just a scream, loud, pitched to break even the deafest of eardrums. It was the cry of an angered animal on its last limbs, attempting to break free from some awful predator's teeth. It frightened me more than I imagined a girl of her age and height ever could had.

"I'm sick of it! You . . . you men are all just . . . just fucking pigs! I'm not a God damn slot machine for you to shoot your credits into. I'm a human being too!" She was fanatical. This wasn't something random, this

211

sounded like it had a long-awaited arrival. And as a ship crashed to the shore, the shrapnel went flying.

"Holy shit," I said, already exhausted and still dire for a quick escape "what's your prob'em anyhow Mariah?"

That's when the tears turned to complete rage, her mascara fogging from her eyes like black blood trickling. Some deranged scene from a Stephen King novel, Carrie standing right in front of me, waiting to light me in flames. Then it happened, right as the other girls walked in.

"My problem is you, is Jack, is my fucking family. It's my boyfriend who - who left me . . ." The tears started to return, only to be brushed away with the black mist and shimmering glitter like stars being swallowed into a black hole. "Nobody . . . nobody really, and I mean *really,* loves me now. I don't know what I've done, and Jack won't . . . And you, you fucker! You'll have Hell to pay someday!" She spoke it as if it were a threat, taking a fist and laying it into my-

"*Auck*!" I coughed out, a boney fist still hits like the tail end of a lead pipe.

Falling to the floor I thought to myself "Am I the only man who keeps getting knocked down by girls, or am I just another one of one-hundred-seventy million? Ass flat back where (I probably) belonged, I watched Mariah march right up the staircase, catching a glimpse of what was underneath her skirt on that final step.

I suppose that would be enough for my imagination to quell my primal desires. But what was it that I felt still deeply burning inside my gullet, an electric flow right past the sternum into my ribcage? That red vision that sets the whole world ablaze?

I stood, not knowing why or if I should care. Maybe I wanted to run up those stairs after her and knock one right into her thick skull too. Or maybe I wanted to stick my tongue straight down her throat until she choked on it.

How dare she act as if she were the only person here who signed up for this. Sure, I felt sad sometimes, but that's what sex and drugs were for, and all the money in the world could buy that much.

"Bitch . . ." I scoured, but Cindy shut my mouth with a single finger lined up my lips vertically.

"You don't know what it's like pal, so shut it." She said and with sass too, as if Jack only hired women who knew how to flick their wrists and wear Christian Louboutin heels to their shoots.

With the anger flowing through me, mixed with my horniness, and suddenly Cindy was up for an attempt at grabs. "Why don't you show me what it's like then, it's been a while. Hasn't it?"

Cindy, looking disgusted by my commentary, gave me a good smack to the cheek like a hard kiss from the palm. Before I knew it, I was back down on the ground, unable to move. Maybe it was because I didn't want to, it was nice down here, the carpeting was soft. Or perhaps I had no reason to rise back up.

Then, like a sudden rain storm passing over me I felt all three ladies spit down onto my face from the staircase. Flinching, as if it hurt, and to an extent it did. Although, I did not mind it entirely. After hours of vein video work and a now limp dick I knew I was out for the count.

Three... two... one... it's over.

Knocked down, I wish I could just black out. It wasn't physical exhaustion; it was mental depletion.

This got me to think, was I really so ambitious to exhaust my physical being on top of my mental stance? Was I willing to deplete what remained of me to simply stop feeling? I suppose I would have sacrificed happiness if the sense of impending disappointment disappeared. But now, disappointment and rage were all that remained and, in a way, I was glad to have at least these two true friends by my side.

– 25 –
K-9 (Part 1)

YEARS LATER I FOUND MYSELF A TOMBOY who was a friend of the Asian girl. I never knew there were rules to friends of friends dating the ex's of said friends until I met her. In fact, I knew nothing about the 'bro code' or anything of the like. It was all elementary-school babble that never needed my attention. A boring scripture of rules and regulations that soon became optional advice.

At this time, I was in a small college town four hours far from the urban city where I used to reside. I thought this was a long-distance relationship, I feel sorry for the suckers who had to travel four-hundred miles to meet someone who amounts to a coin flip or a rolling die.

Between our visits to and from one another, we eventually fell in love. But by this time, she had become the third one, and love was just something that happens to a person. Like an everyday emotion. Don't get me wrong, it felt as real as a wet dream. She and I were perfect for the moment.

But moments don't last long.

Our moment was just under two-years, with torment and pain following. I thought I knew what a broken heart was, but I hadn't even been close to the feeling.

Everclear days, Everclear nights, one-hundred-proof depression and 75.5% suicidal tendencies. Life falling apart, centered around a cluster of events and questions that followed. It was a bitter fruit of a lifestyle that I was meant to swallow. But I didn't want to, I wanted to leave that awful taste in my mouth, as it always reminded me of my mistakes.

I feared she finally had everything with her freedom and I had nothing; I was getting left behind. That's when I decided I needed to catch up. She must've found a guy by now, she must have had him in her bed, in her . . . How could I possibly compete? I had charisma and liquor, an equal foe for the drunk, not the watcher.

So, following through with my cruel intentions, I set out on a quest to shape the odds. To match her with my own count, to outdo her quantity of men with my quantity of women. And yes, I was hurt, so I hurt others.

I had the first girl shirtless with her bra held in her hands as I massaged her bare-naked back. She had been my supervisor at the time, and we always had something to talk about at work. In-person it became something more, or so I had hoped. Unfortunately, she suffered from a similar disease, the disease nicknamed 'sorrow'. I didn't get any from her that night.

Not giving up, I found another. This one was a high school classmate that, back then, I never really cared for. But she was single and cute enough for a suicidal alcoholic like myself. Throughout our night together, I'd sneak more liquor into her glass than was in mine, while maintaining an equivalent amount of liquid between us. It was clever, sure. But all it afforded me was a puking girl over my toilet and napping in my bed for a few hours before having to leave.

Pride dented, but still not giving in, I attempted one last crusade.

This time I was approached by a girl while working the register, she made small talk and handed a small note to another co-worker, who had proceeded to give it to me.

"Text me sometime? <3" with a phone number attached.

Our first date was something simple, a coffee date at a café around the corner of my workplace. This time, a little less cruel, I wanted things to be clean. No hard liquor and no manipulation. I just wanted to see how the world turned with myself balanced evenly on it.

I waited at the coffee shop, arriving five minutes early. Prepared, I ordered a drink and played on my phone for a while. Right on time, she was nowhere to be seen.

Ten minutes passed by, and I shot her a text. Ten more minutes and I was about ready to walk out the door. Then my phone buzzed and I look at her reply.

"Sorry sorry im so sorry!!! Forgot I had a doctor's appointment today!!! Raincheck??"

I got worried: "is it something serious?"

"No no. Just checking for stds. I'll explain next time if there is a next time. PLEASE?? :)"

Shocked by the unwavering truth from her reply, wanting to know the end of the story, I replied: "sure".

Come whatever may.

Two shots of vodka and some OJ for nutrition. A granola bar and some daily shortform videos, watching to improve my own system for overtaking the young minds on the daily.

"How the fuck do they do it . . ." I muttered into my mug. "All they do is yell and scream and act like idiots! And everything they say is a fucking meme, whatthefuck?" I yelled and screamed to myself, acting like an idiot in my own living space. Perhaps I did have what it took to be another monkey on the phone screen.

"Wha's the commotion cat?" Jack said, walking into the kitchen with nothing but a bathrobe tied around the waist.

"Your boy's been goin' on about these online celebs, Jack." One of the girls called out from the kitchen. It must've been Joy, judging by her hoarse voice, years of cigarette sludge lining the walls of her throat. Had I mentioned Joy before? She specialized in BDSM and orgasmic-torture porn and was especially fun to work with.

"Oh yeah? Wanna be a big influencer?" Jack spoke, pouring himself his own poison, whiskey with coffee and not vice versa. "I thought we gave you enough, paid you for your services. We not good enough, bruh?" I could feel him looking over me, but I didn't look back.

I was 'glued to the tele'. Attempting to understand, to focus on what was happening, what was being said. From every hand flip to each head jerk to any vowel upkept or sentence slurred. I was learning from their mistakes, which in turn, became a part of their success.

217

It was surprising how popular these illiterates, misshapen, politically-corrected, barely educated white Irish, Swedish, and American popcorn-stars were. All a bunch of white-as-cocaine serial killers of Likes, Views, Shares and Subscribers. They were vapors, airborne toxins spreading across international flights and sea barren wreckages known as Chrome and Firefox, Google and Bing.

Yet, they were addicting, like a dose of some good molly. The smaller channels online were more like your bottom of the line crack, half snuffed up by flour. Like an addict, I wanted to quit, every day telling myself I wouldn't take another hit, that I wouldn't spend another weary hour watching these buffoons playing games, teaching me how to properly apply eyeliner, or even react to other videos. But like an addict, I kept coming back for more.

Is this where sitcoms came to die or be reborn?

"Hey, Earth to the fucking numbskull sittin' in front o'me. Wake up!"

"Hey-oh . . . sorry, Jack." I was Jack's spiral staircase without an end or a start.

"Good, I got your attention. So, get this kiddo, know that broad from 16th and Yale, that we're gonna' film today at noon? Gotta' slicker plan now, dank ass shit. I need you with me man, goin' to a hotel and . . ." He began to drift, looking to his side and noticing a couple of the house ladies listening in.

But it didn't take a minute past his stare for them to hurry away. Then, in a softer tone he came back to me, "So . . ." Double checking the room to ensure absolute privacy. "We got a new girl that - well, I need 'tested out', so'tah speak. Like a lambo, need'a test drive the bitch to see if she's got tha' promised horsepower. You feel me man?"

"Yeah . . . yeah, I feel ya'." I wasn't sure why this was any different than any other situation I had been placed in.

I'd dealt with plenty of newbies by now. You got your criers, your screamers, your addicts, your runaways. Never mattered by the end, dollar bills tended to wipe away tears, cover mouths, pay prescriptions, and buy four walls with a roof. "*But why*?" I couldn't help ask, I needed to know why this one was so damn special from the others. "You make her sound like she needs Hanebisho toilet paper to wipe after a shoot. Does she shit golden eggs or something Jack?"

At first Jack lacked amusement, I could see it in his apathetic glare. But I learned, I didn't flinch, nor twitch a single muscle out of the forty-three in my face. I kept composure, and sure enough I witnessed him smile.

"You're becoming more and more of a clever fucking prick pal. I like that." He raised his mug to mine, and we drank in the morning buzz. "If I'm bein' honest, she might as well be made of fucking gold for as much as we're paying for her. Top'a dah line girl from the east. Some fucking princess or another, big hit online right now. Can't give that up, video girls barely last . . ."

"Six months, yeah, I know. Just heard Carol left the other day. Wasn't making the cut, eh?" I was getting slick, I had the formula down.

It wasn't just the words we used that defined us, it was our intent, the dead stare and violence hidden behind a smirk or a smile. It was the fear that lurked beneath every pretty face that you saw in every advertisement, talk show host, and service industry

219

worker. It was the wink of an eye before the trigger was pulled. It was everything from Columbine High School to Immigrant gang rapes in Sweden. Blue irises can still bleed red from a broken vessel.

He laughed; it wasn't his regular laugh, however.

For a second he appeared hesitant. Not because I was outgrowing him, but because I was growing into someone like him. "No, she wasn't." He grinned, but it was fake. "Anyhow, kiddo, this lady's making the dollar bills swim like silver sprats in a frenzy. I'm havin' JW break her in or whateva's left to break in today. Six inches should be more than enough."

"Coo', when you need me?" I asked, we shared specifics and I traveled back into my new, cruel, short-term realm of entertainment.

I doubt he even noticed my transfinite change, my altercations. I was a cocoon ready to burst open, an egg ready to crack through my shell. The black powder in a fifty-caliber bullet ready to explode. Each movement, reaction, inaction, indecision, every precision, precaution made every difference in how I saw myself. Soon, I was seeing myself in a third-person view, always wondering what *made me,* me.

Thirty years back, three decades behind we had Seinfeld leading the way toward the true American image. Hell, people across the world were watching Seinfeld, listening to every Jerry-rigged line.

But this wasn't just American, it was the leather to a Hermes Napoli suede calfskin derby shoe. It was the Ylang-Ylang nectars from Madagascar put into each bottle of J'Adore. It was a five-million-dollar Koenigsegg CCXR Trevita. It was money that could house over a thousand or more homeless individuals in their own tiny homes. It was money that could feed one-million and two-hundred and fifty thousand children in third world countries across the globe. It was money better spent on cheap laughs and clever commentary. Money that I'd rather have flowing into my pockets.

Even with the porn industry at an all-time high, it still didn't satisfy my tastes. When I started, I started with a sign that read "*Looking 4 Amateurs*". Now, I was the one filming both amateurs and professionals. I still had the camera, but also had the image, the video, the top quality at the top dollar.

I was the hard earner, the dream maker, the American Fantasy. But I wanted more; I needed more. I wanted what Jack had, every little bit. The control, the power, the background businesses. Handing a gun to my own protégé and telling him or her to keep guard and to back me up. To give the orders and herd the whores. I wanted that insider information, that drug-deal gone right, that studio setting with great lighting and preferred acting.

All because of me.

I wanted it, needed it, and if it was in porn then it must've been destiny. But if I become more than that, more than Jack, how could I be happier? I couldn't be, or so I assumed. Always basing my actions on assumptions was something I noticed. Why was it?

Am I talking to myself again? Judging by Cindy's look from across the room, I knew I was, in one of my self-help moods spoken aloud.

"Four'o'clock, we'll be there." I assured Jack, he seemed satisfied and left with his half-draped bathrobe back upstairs into his room.

Funny how a page of thoughts can wipe away a few flickering minutes of time. One more sip and I felt a warmth through my veins and numbness crawling around my lips. But my glass was empty, and I knew I'd need one more good dose before setting off. There was work to be done, lots of work. That online fanfare that I had been so hypnotized by wasn't waiting any longer.

Pouring myself another drink, I wondered: "*Do I show off my car, or the money I bought it with first*?" Then, as the liquid touched the glass and became indistinguishable, I heard Joy's voice attempting to whisper right next to me.

"He's testin' out a girl, huh?" She said, the smell of morning tobacco mixing with scrambled eggs and last night's cock-suck was overwhelming. I wished she would have brushed her teeth first.

"Fuckin' shit, Joy." I wanted to act surprised, but in all honesty, I just wanted away from that putrid mouth. At least the smell of my breath was consistent, stale vodka from the night before and a lick of toothpaste across my whites. "What're'you even listenin'in for?" Everything was scrambled, much like the eggy smell of her breaths, heavy and deep.

"I know, you haven't been around long enough to know, but I know."

"Know what, God-damnit." My inner profanities were surfacing.

"Joy," Stacy called out from the living room, slipping into the scene like some shadow with her dark complexion. I was surprised, at the moment, that I could recall any of their names at this point. It seemed like we had a new bundle of girls after every blink of the eye. "he's not worth it." She said whole heartedly, "He wouldn't care. Now com'n, gotta' pretty up before the studio." She said, with apathy.

Joy, without another word (thank God) turned away and followed Stacy across the living room, to the other end of the house and up the staircase where the girls always freshened up. I would have been offended if I wasn't already feeling the buzz. Without another word myself, I began to wonder, maybe I should show off the house.

People like seeing what they don't have. They value other people's valuables against all else. Watching the trees swaying in the wind, the newly cut grass evenly shaved in a bright green shimmer of dew, I knew at that moment I would have to start small.

Maybe do a selfie-like shopping spree video, find the hottest garbs, the dopest gear. Then, at the end of the video, set it all ablaze in some brand-sponsored pyre. Money wasn't an object, and the objects I bought didn't mean much either. Was that really the message I was going to go for? Did a message really matter? People like money, people like fire, a message wasn't needed.

I was here to burn the world down.

Then it hit me, the world in front of me was made of money. Drug money and liquor money, start-up cash and green bills moving fast across tabletops and women's tops. Yet, here I was, still unable to afford true happiness. I was only able to afford the medians in between. And now, somehow certain, I thought *how could this change that*?

Putting my face on every public scene. Everyone's friend was the idea I suppose. What's the fortune without the fame, was it half empty or half full? I never understood that, why can't it just be half? Half sober, half sane. Half angry, half regretful. Half you, half me, maybe that's what it came down to. And for that moment in time, I stopped sipping against the glass, turning my eyes away from the computer screen, I looked up into the ceiling and drifted off.

From existence to non-existence, from this world into the next, I was a space captain driving my ship back into unknown voids. That's where I met her again, like the first time, Abby.

She was just as headstrong as we were stupidly confident, perhaps we were one in the same. She was a soft laugh that spoke echoes of words that formed a story that even we were never told. We were a hard crashing wave dissipating as soon as we reached the surface of her beach, where we gently caressed the soft sands that formed her skin. Her skin.

Through all the footage I had gathered, the HD, 4K, Ultra-apparent and hardly subtle realism of reality we built together by past misconducts and present propositions, little had changed. However, sometimes little meant a lot. Abby was a lot to me, was more to me than the little things, was the tiniest blink of light in a universe devoid of stars. Yet her shine still carried on, and through my memory bank, as if it had never been robbed by this disgusting industry.

I awoke from my drunken drift.

It must've been a midday nap, the alcohol playing with my head and heart again. It was then that I knew that my video shouldn't be some comedic commentary on some trending bullshit, nor bullshit trends like another reaction or challenge video. I wanted to do something real, whether it met the algorithm's motives or not. For once in a long time, I wanted to *be me*.

So, I turned the camera on, set up some lighting and paused for a moment to think about what I had to say. But that was my first mistake, and I knew it. So, instead, I gave up to giving in, and spoke . . .

"All of my past mistakes . . . they've been bricks used to build a house of regret and torment." It felt right with how wrong it felt to give myself away. "But . . . I suppose, if anything, these bricks only built the foundation to the house, perhaps even a cellar or basement of sorts. For context, if it matters, I know I'm new here and should be askin' for Likes and Subs. But that ain't the case. Instead, I'd like to tell you about a girl . . ."

About a girl, like I became Kurt Cobain.

Then through dramatics, and some wiped tears, from soft edits and limited tags, I uploaded the video onto my page. Immediate fear swept in, call it *butterflies in your stomach* and yet it felt more like flies feeding on the lining.

Whatever happened, whatever the case may be, I was on and uploaded, my face just another digital donation to the realm of the new reality. I closed my computer, gave a breath of exasperated content, then looked at my phone to find that the time was close to three. I freaked for an instance but called an Uber my way.

"Can't be fuckin' late, can't be late, can't be late." I muttered, a few of the girls viewing me from the living room window as if I was a part of a reality TV show. Then, Stacy called my name in slight dread. I looked behind me and she approached my toes, our faces separated from an inch between our noses. She smelled of daffodils and cheap scented candles. Her lips had never been so tempting, so blush with red hues and barely parting. Back up to her eyes, they were sad.

They were always sad.

"Listen," she began in a deep, reconciled gasp, "whatever Jack's got you doing today isn't good. He's done this behind doors-shit before, and it's almost taken us all down. Not that I care about you, but you better be careful."

"Stacy, you were with a different guy every day last week and I had filmed every second of it. Who are you to tell me-" that's when I felt her finger on my lips.

"Shut up, idiot." She began, the sweetest her voice has ever sounded. "I know I'm a little fucked up, but believe me, Jack's up to no good. He ever tell you about his track record? His time in prison, his side hustles?" Her finger left my lips and all I wanted to do was to kiss her with every ounce of passion I had left inside of me.

But it wasn't possible, with the sounds of my Uber pulling up and her sad eyes now holding tears back between a smile and a wince. "Just please, be better than we are. I know, the ladies here want to be better. But some of us have debts, have kids, have hard lives and . . ."

I touched her shoulder, whether it was the right move or not, I felt a connection. It wasn't apparent and not completely sexualized, but to a degree I was a third-degree heart ache to understand her. Behind all the footage and editing, somehow in this moment I felt a pulsing in my heart. She was a person; she was human. And in a way, I had become less than such. "Stacy, I - I'll look out for trouble."

She reminded me of Abby.

This was the wildlife, the separation between sex and friendship, the dichotomy of human confliction. Our lust and our love, the dissection of the human condition was shattered and laid out in pieces. In this moment, before my car ride out onto the edge of town,

I looked past Stacy as a woman and saw her as flesh and bone.

Seven-trillion nerves in a slow thaw of existence. And from the rearview mirror of the Uber, she became a phantom and I, like a shadow hidden in a bright-lit room. What were we, where were we, and did it matter if we still spoke and saw and tasted and felt? Did she feel like I felt?

Are we the same?

The memory weaved itself into the deep consciousness of my brain, stapled shut and nailed to the floor of my hippocampus. That moment will never leave me and should never leave me, even if I wanted it to. It became the anchor that would someday sink the yacht. It's why celebrities committed suicide too soon.

It was a bitter fruit.

I made it to the meeting spot. The fucking driver told me to leave a good review, but he was ok at best. Outside there was an old warehouse, broken with dirty windows that grew long and rusted from years of abuse. The outer walls were also rusted, tainted metals set in that triangularly ribbed form. It reminded me of an old sea-side dock fishing building. But there was no ocean here.

One door, off to the corner of the building was the only entrance I could find. It was a post-apocalyptic persona resonating from the painfully perpetrated form of the barely functional facility in place. To put my words straight, it made me uneasy.

This wasn't our usual hotel or meet up. This place was off, off our usual schedule and set-up-shoots. This was the H.H. Holmes of meet up spots. I didn't like nor agree with the location. And yet, all these thoughts had been repeating and orbiting me since I first grasped the handle of the door. Standing cold, silent and uncertain.

I've trusted Jack thus far and so, I turned the handle and entered, knowing all too well that this was my greatest mistake.

Inside, I was late. Inside, there was Jack and two other crew members. Inside this empty building was a fancy carpet bleeding underneath a cushioned couch. And on that couch sat a small Vietnamese girl, who looked underage, with her legs held open by another man examining her parts. It all would have been appropriate, with my camera in hand and the focus on her exclusive parts, if it wasn't for the cage nearby being open.

At that time, I watched a Doberman emerge from the bars, a drooling mouth, paws covered in mittens, and a full erection throbbing. It was then that I understood Stacy's words. And I grew in dread.

It was then that I knew that I had dove too deep into this industry. Every moment and memory now contacting me, haunting me, and now residing in me. My words were repeating from my friend's, my family's words ripping. I was made of minor shreds of a man more fortunate in fortune, yet less luck in the end game, to realize that children and beasts make money too . . .

– **26** –
K-9 (Part 2)

BETWEEN THOSE TWO YEARS her sister's wedding was happening. Being a baker, she was the designated wedding cake producer and designer.

From flour to floral edibles, she was in charge. But the weight of the wedding started to conflict with her judgement. I recall some yelling, some demands and the like. The stress was a variable factor in an equation set to a negative denominator. In hindsight, we were both fucked from the start.

Driving back to the apartment I knew I was done. Not for the right reasons, I guess I was just sick and tired of being "tied down" by a ball and chain made of copper better sold at an underground auction. In that moment I was a man, I didn't need a woman bossing me about, I didn't need to be stressed by the wedding like she was, I didn't have to be obligated like she was.

I didn't have to be anything but buzzed by alcohol and free from the shackles of tyrannical oppression, known as "going steady". As soon as we left the car, I walked out that day, towards the staircase and up to the apartment for a few drinks before driving off to my shift. Pissed, blinded by rage, engaged in self-pitiful-pain and a casualty of self-serving ideas. It was then that I heard her voice.

"Please, don't go. I need you. I can't do this on my own . . ." she sounded pathetic.

I looked behind me to see her knees shaking, tears falling, and hands held up in prayer, as if that meant forgiveness. In that moment, if I hadn't been so stupid, I should had felt something other than resentment. I should had turned around, embraced her, wiped the tears away and said "fuck it" to work.

On that day I should have dropped to my knees, bled my own set of tears, placed my palms forward and thanked her so much for believing in me. For giving me the justice I always needed, for providing the love she always had. I should have crawled on all *fours like a beaten dog in the snow looking for a warm place to hide and then collided into her arms and begged for just one more day around her leash.*

But instead, I was more concerned about acting like a "man" then being one.

"No." was all I could say, was all I cared for before turning and leaving her.

It was the beginning of the end, all downhill from this point forward. Funny enough, it's easy to ride downhill. It's hard to go up that same hill, repair, replace, and respect one another. But when you're going downhill, all that's ahead of you is the bottom . . .

Entering further, I was hesitant and nervous upon approach. I could feel my palms sweating, my knees buckling, and a pain in the center of my neck. It was now that I had wished some horrible thing upon myself, a tumor breaking my blood vessels, or the baby boomers killing another tree for cheap merchandise at a future thrift store. Something to take me out and away from what was about to commence. But nothing ever happened, as Jack pulled me to the side and whispered into my ear:

"She's the hottest thing on the Vietnamese market and we got a deal on her. She's fucking young man, like . . . fucking young. But as long as you deny it in the meta, you're good bruh. She's gonna' take that dick like . . ." I watched him lick his lips, salivating over her open entry point, then repeating: "she's young man."

In the embrace, somehow suffocating in Judas' arms, I knew he was an animal contemplating his prey's demise. Everyone else there was so normal, desensitized, saturated. Blanketed eyes glazed past me, slouched bodies wavered over me, useless apathy concaved around me. I was my own animal trapped in my own trap.

What fucking irony.

"Jack . . ." I thought, but for a moment in time, adjusted and became aware of those around me. My body unsteady, my nerves going haywire for the first time since – since – since Goddamn Abby.

Since that fucking time in my basement, when I was scared, when I couldn't get it up, when I was weak, when I wasn't a man, when I was in love, and when I hated her.

When I loved her, I never knew her. When I was just a boy, I've now become a man, though still a boy. Can I ever change, or can I change the world, or is change even possible, or is it even up to me?

Is change like the color of the rainbow, or is it the whole rainbow? Or is the world just set in white and black and grey, and we need to discover where we exist? Then it all came crashing down, as Jack's arm left me and the dog trainer led the poor mut and his obligated erection over to the girl.

"Get that camera rollin' bruh." Jack commanded.

But I didn't feel the same, I almost felt indifferent. But I knew it was the alcohol and drugs talking. Suddenly, this industry reminded me of all the things I had been fighting against. Control, demands, a cage in a dark room set in solitary.

My parents' shadow, living up to the past generation's values, undertaking extremes that, in the end, didn't mean much more than devotional lost letters. It occurred to me now that my parents had never lived up to their parent's potential, and so the blame was transferred onward.

A generational abomination of war-propaganda-paranoia, commercial cartoon sales and a guilty-as-gold generational gap. The money I lacked now had driven me to watching this poor Vietnamese girl be forced to spread her legs, have watched this dog sickly drool, have watched my boss resuscitate over the idea of one more viral video raking in enough content to pay for his over-exasperated mansion.

And in the end, his mansion would finally form the mausoleum in which all his women would be buried in. A lonely grave of land on a monetary market meant for buyers to conform, formulate and sell to lesser men like us, like me.

In this moment I was truly me, and Jack was truly himself, and this girl was truly made to be broken. I couldn't stand the thought.

Turning to Jack, with a sort of faded confidence I asked, "Hold up, I need to change my lens.".

At first Jack looked at me with a very conjoined look, but after a second thought did not speak but waved a hand. The dog handler and other crew members halted their actions. It was, at the very least, a little bit of time I could spend saving this poor girl from the beasts' impalement.

In the seconds I spent switching out lens to my camera, I knew there was only so much I could do. Looking at the room, there wasn't much the lighting would interfere with. The rest of the crew, by looks, were new and cowardly in the business. In a sense, this was my advantage. Then there was the dog, something must be done with this carnal canine.

Standing to the tallest I could reach I raised myself to Jack and demanded: "I need to get the white balance just right. The damn lights and all in this dark place, fucks with the imagining, you know?"

He almost immediately gave his resentment, stating, "I have already given them orders, Chief. What more do'ya need?"

It was then I knew I could exploit him. He knew how to order, not how to deliver, he was half of the job.

I became the other. "If you want this perfect or nearly to, if you want the money you deserve, then you'll let me set this production up." He was unnerved, but I had a plan. "Let me get this just right, just how you've trusted me to do. Trust me Jack, I'm the best you got."

And he nodded, going off to drag a smoke as I carefully approached the Vietnamese girl. But the closer I got, the smaller she became. God, she must've been young. It placed an ulcer in my stomach where, before, there was only booze and the nausea thereafter.

And as I angled my camera, she shrieked, as if I was going to do something else. I didn't want to hurt her, and it made me realize that I was hurting everyone around me. Including myself.

But as Jack was distracted by his chit-chat and drag, I pulled out my phone and dialed 9-1-1. I knew that I could be in trouble, mostly so, but I felt the need to help this young woman. The feeling overcame me, some parental protection embodied by instincts, as if she were my daughter.

I had never felt this sensation before.

And as the call was made, I heard the operator speak. But all I could say was "I need help", and after the whisper, I hid the phone within my pocket, the police still on the line. Then I fiddled with the camera, but I knew it wouldn't buy us enough time. As she sat their, naked and bare, waiting to accept the dog's lower tongue, I tried to convince her.

"It's going to be ok, just hang on, will ya?"

That's when Jack must've overheard me.

"Wha's that kiddo?" and I knew, time and time again, that I could play to my own advantage.

"I need those lights moved back. That shit's gonna' light her up like a white ghost on the fuck'n cam!"

I saw him appalled, now becoming stressed. But I had worked for this man, this disgusting abomination, for years now. I knew that he'd have the crew move the lights, buying us a few more minutes of time. If the crew wasn't so elementary, I wouldn't have even tried to fake it. Then, in my own head, I was certain that I would've become just like Jack. Dissolving, and changing into some chimera of all that was wrong with society.

I didn't want to become that, not any longer.

As the crew began moving the lighting, following my waving hand as I waved them towards indiscriminate and outlandish places around the stage, I could hear the operator on the other line from inside my pocket. I could even hear them muffled beyond the heavy breaths of the girl to my front. But I couldn't help but give a smile. Not because I was happy, but because I wanted her to understand that it would all be ok in due time. But time was running out.

"This fucking light'n o-k with you bruh? It's neva' been sush a hassle before? You fuck'n with me bruh? This some sort of fuck'n game for you?"

"No, no Jack, I just want to get it perfect and-"

"Perfect? Fuckin' perfect, he says." As he pointed down on me amongst the rest of the crew. "This fuck'n pricks been wantin' perfect'n for 'is one shoot all'oh sudden. The fuck's wrong with you bruh? A dog dick in a slut ain't nothin' these days! I think you just fancy yourself a long fuck'n glance at her pussy, bruh?" as he walked on towards me.

Then, as he reached me, he held me tight by my shirt collar and barked louder than the fucking dog did. "Don' get smart with me, bruh! You can have this little slits' slit the second she's done with the doggie!"

My camera was swinging around my neck like a noose yet to be tightened. And all I could do was grasp his wrists to keep from choking me out.

But he set me down and forcefully ripped the camera from my neck, its strap running burning lines up across my neck and hairline as he did. He started to look at the camera screen, but quickly noticed that I hadn't even turned the damn thing on. Jack acted like it was some sort of joke, yelling at me that time was precious with this one. But then, the muffled voice from the phone reacted once more, and I could tell by Jack's wide eyes that he knew that something was amiss.

"Where's your phone, bruh?"

"*I didn't know, or, I didn't want to tell him.*"

"Excuse'mah bruh?"

I did not know that I had spoken aloud.

He reached for my pocket; put I held back. I yelled at him, stating that he had no permission, that he was getting paranoid, that he had no right. But based on the girls he had in his house, that only made him more aggressive. Anything and anyone in his house are what he owned, and I was no different. And now, I finally understood how the other girls felt beneath his control.

During our struggle, in the background the Vientenese girl was crying and sheltering herself. The crew was surrounding us, uncertain of what to do. I couldn't blame them, as Jack and I tussled. For a few moments, he was laying fists into my sides. I was grappled, with Jack on top of me like some alpha male dominating my poor, particularly petite body. But it was all violence.

Then again, porn was violent.

We struggled for some time, while another man, the likes of which must've been the provider of the girl had started to argue with the dog handler. At this point my camera had been smashed to pieces, with others in cases in need of backups. But that wasn't the point.

I was the point.

The point of impact, the point of manipulation, and currently the point of Jack's abuse. We had run out of time, and all I could do was yell to the girl to "Run! Run now!" but it was too late. As soon as I yelled, Jack got the message. He was pointing at his goons, making sure that the girl wouldn't leave the room. And then, to the side of my forehead I felt something cold, metallic, and deadly.

That's when I had realized that Jack came loaded, with a 9mm aimed straight into my temple.

"You're gonna' die tonigh', you betraying fucker. You're gonna die, along with that girl if you don't die quietly."

But before that trigger was pulled, an alarm rang out. It wasn't within the building, rather outside of it. As the gun left my head, we each looked out to the windows barricading this Hell hole and saw blue and red lights flashing into purples. An officer had arrived on the scene, and Jack couldn't have a dead man bleeding along the concrete.

At least, not for the moment.

And as he rose, I kept to the floor. Then he demanded that I rise, and to "*act coo*" before proceeding to the entry point. His pistol neatly tucked in the backside of his pants.

– *27* –

K-9 (Part 3)

LOUD KNOCKING AGAINST THE sliding metal door echoed throughout the room. Everyone stayed quiet, while the crew forced her and I behind the couch. Turning the lights off, Jack flipped a switch nearby, illuminating the room in some awful, dingy orange luminescence. Then he unlocked the door and answered.

"Oh, well hey there officer. What can I do for ya'?" I heard him speak, knowing that he was giving the officer his biggest and brightest smile. That damned smile.

But at first, there was no response. I was wondering what the officer was doing. I wanted him, or her, or whoever to barge right in and save us. It was becoming more of a struggle keeping the girl's mouth closed. I could tell she wanted to scream out. So did I, in fact.

But the time was imperfect.

I looked around the backside of the room to see what there was, if there was anything that could be used to help us escape this situation. Then I glanced up at one of the lighting fixtures and could barely make out the image at the door against the glass of the large bulb. That's when I noticed the officer peaking in and around Jack.

"We got a real strange phone call from here. Is everything going all right?"

"A phone call eh?" I could hear a small crack in Jack's voice. That was the first time I ever heard Jack slip under pressure. "One've us must'a butt-dialed ya'll or – or somethin'. Isn't tha' righ' gentlem'n?"

And from the bulb I watched them each nod in compliance. All the while I could feel drips of saliva falling from my hand, the girl's humid breaths growing insatiable with each passing minute.

"That so?" I heard the officer reply. By the sound of his voice, it didn't seem like he was buying it. This was probably the first time too that Jack couldn't sell a lie, unlike the porn he was producing. "Mind me askin' what's with all the lights? And the dog?"

"Ah, yeah well, we're setting up a scene ya' know? For a short film, be'n played at the indie film fest an' shit this year. Short film 'bout, oh you know, classic dog movie an' all."

"Ah, I see, like Ol' Yella?"

"Yeah, buh more like Reservoir Dogs."

"Huh, I don't recall Reservoir Dogs being about dogs, or even if there's a dog in that movie."

"Well, is like Resv'oir Dogs, but with dogs. Like a play on words, you know?" Jack was out of his element.

"All right, what's it called?"

An immediate silence overtook the space. For once, I felt like the smartest person in the room. We were all waiting for Jack's reply. Hell, I would've laughed out loud if I wasn't so scared shitless.

"River Dogs." Was the best that Jack's tiny imagination could conjure.

"Right . . ." the officer stated. I watched him move in past Jack to examine the room further.

Then, from the reflection of the bulb I noticed Jack attempting to unholster his pistol from the backside of his pants. It was only a matter of time now. But the handle seemed to be stuck against his belt, and I knew that I wouldn't get another opportunity like this one.

Letting go of the girl, she started screaming through her tears. She startled everyone, as I lunged myself above the peak of the couch and yelled, "He's got a gun!"

That's when the officer drew his weapon. The crew members all scurried against the walls of the room, but Jack had already unlogged his pistol from his backside. Jack fired first, and I heard the bullet ricochet behind me.

As the officer began to fire, is was utter chaos. But in the moment I panicked, lifting the young girl from her feet as the dog wrangler let go of the leash. There was a lot of yelling, and gunfire encircling the room.

Somehow, as both the girl and I ran hand-in-hand together towards the door, I watched Jack's pistol ignite before my eyes. Blinded for a second, I threw my body against his, sending him flying back into the corner.

As we ran from the room, I briefly stared back to see that the dog had a crew member in its jaws, that the officer was calling for backup, with Jack nowhere to be seen.

Heading back into my Lambo, I quickly sat the girl down in the passenger side seat before driving off. A hot sweat filled the cabin of the car, as I roared down the road, thinking out loud to myself, "Where am I going?"

I wanted to put the windows down, let the churning heat and sweat from the two of us extinguish itself in the nighttime. But with the girl still yelling and crying, I couldn't risk it. Then I realized I had to slow down.

I was travelling eighty in a forty. If Jack didn't catch us, then the police would for some speeding infraction. Not knowing how that would play out, I simply wanted to keep us from gathering any more attention.

Miles down the road I spotted the neon lights of some shitty motel. The kind you find hookers stamped outside of on any given day. Screeching into a parking space, I kept the engine humming. Then, looking to my side, I saw the girl shivering.

I begged with her, "Please stay here. I'm going to help you. Just, don't do anything stupid, ok?"

She looked at me with a plain stare. Not understanding a word, she must've seen something in my own eyes. The same fear that she had was also mine. It was communication without words, as she reached a hand over to brush along my cheek. That's when I knew I could leave her, if only for a moment longer.

Exiting the car, I made sure to lock it. Checking my phone, my heart skipped another beat. The 9-1-1 operator was still on the line. I quickly hung up, seeing that the time was half past eleven.

Walking up to the motel's service booth, I knew that I'd be lucky to find a room at this hour. But below the neon board was a smaller sign that read "Vacancy", so, I had hopes.

Not much hope, but hopefully enough.

As I approached the counter, a man reading a magazine slowly but surely bookmarked his page with an unlit cigarette and turned to look at me. He was the type of crusty, down-on-his-luck type of person that'd be working the graveyard shift at this motel.

"Whatcha' need hot shot? One hour, half-an-hour?"

I ignored his comment, "I need a room for the night, maybe two, maybe more."

"Yeah so, this ain't the Hilton pal. And you don't look to down on your luck judging by the ride." That fucking Lambo was starting to become a curse. "If you head a bit further north I'm sure you'll find the shoe-spit and shine type of establishment your lookin-"

Then my phone rang, it was an unknown number calling back. I knew it was the police, so I ended the call and turned my phone to silent. That's when my stress reached a boiling point, and the mother-fucker in front of me was about to get a mouthful.

"I need a fucking room pal! I ain't in the mood for your shit right now." My hands were still shaking, I was covered in sweat and freezing, and I had enough bullshit for the night. "First floor, near to *my ride*," I condescendingly ordered, "and make sure it ain't no shit-stained, cum-rocker."

At first, I saw him ready to just call the cops himself. But a handful of Benjamin's looked him in the eyes and told him otherwise. Unfortunately, I handed him my wallet for this room, so I hoped we would get to stay for longer than the hour he figured we were doing the dirty.

Thankfully he was a man of his word, giving me the key to room 106, right in front of where I pulled in. Leaving him to count his cash, I quickly unlocked the room.

It was dingy and smelled like cigarettes, as was to be expected. The funny part of it was, this probably was their premier suite. Not thinking on it for too long, I ran to the bed and tore the comforter from its rest. Then, back outside, I unlocked my car and, as the girl began to move up, I wrapped her in the comforter before leading her into the room.

I pressed my keys once more, watching the lights of my Lambo blink twice, knowing she was locked for the night. Inside the girl simply sat on the edge of the bed, wrapped tightly in the comforter. Compared to Vietnam, I figured, this establishment seemed high class in comparison.

Then, as I took a seat beside her, something awful occurred. She let the comforter slip off from her body, and she began to make moves across my own. That's when I gently pushed her back, bringing the comforter back around her. It must've been instinctual, as if she were an animal trained to do so. Whether she was thanking me or not, I didn't want to. We weren't quite out of the clearing just yet, as I felt my phone vibrate with another call. And sex, as it was, was the last thing on my mind right then and there.

Especially with her, especially after Myra.

It was now that I realized, in pandemonium, that in the last year and a half of my life had all developed into this. Working with Jack, the fucking shoot-out, and now this shitty motel on the edge of town. With an underaged Vietnamese girl who didn't even speak a word of English. With the police calling me every other minute. And who knows what else went down back at the abandoned building. My hope was that Jack was at least arrested, if not gunned down by now.

I was pacing the room now in thought, I hadn't even realized that I stood up. This level of panic, the stress of my anxiety, and the fucking adrenaline flowing nonstop through me. I was being consumed by questions and ideas, pacing and pacing, thinking I could walk it all off.

I couldn't.

That's when I realized, I needed to say something. But to who? The Vietnamese girl? She probably already thought that I was crazy. I guess I was at this point, that was no longer in question. But I needed to speak to someone or something just to get it all out. To quiet my mind and set free all my repeating words and statements, just to gain an ounce of sanity back.

And as my phone buzzed another time, I almost chose to huck the thing into the wall. That's when, in my own reflection, I saw myself mirrored in the screen. I finally had something to say, that I wanted to say weeks ago. This time, however, it wasn't for views or subscribers and the like. It was for me, especially if this was my last night on Earth. Either as a free-man, or a still-alive one.

So, I opened the camera on my phone and set it to video-mode. I didn't no how much time I had before being found by the police, who had probably tracked my location already. But with my insurmountable panic, I quickly sat myself down against the bed, watching the girl's feet kick next to me for a second before hitting record.

I talked, talked more than I ever had in one sitting. Speaking to the phone, watching myself on its screen, I had no choice but to explain it all.

From the very start, when I was holding that cardboard sign. To my times with Frankie and Abby. I even talked about Myra, knowing that it was probably a mistake to do so. But I wasn't ready to leave any details out of the picture. No, I wasn't very exact with the overall story and, yes, I was speaking quite frantically. But it wasn't the details that mattered to me then and there. I just wanted to have a voice left over for someone to hear.

My love for Abby, my melancholy through Michael, my admiration for Frankie, and my hatred for Jack. I explained it all, as if speedreading through the past twenty-six chapters of my life. And when I was done, I noticed that my eyes were watering, lips quivering, and the room had gone silent.

The girl had fallen asleep beside me, and before ending my twenty-six and a half long minute recording, I made sure to tuck her into bed. Then, at the very tail end of everything, as if I knew my time of death was approaching, I looked at the camera one last time and said.

"I love you, mom, dad. Even you, Frankie. And . . . Abby, I think I love you too. And Myra, I'm sorry for what I did. And Kyra, just know that I think about you a lot too. I love you all, in your own, weird ways." And then I stopped the recording.

It's funny to think how a man like me could record the most private parts and functions of the human body without a care. But when it came to having my own camera pointed at me, it felt like life or death.

And as I got up, I began to upload the video online. Being so long, it would take some time before the world could view it. But time had run out for me, and I was ready for the next chapter in my life. Even if it became a very long chapter.

At least that's what I was prepared for when I heard a loud knock against the door. Afterwards, I noticed the police lights flashing from behind the curtains and knew that my time had come. So, with the girl still asleep, I walked slowly towards the door, preparing my wrists for a pair of cuffs.

Who knows, maybe it would all work out in the end?

That's when I opened the door and was immediately shoved to the carpet inside. I heard the door slam shut afterwards, and the girl waking from the bed. She was screaming again, but I didn't know the reasons why until I looked up.

And there was Jack, with his pistol aimed at me.

- 28 -

Misery Loves Company

IT WASN'T HIS GUN, I noticed, but instead it must've been the officer's pistol and I feared the worst had happened. While attempting to get back up, all I could feel was his damn foot slamming me back onto the carpet, with the gun waving between me and the girl.

She did her best to keep quiet, while I was barely holding onto Jack's foot above me. He was compressing my chest, I could feel a rib or two snapping in the process. Then I began to yell some half-breathed yell, and he didn't like that.

"There'ou go, crying out like'a lil' girl again. You two must've been made for 'nother." As he removed his foot, lifting me by my shirt's collar before pistol-whipping me straight across the forehead.

I was lucky that his aim wasn't great, but the fucking butt-end of the pistol still hurt like Hell. Everything went black for a few seconds before I could see again. He had made his way onto the bed, next to her and his arm constricting around her neck like a fucking snake.

"St-s'op it F-Jack . . ." I managed to cough out. But it was no use, as always, Jack was in control.

And I was Jack's red carpet into the end.

"St-st-stop it!" he yelled out in amusement. "You fuck'd up everythin', every last fuckin' thing kiddo. Bruh, like, I thought you were one of us? But you let this nobody lil' slut get the best of your -what- morals? Fuck'n pathetic, bruh."

"Fr-Jack, you know that . . . that this was wrong. Why – why the fuck would I ever . . ."

"Why what?" he questioned insentively, still strangling the girl in his arm. "Why you gave up the perfec' gig? Why you gave up the perfec' life? If it wasn' for that stupid fuck'n Lambo outside I might never'a found you two."

That's when I knew the Lambo was a curse.

A curse from the gig, the job, the shoots. My trust in Jack was too real to be true. There would always be a breaking point, a line that I couldn't cross. And that line was almost washed away with the tide, as if it had been drawn in the sand. Washed over by the alcohol, the drugs, the women, the money, everything I wanted. Now, everything I wanted and everything that came true became my greatest nightmare.

"We don' have long, bruh. Police'll be here shortly, I'm sure. It's time you faced the consequences of your actions."

And as I watched the girl's face turn blue, I let myself go. To rage and the fire building in me. I couldn't hold it back, not even in the face of death itself.

"Consequences?" I asked, rising to my knees along the floor, "You're one stupid sorry son-of-a-bitch for asking me to face *my* consequences pal."

I knew that would get Jack fired up, and it did.

He let go of the girl, who collapsed onto the bed without a squeal or a sound otherwise. As I moved to the wall, I watched Jack come right up to me. He didn't grab me by the collar, nor did he aim his pistol right towards me. A man like Jack feasts from his pride, and when his pride is hurt, he acts like a wounded animal. This much I knew was certain.

"My consequences!" he shook the room. "I've been in this shit longer than you've been alive, bruh! My consequences didn't exist! It was do or die all the time, no fuck'n in-between pussy bullshit excuses or otherwise!"

"Is — is that why you're here, now?" I understood I was about to die, so at least I'd die with a smile on my face as I laughed at my own words. "Is that — that why you're here with me and her now, Frankie?"

But I didn't mean to call him "Frankie". I think that there was just too much resentment from the two that I've held onto for far too long. It's ironic that, at the end of everything, we start to think about things that mattered to us the most and how we never used our time to say what was truly on our minds. Yes, I resented Frankie, but more so I resented the bastard holding the gun in front of me.

"I think its 'bout time we stop the talkin', bruh." And that pistol of his looked me in the eyes straighter than any girl in my life ever had.

But before that trigger was pulled, I watched the flashing lights multiply through the curtains. With all the noise ringing inside of my head, I could still make out sirens outside. So, I kept on smiling. I wanted to die with one last word.

Something that most of us will be refused.

"Jack, but I think that you're ab-"

Then, I watched the barrel ignite, but only after the Vietnamese girl had jumped from the bed and laid her own teeth into Jack. As he fired, I felt a quick shock travel through the right side of my chest. It must've been the adrenaline again.

And as Jack struggled with the girl, bullets were being shot in every direction. That's when I stood up and began to make my way towards the two. I was ready to take that gun, point it point-blank at his face and fire one off myself. Then, while leaning against the front door, preparing my attack, the fucking door shattered at the keylock, and I was sent spiraling down again as it opened.

More shots were fired. All I heard were loud bangs, the smell of gunpowder acting like an inhaler as I gasped for breaths. Next, I felt a foot cross over me, then a black boot accidentally stomping my leg. Police officers filled the room, but not before one last bullet strayed my way.

Things were, as you could imagine by now, getting real dark. Not just within my story, but more so my mind as I began to feint. It couldn't be helped; I was losing blood. Blurs and swirls and light-headedness overcame me, and the next thing I knew was that the world was disappearing.

Finally . . .

. . . I woke up.

The world around me was still a maze of poorly drawn lines, with some dickshit having colored outside of them. There were voices, but nothing tangible was being said. At least, I couldn't understand what was being said. It became complete vertigo, early on-set dementia taking form. I hadn't known where I was or if I was even alive. This could've been limbo for all I knew, but a part of me reminded itself that I'd be sent to Hell before any purgatory, if that shit were real.

I wasn't religious and was the last thing from a saint at this point. But worse people had been forgiven for their sins, I supposed, so perhaps I was lost in a void. Like a ghost wandering the space in which I had died.

Too bad it was that shitty motel. Years after my death, it would probably be featured on some B-grade ghost-hunting show, televised to the world. The story of the young man and his underaged accomplice, and the porn-king who shot them both dead to rights. Wow, what a thrilling fourty-five minute episode that would make, with commercial breaks in between. If a ghost hunter had an EMP out, what would I tell them? *That I was framed*? *That it was Jack*? *That my dreams had divulged into sinister outcomes*?

Or could I just say, "*I'm sorry.*"

"*Doctor . . . he's still with us . . . he's awake . . . he kid . . . what's your name? . . .*"

"Oh shit." I couldn't believe it was real. "*Is this going on Discovery? Or HBO?*"

"*. . . what's your name? . . .*"

Persistent fucking ghost hunters. "*I'm . . .*" but I was fading again. I didn't even know that ghosts could feint.

Soon I felt my body being lifted, my head was swaying to either side beyond my control. There was pain at points in time, but they would subside as soon as they started. I was cushioned against a cloud, the walls were white, there were numerous faces of strangers staring back at me. I thought I knew them, I had to know them. Perhaps they were my ancestors, or I was still dying and was replaying my entire life out. My childhood, teenage years, and most of college however, never really played out. As if my reel had been snipped at the start, and all I had left were the past two years of my life to look back on.

What a shame, I thought.

"Frankie . . . Abby . . . Myra . . . I'm . . . I'm so . . . so sorry . . ." was I really this full of regret?

I felt a needle puncture my arm. Was Kyra somehow with me too? Looking around in my dazed state, I recognized a hanging bag beside me, some strange monitor that kept on beating to the drums of my heart, and god-damn white-coats scattering around me.

"We need to sedate him . . . the bullet wounds are too deep . . . contact his family . . . does he have any contacts?"

Contacts? Was my phone still with me? How was my video doing? Had I reached an audience? I needed to know, right then and there.

But my arms had trouble moving themselves. I could picture them fleeing into my pocket, but I couldn't move them. It was a phantom sensation that I truly didn't like. Then I remembered the girl, her feet kicking next to me while recording. Then, me tucking her in before Jack intruded. And if I was going to Hell, then I was sure to meet Jack there as well. So, in the last few glances I made, I awaited Jack at the edge of

. . . I came to.

My eyes blinked rapidly in the harsh sunlight from the window nearby. Laying in a bed that was neither my parents, my own, nor the one from the mansion, I began to wonder where I was. And looking at the windowsill, I saw a few vases with flowers soaking in the sunshine. There was a stuffed rabbit, and some cards attached to each gift.

Though when I moved, my hand had accidentally landed onto some remote of sorts. Suddenly, the television overhead turned on, and the volume was loud. There was a football game underway, but the cheers from the crowd on live television drove me insane. Cocking my head to the side, my eyes followed down to the remote and I began to press every button imaginable. Anything to shut off the annoying cheers of my rude awakening.

God, I was weak. My arms had barely moved, but I felt exhausted. And my legs, I kicked them a couple of times to ensure that I still could. Then there were the walls, painted white, the color of disinfection, surrounding me.

It wasn't a minute later that I saw a nurse reach my door, with a crowd of people conglomerating behind her. She tried her best to keep them at bay while attempting to reach my bedside. But it was no use.

The second that door cracked open, a swarm of parasites with cameras and questions entered my room. All at once I became surrounded by my bedside, and the questions began to flood the room.

"Tell us why you're here?"

"It's said that you're in the porn industry?"

"We saw your video online. How do you react?"

The flashing lights around me were nauseating, but the worst was knowing that I was now on the other end of the camera. It was true, that misery loved company.

"Did you aid in the murder of officer Vandez?"

"Who is the Asian girl that was found with you?"

"Are you a part of Jack's unruly practices?"

I saw myself in every lens that faced me. Bandaged, dressed in a hospital gown underneath a sheet, wide-eyed and uncertain where I was.

"Did you make the call to the police?"

"Were you the one who saved that poor girl?"

"What's hidden inside of Jack's mansion?"

The questions were never-ending.

Eventually, security made its way into my room and pulled every media-cockroach from my bedside, back into the hallway. As they did, I watched one officer in particular spit down to my hospital bed as he left me alone.

After a few minutes and continuous arguments from outside of my room simmered down, the nurse came back in. She definitely wasn't paid enough to deal with the media in L.A. And after checking my vitals and ensuring that I was all right, she looked down at me and asked.

"Was it worth it? Taking advantage of those girls and all?"

And for a moment, she was completely right. But, in my situation, I no longer wanted to play the bad guy. I wanted to be good again, as if I had a choice. So, I replied back.

"I was trying to save them. There was no other way, except to become the monster. But the monster isn't always bad, just scary to those on the outside looking in.

– 29 –

Trial By Fire

*I'VE CHEATED AND HAVE BEEN CHEATED ON. I
guess that's what they call karma. That Asian girl I lost
my virginity to, through her parents' expenses she had
taken a trip to Vietnam for three months to be reunited
with her family. It was sweet for her, and sweet for me.*

*You see, we hadn't been doing so well. The
connection that we once had, well, was becoming lost.
And during her three-month escalade to the east, I
started looking at other opportunities. Though, most
never amounted to much. Not but one girl in particular.*

*She was my supervisor at my first job, even
though she was the same age as me. An average girl
at most, average breast size, average charisma,
average height, and an average personality. But she
was nothing special. Not until we decided to hook up.*

*One night, we met at a restaurant together.
Nothing fancy, just your usual run-of-the-mill burgers
and fries and bar-food type shit. Corporate, of course,
with hundreds of locations across the nation. Yet, in a
sense, that made it more degradable than a mom-and-
pop food stand.*

*Nonetheless, we sat and we ate. I could tell that
she was seemingly off. She'd sway across the booth,
eat delicately, make small talk about work and the like
before she invited me back to her parents' place. Once
there, she revealed a bottle of vodka from behind the
couch, had claimed that her parents were gone for the
week and just wanted to have fun. And golly, did I
want to have fun.*

But I was a straight-edge kid back then. Funny how that persona changed so drastically in later years. But I refused to drink, and at one point I pressured her, claiming that I would leave if she didn't want me around. That's when she must've made up her mind, inviting me up into her bedroom.

Once there, it didn't take long until I had her pants off. And from ten until two, I was finger-blasting her into absolute orgasm. She was a screamer, which I never experienced but thoroughly enjoyed. And her insides were so ribbed that, to this day, I wonder what it would be like pushing inside of her.

The morning after was more comical than it should've been. I recalled us waking up around six, but I pretended to be asleep. She had rushed into the bathroom, and all I heard from the bedroom were the most horrendous, mind-blowing shits taken. My father couldn't even compare.

And as she snuck back into bed with me, after the vodka-shits had made their ways out of her, she snuggled gently against me and in my ear she said:

"I'm calling out sick today, but you still should go in. Just so nobody knows that we were together last night."

And I did, and I worked my shift. And I said nothing to no one in regards to her and why she called out. I didn't mind; I got my little fling. And years later she'd messaged me, asking what I was up to.

But I never saw the message, and so I never replied.

Then, years after her, and years after the tomboy and the Asian and all other women, I was cheated on in college . . .

A few days more in the hospital, and one nurse decided to show me the bullets. Not "*bullet*", but "*bullets*". There were three in total, one in my right leg, another in my collarbone, and the final and most deadly one was buried next to my heart. She said I should be thankful, that God must've been looking out for me or some shit. Because, if that bullet had inched any closer, then I'd be a dead man for sure.

I also learned who fired the bullets. No, it wasn't just Jack, though he had landed two shots into me. The first was the one closest to my heart, which he fired before the Vietenese girl had attacked him. I guess I should've been thanking her more than God for her service. Then there was a stray bullet that landed in my leg from Jack's furious gunfire after the police had entered. But the final, mismanaged bullet to my collarbone was shot by one of the entering officers.

Even though I was crawling on all fours after being knocked down. Even after being shot once, then twice. Even though I didn't pose a threat, the damn officer still shot at me.

I was recommended to seek out a lawyer at that point, though that fact was obvious.

I was in a shit-ton of trouble either way, having been a part of the porn industry, having followed Jack's orders for a year, after having evaded the police that night. I was in serious deep shit for what I've done. But luckily, I was being painted as a hero.

My video, the one I had uploaded at the motel, was gaining traction. Not just traction, but it became a God-damn highway for viewership. Yes, you had the haters who never agreed with your motives or story. But more so, you had those that were willing to listen, interpret, and come to their own conclusions. They were the ones, the content creators that I once despised, that lifted me up from negative press hearing. Although, there was still a great amount of negativity to overcome within the public sphere.

Even though I was branded as "uncertain" amongst the general public, many online creators came to my aid. Hell, I didn't even ask, they just did what they felt was right. Or, rather, what they thought would garner more views. And after a translated statement from the Vietnamese girl, who I now know to be Mai, I became publicly accepted as the savior of the trafficked woman.

Of course, this was an oversight of the media. In my mind, I was just helping one single sex-trafficked individual who I felt strongly about, not in terms of attraction but in terms of empathy, as she helped solidify my case. My case, in which, was being held in a month.

Like the Depp versus Heard case, mine was also reaching notoriety. Not only because I had obviously saved a sex-trafficked individual who was underage and illegally imported into the United States of America, although those facts did help my cause. Instead, it was also about Jack and his ring of women, the drugs he bought to keep us all content, and the tax-evasion which the government cared about most. No surprise there, after all.

When speaking with the media, I always had my lawyer by my side. Did I mention that I found a lawyer? Or, rather, a lawyer found me. He, in particular, a William Grand Walker the Second, was used to complicated cases involving high notoriety and acclaim. He said one sentence to me:

"*You wanna' win this mess and make a hundred mil?*"

And suddenly, I was hooked.

As the media surrounded me, whether limping out from the hospital or to and from the hotel I stayed in temporarily, he was always by my side. I called him "*Walker*" for short, and he somehow appreciated the sentiment.

Anytime I spoke, whether it was live on television or on some creator's podcast, Walker would be with me. We did amazing things together. Even if he wasn't in the camera's frame, we'd share gestures and face-signals to indicate what not to say, when to say something, and how to say it.

I was his puppet, but I was paying for his strings. It was almost parasocial, except for the fact that he existed right there with me. I must've been a probable case, otherwise he would've left the day after my release from the hospital bed.

Whenever the media would ask me, "Did you do it?" I would ask "Do what?" And anytime they pressure me about living in Jack's mansion, doing his bidding, performing his outlandish jobs, I'd say, "He forced me, drugged me, threatened me. I had no way of escape. I was just another victim in his insidious schemes as the girls I worked with."

Then, sometimes, the girls from the mansion would be interviewed. Not as popularly, but just as importantly. My name would come up, but Walker would already have the check in their names, and so, things were kept quiet.

It was really up to my old friends and companions who, if worst came to worst, would spill their guts about me. When Myra was contacted, I was fortunate that she had nothing to say. And I admired her greatly for that. Then there was Abby, who refused outright to be a part of the controversy, probably due to Michael who kept her on a tight leash. In a sense, I was thankful for his abusive control over her. And yet, I knew that, regardless of whether she would speak or not, that she would have nothing bad to say about me. Or, at least, that was the wish.

But then there was Frankie. My best friend since elementary school, who lived a block down from me. We ignited his sister's dolls with lighters and blew up gun powder when his father wasn't home. He had led me through some tough times but also caused some of his own. But so did I.

I guess I never mentioned his sister.

It didn't matter now, because as soon as the media got ahold of Frankie, he became full of hysterics. He mentioned how dishonest I was, how I had betrayed him, how I left him behind for California. How I was destined to be in the title page of ever news article, and not for the right reasons.

Even a check sent in by Walker didn't calm his decent. He was a raging bull, furious by the fact that I had made a name for myself, even if it took three bullets below the flesh to do so. He was mad, and so was I.

But I kept my game face on, pretending not to know who exactly he was except for an accompanying tool towards what I thought was grandeur. And between the soft-sided voice that was Mai's, the heart-felt outtakes of the ladies at the mansion, and Jack's own upcoming conviction, Frankie himself was lost in a stream of biased news.

Fuck the man.

Frankie had fallen, just like Jack.

In a court hearing weeks later, I was called on as a witness to his testimony. I claimed, without a doubt, that Jack had been manipulating me from the start.

That all the sexual encounters with the women from the mansion had been prioritized by him. That he spoon-fed me drugs, molly, alcohol, or heroine, and especially coke, to keep me complacent within his business. I stated that I sympathized with the women in the mansion, even mentioning Kyra's name to the public, as Jack had threatened her before her leave. He did. But, not in the ways I fabricated the truth.

I told the judge and jury that Kyra, a once proud girl from the lower-class establishment, had sought great fortune from the insufferable Jack. That he fed her with pills and shot up her arms with dozens of amphetamines beyond her will. And on that final day, when hospital records had shown that she had overdosed, Jack had kicked her to the curb instead of helping her with her addiction.

It was all viable, to a point. I couldn't fictionalize the truth, only fabricate it to an extent. And given Jack's history, and the profound fact that he had shot a cop dead, nothing and nobody was taking his side. Then, looking at him from across the court room, I smiled again. And I knew that he hated it within every cell of his body. He hated me.

And on the day that my trial began, Walker assured me that this would be a walk in the park.

I pleaded innocent to every insurrection that was placed above my head. Like a Sim's character guilty of using every cheat code in a video game to get ahead. But my halo was bright, shining in the lights of photographers and videographers alike. Even if it had gone black, I was still portrayed as the "*good guy*" that was helpless under the tyranny of the porn industry.

"Jack forced his drugs onto the girls, then onto me. It was very selective. He wanted to keep us under his control, to ensure that we became addicts. To ensure that each and every one of us would go to him if we ever faced a relapse. And he kept us compliant.

There wasn't a single shoot I did where I wasn't under the influence. Jack made it that way, his way. He used drugs to control us and abused us through the drugs. And if it wasn't the drugs, it was the alcohol. And if it wasn't alcohol, it was money. Dirty, filthy, blood-soaked money that I, unfortunately, accepted under his rule.

He'd turn a gun on us with a blind eye. He showed no mercy. Jack had forced us all to abide by his command, and when doing so, we had no choice but to accept our demises. He's a cold-blooded killer and a tyrant, and I wish for nothing more than to see him behind bars for the remainder of his life.

Yes, I understand that I have done terrible, atrocious, and even malicious acts under his assertive power. But every day I would regret my choices, and every day I felt like taking my own life by my own hands.

All because of this man." I pointed from the podium to him; eyes watered on purpose.

"I wanted to die, nearly every single day that he had me under his control. I just wanted to escape. Yes, I knew what business I was getting into. But I wasn't smart enough to comprehend the decisions that I made."

That's when Walker whispered an ear-full to me, telling me to lay loose and calm my predispositions.

Looking back at the judge, I finished my statement.

"If it wasn't for Jack, then I wouldn't be here now. I was a young, stupid, impressionable kid who didn't know any better. If I could take it all back, if I could of saved officer Vandez on that night, then I would have.

But hindsight is twenty-twenty for a reason. A reason that I understand now. And so, your honor, I'd wish to conclude my summary of the man who, not only murdered officer Vandez, but also had murdered the innocent lives of illegal sex-workers and men like me in the process."

And the jury applauded but was quickly silenced by the judge. I knew I had won the popular vote, from a bunch of nimrods who probably had "TRUMP 2024" bumper stickers on their trucks, at the least. Thank God for American idiocracy, I suppose.

Even if there was one or two liberals on the stage, they'd too be casting a vote for me. I spoke my lines perfectly and my reasoning was definite. I was sure that I had won the popular vote, with it being streamed across different platforms of the like.

And in two months' time, with more bickering, more evidence, and even more statements, I was finally a free man. Jack had been convicted to twenty-five years of imprisonment without parole, and I was given a few infractions to pay off before leaving the courthouse.

Just then, at the booth where all courthouse bills were paid, a man approached Walker and I. He was well dressed, if not in some hipster new-age fashion, but acceptable enough. Coming up to me, one guard from the gallows began to move forward. Even I was concerned about a gun being fired my way.

It wasn't right when Charlie Kirk, a right-wing progenitor got shot and killed in front of a live audience had to die. I wasn't a fan of his, not by a long shot. But simply speaking your mind shouldn't have meant the death sentence. Though, that fucking cunt, Brian Thompson was well deserved.

But my life wasn't. At least, I didn't think it was.

And before the guard could apprehend the man for reaching into his suit-jacket, a business card was revealed.

"Talk to me if you want a best-selling book later."

And with that, I held the card, like a precious Christmas gift of sorts hand delivered to me by Santa himself. And after meeting Jack, and after having been used, I was ready to apply my fullest to every possible avenue.

I was the whore of my own mansion.

– **30** –

Oral

MY FIRST YEAR OF COLLEGE, I met a girl. She wasn't as attractive as the other girls I had set my eyes on. But she was willing and pretty enough, so I gave in.

Our first date was at a clothing store, some retail-named brand that has been struggling financially since the stocks had dropped in 2009. But it was still holding on, title and all, as we entered and started searching through dresses and lingerie. It didn't take long until she found something that she liked, before pulling me towards the dressing rooms and asking me to come in with her.

I asked if it was all right, being a gentleman of sorts.

She approved and dragged me through the curtains. Immediately she got down on her knees and pulled my jeans off by the belt. Next thing I knew was she had her mouth wrapped around my member like an anaconda swallowing it whole. It didn't take too long before I was ready.

Thrown on top of the dressing room bench, she maneuvered herself over me and, before I could react, had me within her. A few minutes later, she was begging for me to come inside of her.

Suddenly, I was locked in a place between fear and bliss. And when I let go, I moaned so loudly that she had to muffle me with her own two hands. Afterwards we walked around the store. I was still in a state of shock, satisfied but also nervous about what I had just done.

She was the last girl I'd want to have a child with.

Fortunately, she never got pregnant, at least not with my kid. And when she did, it died in the womb. You see, she kept on telling me about her ex and how he was always asking about her, wanting to meet up and the like. Then, a month went by, and I heard through rumor alone that she was seeing another dude.

I left her shortly after. Then, when it came to that guy, she found another one, and as she was fucking him, she was also fucking another. It was a game of Dominos, except men like me were the Dominos and she was the prissy little finger knocking us down one by one.

That was the first time in my life that I had been cheated on. Funny, though, that her supposedly obsessive ex was just another boy like me. Some other smuck was cheated on by her and I, while I never was able to connect the pieces at the time. And when she cheated on me, I was sure that I had become the obsessive ex, always reaching out.

Just a scapegoat for some nymphomaniac. That was the problem that I saw in our society, from the "me too" movement to women's rights. Pussy has always held power. And somehow, it wasn't enough.

Steven was the wizard behind the floating green face surrounded by smoke and lights. I must've been Dorthy, Mai was the lion, Walker was the tinman, but that only left the scarecrow. That was until Steven became my agent, both mine and Mai's in fact. He could pull strings, find loopholes through algorithms, transform a smuck like me into a well-positioned and charismatic headliner.

That's when I was assured that the scarecrow in it all was the audience we'd attract. And he was right, was most certainly right. Steven picked up punks like me all the time, but my story was a blue moon for him. He was as excited as I was for this continuing venture.

My first novel was titled "Behind A Red Curtain – The Story of a Porn Director Gone Horribly Wrong". It was placed under the tags of "romance, morally grey, and true events" which I found all to be somewhat comical. Especially since I wasn't writing the book, Steven had a ghost-writer for that. A few interviews over the phone or by email, and the ghost-writer had all the details that they needed for the next few chapters. And within two months, I was a published author. Or I was allegedly.

But between the novel and up to now, Mai and I had been conducting an online circuit of sorts, or rather a circus show. Although I had won in court and Jack was locked away, Walker still had some leverage to pull, and we were making headlines across the country.

Mai, the poor underaged, sex-trafficked Vietnamese girl saved by the poor bastard who got manipulated into the porn industry. That was the story, anyhow. I never admitted my faults, I couldn't, not with Walker watching my every word. Even in the courtroom we made it seem as though, through the forceful injections of drugs and alcohol, to the abusive nature of my quote-end-quote employer Jack, that I became as much of a victim as Mai. It hurt me sometimes thinking about how I always wanted to become a part of porn, an easy paycheck and free girls and the like. But the way the story was told, well, I might just have to die with that lie.

At least, if I wanted to keep my composure in the public eye. Funny, how one day you'd be filming other people naked, exposed, and violated, just to end up on the other side of the lens. Mai and I had a whole eight-month long stretch together, becoming headlining features for television shows, podcasts, and the like.

We shared the same tour bus, but slept in separate spaces. Obviously, after Myra, I didn't want to test the fates any longer. But even with that thought in mind, I had no interest in Mai, not because she wasn't beautiful or nothing. But because, after I had rescued her (and myself) from Jack, it didn't seem right. Not in the slightest.

We were the same victims to the same industry, again that's what the story was. And eventually one evening, after a live show broadcasted to hundreds of thousands of viewers, she approached me backstage. She still didn't speak much English and always had a translator on set with her. But even without the translator, she told me in the sweetest way.

"You are big brother to me."

It wasn't only her broken English and Vietnamese accent that made it that much more heartfelt, but the headlines would say otherwise if permitted to. Eventually they were when she said it again a few shows later, on air. Regardless of how the media made it out to be, it was the fact that she saw me as a brotherly figure that brought me to tears, alone in the tour bus shortly after the show had ended.

It's funny, when she met me inside of the bus, I had already dried my eyes. Though, I'm sure she could see the redness from my lids. And that night she didn't speak a single word until the next morning.

She just came up to me, smiled, and hugged me tighter than I had ever hugged a friend, family member, or lover before. And damn, I wanted to cry some more.

But there was no time for tears on the road. My "book" had just come out, just before the holidays and I was meant to capitalize on that fact. And capitalize I did, as Mai and I began a book tour during the same time we were meant to tell our tales to millions of people who had no clue who we were, what we stood for, and what we wanted, outside of the generative press.

All in all, it was a great success.

But before our eight or ninth appearance on another late night televised show, something happened. I heard a knocking against the glass window of our tour bus. I was the only one in the bus at the time.

Unlike my colleagues, Mai, Steven, and every other minimum wage worker, I was taking a few shots of Jack Daniels to prepare myself for another night on stage. Irronic, isn't it, that I'd be sipping through a bottle of Jack's like a reminder of the man who tried to kill me. Misery was funny sometimes, and sometimes misery was the only thing that I could laugh at anymore.

So, I strutted myself to the bus door and opened it. Looking around I found the culprit, some douche-bag dressed in Gucci sweats, with a Louis Vouton sweatshirt and a pair of the latest Jordans tied around his feet. I was sure that he thought he was impressing to those around him. But I was never one to recognize wealth through brands.

Regardless, I walked over to him, carrying myself confidently through the 40% liquor injection. But he didn't smile, only smirked, as he asked me one single thing.

"Yo, my man! I'm hot parta' town and you know, I been hook'n up with the newcomers from time to time. And your ass has been making the headway since that court shit, so, like, you wanna' hit of somethin' or what?"

It reminded me of Jack's mansion, his escapades, only this time it felt more dirty but more inviting. Like a delivery driver at your doorstep before even placing the order. He had all kinds of shit too, stashed away inside of his Dior bag, hanging from the side of his shoulder like a slinger should usually do. Anything from crack, salts, Mary Jane, to uppers, downers, and left to rights.

I asked if he had any of that Cali snow, that shit I once hit with Jack. There was something memorable about the memory, though the memory was jaded at best. Maybe that's why I wanted a hit of it, for old times' sake.

He must've known that I had the dough. Otherwise, why would he be banging on my tour bus while my security was on detail elsewhere. Yes, I received a lot of hate mail and death threats, even after my motel video hit the stream. Twenty-two million views now, and no media station had made it close to what I had admitted to -what I had produced in completely honesty- up till now.

But he still asked me to show him some bengi's, and I obliged. It wasn't like I was running out of dollars any time soon. My books sales were making me thousands, if not tens of thousands per quarter. And with Christmas and the New Year vastly approaching, I'd be seeing millions in no time.

So, I forked over four hundred in cash for two eight balls. I didn't know if it was a deal or not, and I didn't really care. Consider the leftovers as a tip, I thought. Scum like him deserved less than the three bullets I paid for.

He was smug after our transaction, and I was smug while in the bus, getting paid my dues. Those white fucking lines, I cut them up with my premier credit card made of metal, not plastic. Then, just as I had seen in rap music videos and the like, I stole another hundred from my wallet and wrapped that bitch up. And not before long I hand snorted three lines, plus the germs of over several thousand people.

But if I became contagious, I had the money to cure it.

And God it felt good, bleeding through my nostrils with some intangible fire igniting my senses. I was in the tour bus, just pacing around, wanting to destroy everything in sight. Wanting to crack the windshield with my own fists, drive myself off a cliff just to see if I'd survive. My adrenaline had never been higher.

Then I got a text. It was from Steven, asking where the Hell I was at. It was five minutes before my time on set and so I rushed from the bus, through the backside of the venue, into the backstage to meet him, with a few minutes to spare.

But the bastard had stopped me, had noticed something different about me. Then he wiped the blood from my nose and asked me.

"You on some shit right now?"

I didn't want to lie.

Sorry, I *did* want to lie. But with Steven managing my money, while Walker managed my liability, I had no other choice but to admit that I . . .

". . . I just snorted a lot of white."

I expected him to be disappointed, like my parents when they made that first call to me from the courtroom. But, instead, he held his ground.

"Just stick to the fucking script kid, keep your legs unbuckled, and your head from swaying. Tonight's another big night, and we can't let them know that you're on some serious shit. You got that?" He held me by my arms, though I wanted to resist and break his. But I couldn't, he was right, after all the speech classes and interpersonal lessons I had taken due to my acclaim, I couldn't let this show go a-bust.

"I'm cool, I'm coo." I said, though something was off.

"Good, you're an American Hero to the public eye right now. And I know that you wanna' keep that. Just know that, no matter what you're on or what you're going through, we can make it work to our advantage. Just . . ." he seemed disparaging, "just don't fuck it up just yet."

And I nodded my had, probably more violently than I meant to, but did so anyways.

Shortly after, my name had been called out and I met Mai on the stage, in a seat just beside her.

The show was full of the usual questions: *What got you into the porn industry? Do you regret your choices? How much did Jack actually manipulate you?* It was all the same bullshit, followed by the same bullshit answers.

"*I was a desperate college student with an abundance of dept, looking for an easy way out. I regret most of what I've done, because I know now that I've hurt many young women and men in the process. Jack was a mercenary; he always fed on my weaknesses and, through substance abuse, was in complete control of me.*"

Most of what I said was true, but there was the little white lie that always turned the blacks into grey areas for debate. And debate online is what kept my career standing, somewhere between the bad boy and the good guy. And, while answering, I couldn't think of anything better to do than to rise up to the show host and put a five-finger bullet against his smug, fake, fucking mouth.

But I kept my cool, controlling my jitters and clenching my teeth anytime I wanted to scream out at the world. "*This isn't my fault that the world is bad, its yours!*" but I kept my cool.

It was only when Mai looked back to me, from her seat on the stage, that I truly saw disappointment form in the eyes of an innocent left to conjure the words "you're guilty". I know she had said it without speaking and knew that she had meant it. In a sense, I became furious. But in another sense, I was disheartened.

Mai, the girl that I had rescued. Was saving her more for my own longevity? I supposed that I didn't save her on account of my own possible murder that night. That wouldn't make sense at all. But why did I save her? What was the reason, besides a line in the sand becoming crossed? Had the beach that filled our own subconscious been so vast that I couldn't find another way across the line in the sand?

"I'm just as guilty!" I yelled, though, I didn't mean to.

But the entire audience had heard it, right from the front row into the back. And suddenly there was no applause, no sentiment or sorrowful whispers. There was only the darkness, bleeding against the bright lights of the stage, a stage that I always had known that I could never leave.

It wasn't the show, or the production or the crew, or Mai or the show host that contradicted me. Not even Steven, who looking from the corner of the curtains, had given me a stare of disapproval. But it was me, at my high, caught between the guilt, that wanted to forfeit everything.

And then, at center stage I rose and, reaching for the one camera that had its lens swapped over me, I pointed and spoke for all to hear.

"I'm no hero, so please . . . let me go."

- 31 -
Serial Fame

I HAD CRACKED, but that wouldn't be the picture on the front covers of news articles and the like. No, instead my agent had painted the picture of a young man faced with post-traumatic-stress-disorder. And boy, did I feel like shit because of it, like stolen valor that I never asked for.

It might've been the drugs, but there was something deep inside of me keeping me from a normal life. Perhaps my agent was right, maybe it was a form of PTSD?

Or perhaps I'm still just as fucked up as before.

Regardless, book sales only increased, and my fame online was rising by the day. However, Steven suggested that, before rehab ever becomes an option (due to negative press), that I should take a break from touring. He assured me that Mai had it under control, and my break would look provide some positive insight into the "truly haunted individual" that I was now labeled as. Before, I was the "manipulated cameraman", and before Jack I was the "boy standing with the cardboard sign". I was used to changing labels, but never this quickly. It really did show how fickle we all became when judging others.

And don't get me started on the hypocrisy of that statement. While alone and board, spending countless hours of the day in my presidential condo on floor 33, I had nothing but time to think.

I thought about a lot of things too. I thought about my public perception, as well as my perception of the public. Realizing now, while reaching my mid-twenties, that I've always found something to hate about people. And that hate might just turn into karma someday, if not already.

I thought about Abby sometimes, and not just when I was feeling frisky. In every sense of the word, I *missed* her. There was this idea of loving something that you could never have that drove me nuts somedays. She was that something.

Then, after a few days of lying around and *thinking*, I finally decided to *do* something. That video I had captured on my night with Mai at the motel, it had garnered an incredible amount of attention. Twenty-two million views and counting, the jury even had the pleasure of watching it several times during my court hearing. It could have been a dead end, and I would've locked away just the same as Jack.

But I got lucky.

Funny thing was that, even with 22,000,000 views on a single video, my channel had only gathered around three-thousand subscribers. But I was bored, and my subs hadn't seen into life since then. So, I started filming in my free time. No longer for attention and ad revenue, but instead to relieve myself from the boredom of my break. And it worked.

Again, the views didn't matter. But the hours spent setting up some proper lighting, a green screen, script writing, then filming, adding effects in post, editing the files together, creating a cohesive video, exporting, uploading, tagging, titling, posting, the works.

A lot of people think that content creators don't do much, and for a lot of big names they don't. They have hired helpers for most of this bullshit. But when you're doing it all alone, there's a lot more to a ten-minute video than you may recognize after your first watch.

Steven hesitantly called me after he watched my first few videos. He told me to get with Walker next time, have him go over the script before filming it. But otherwise, he was happy that I was keeping myself preoccupied. Then, moreover, he was happy that I was keeping up with my positive press.

Men like him are always 50/50, blacks and whites. It's either success or failure for them, which is the line that I needed in the sand, along the beach of my own brain. There was no gray area, it was do or die. If a younger me sat down and listened to me spew that shit to him, he would've raised a middle finger and told me to "*fuck off*". And that's what we call evolution, looking back and recognizing how absolutely stupid we were once upon a time.

So, a few weeks passed, one more and Steven would have me back on numerous podcasts and talk shows alike. He didn't even mind if I was drinking or on some sort of "prescription", as long as I didn't overdo it again. If I kept my cool, then everything was *coo*.

Wait a second . . . had Jack highjacked a part of me?

Nevermind, it was a mistake, a small implicit whisper from my brain. A reminder that I wanted nothing to do with the man; much less be anything like him. And with my face facing every camera, now back on the circuit, I knew that my life was better without him. Better than the cellblock he'd live in, eating better food than the slop that he'd be served. And the girls, they were real. Not that the ones in the mansion weren't, but they always had ulterior motives.

Take Kyra for example. She slept with me, sure, but always wanted a hit of something. And I always happened to have that something, mainly because I knew it would keep her in my bed day after day. But more so, she wanted something else, something that nobody can buy, let alone afford in the wrong situation. That something was my time, love, and companionship. Even though it felt right at the time, looking back now I can tell that it wasn't recuperative. And you better bet that was the script I ran through Walker, before posting it online. Kyra No names included, to keep things private. But anyone who knew me from the mansion would know who I was referring to.

Thankfully, they had all been paid off, signed, dotted and dated on paper all the same.

And everything was going swimmingly. I kept my dosages, my usage to a minimum if I knew I had a show later. Nobody can tell, really, from the bright spotlights above naturally dilating your pupils, to the inconsistent movements from your fingers and toes. Everything was kept secret, behind red curtains and flashy screens.

Then, while on a podcast with some creators, it all went downhill. Not because of anything I had said or done, but because of the headline and the person behind it all. "*Once a Misogynist, always a Misogynist – Close Friend Opens Up About the Abuse NOT SEEN on Camera*". The headline was read to me during the midst of an interview. One of the creators just happened to check his phone, search for my name. Apparently, he had become ill-prepared as a co-host.

But the second my name came up in the search engine, and on recent news, that article appeared. And it didn't just appear once, but five times over by separate outlets covering the same story. That's kind of how the news works these days, someone gets a lead and other copy and paste it.

The article itself then came up in our discussion. It's sad, really, because the interview was going so well before then. The co-host (whatshisname) brought up the website and the author to my attention, live on camera. That's the problem with podcasts; they aren't as scripted as one may think.

Though, neither the publisher nor the author of the hit-piece rang any bells. Rather, it was the name that followed, the person who they had interviewed.

And to my surprise, it was Frankie.

Good ol' fucking Frankie at the helm, divulging the b-rated media with doubt, sending my name through the gutter and attempting to cash in from my misfortune.

He brought up that very first day while standing outside with the cardboard sign, telling the story as though he was manipulated into the idea. Then, when we had Abby involved (whose name had been retracted from his statement) he claimed that I forcefully insisted he be the one on camera, not me. Later he discussed the crappy motel we were living out of, with no mention of his family ties being involved. Lastly, with vigor, he described in detail the night he came home to the motel alone, when he never saw or heard from me again.

That last part was true, but he was definitely swaying his intended audience. Not that I hadn't, of course. When I made my own video in the motel, I knew that I had left out some savory details. But what he was saying, some of it was a straight up lie.

So, there I sat amongst my host and co-host alike, begotten of words and in utter shock. They asked me for a statement, but I told them I needed to leave. Insisting that I stay, I refused. I needed Walker on the phone; I needed Steven on the third line. I needed some way to turn this around, because not long after the article had been posted and reposted, I saw the notifications on my phone explode.

Hateful comments on all my most recent videos, by bystanders who didn't have the full picture, nor needed one. They just required a taste, one bite, before becoming savages. Like cannibalism online, it only took one bad bit of press before the world started feasting on your image.

In a way, I suppose that makes us all cavemen.

And by the time I was outside and walking towards my ride, I hopped in the backseat with the driver ready to take me home. Even he knew that the paparazzi would swarm me at any second. Then Walker finally rang in, and I answered.

"This the same Frankie we discussed?"

I told him yes.

"Then we might have a problem." He didn't sound frightened, but instead sincere, the softness in his voice telling me that we had a fight that could still be won. "Frankie's the closest one to you besides your family and ex's. But he's the only one who never excepted our bargain. I guess we have an explanation now, as to why."

"That's lovely and all." I wasn't in the mood for wordplay, "What's next for us then? Can we sue the motherfucker for defamation or something? Can we at least have that article taken down?"

"Doesn't much matter if the article is gone or not. These types of posts remain online in some back catalogue or hard drive somewhere." The miracles of technology were manifesting right before our eyes, "We could get him in a courtroom, sure. Or we could let this simmer down, take another break . . ."

"I don't want another break! I want to keep the ball rolling! These are the best times of my life and I'm not letting some son-ov-a-bitch take advantage of me!"

"Frankie's your friend – best friend – it would look awfully bad if you acted this way towards him."

"Get Steven on the phone then." I was full of rage.

My best friend – or – used to be "*best friend*" was waging a war against me. I couldn't let that stand, not after what I had been through. Three bullets through my body, and Frankie had the absurdity to access me as the villain. I know, I had some second thoughts on whether I was a savior of any kind or not. And I still don't believe that I was, in any regard.

But to be labeled a "*villain*" was going too far.

"All right, I'll get Steven on the line. But just know, he was your greatest friend. I know that means nothing to me, let alone you any longer. But it matters to everyone else except for you, and that's what's gonna' win this."

Maybe he was right, he usually was. When the car stopped in front of the tower in which I stayed, sure enough the press had gathered. My bodyguards had been awaiting my arrival, as they fled to the door and shielded me on my way out. All around me were flashing lights and the sound of a thousand lens shuttering at my exit. I was on the phone still but could barely speak a word over the commotion that was forming in the background.

"*Did you manipulate Frankie*?"

"*Was this all your wrongdoing*?"

"*Has everything been a part of your plan*?"

"Did you manipulate Jack too?"

That last question sunk in like a dagger to my backside, as I turned around to face the man responsible for asking it. "Did I manipulate Jack?" I responded, disgusted by his own name fleeting from my mouth. "Jack was a despicable wretch, and you're a fucking lunatic if you think that I could . . ."

But then I heard Steven on the line, telling me to calm myself. "*Don't say another word*." He asked, and I obliged. For a minute, I thought that I had said too much again.

But in the weeks that would follow this incident, my cursing of a media roach would be the least of my worries. Suddenly, unknown users and unknown names started digging through my history. I had no choice but to pause all of my social media accounts, keeping everything private. I wasn't exactly certain how this event would play out.

All I knew was, with either ending, that Frankie would be paying for his mistake.

– 32 –

Frankie

THE DEED WAS DONE, and it had been settled. Walker had sent Frankie a cease-and-desist letter, before my friend gave up on his smear campaign. But the fallout was extraordinary, and again I had been placed on a break. It was embarrassing, going from one break into another. My stress levels had never been higher, not since I had a gun pointed straight my way.

Yet, I wasn't done. The situation had come to a close, but I still was without complete closure. So, I booked a flight out to Denver from LA. Walker insisted that he came, so another ticket was purchased. And on that flight, in first class, he texted me while sitting right by my side, to keep things confidential.

don't say anything youll regret later even if its just the three of us together i cant keep you from burning down everything we have made so far

As I replied, still full of fury.

my best friend betrayed me, how should I act??? this was out of line even for him

And I could tell by Walker's face, now staring back at mine, that he wasn't pleased.

*we have a multimillion dollar empire on the line if
that isnt enough to convince you then go ahead and
burn it down but i wont always be there for you if all
that's left are ashes*

Again, he was right. I wondered shortly after, as
the plane took off and I grappled the arms of my seat
in panic, whether I'd ever be the one who was right of
the wrong. In a sense, I thought that I had everything
figured out by now. But in the end, I was still a catalyst
for greater prospects, the tuning rod pointing towards
water, and so I couldn't let Walker down.

But not just Walker, but also Steven, and my
publisher, my bodyguards, my DEI assistant, my crew
members, my tour bus driver, Mai, and everyone in
between. I was no longer a singular entity, but instead
I had become the sapling of a tree that sprung
branches and leaves in my growth.

It was no longer just about me, but the empire I
had formed from my unfortunate appraisal. Even a
priest or a pastor was the shepherd of their own
community, and mine was much the same. Only, my
taxes were higher.

Regardless of my immediate thoughts on the
situation, I had assured Walker of my full cooperation.
With a nod and a handshake, no paperwork between,
it had been enough to ensure us the success that we
awaited.

It was difficult though, distinguishing business from
interpersonal affairs. I knew what I *wanted* to say to
Frankie but also understood what *couldn't* be said.
And there it was, that line in the sand, a border I could
no longer cross. But from my side, I could still maintain
my dominance.

As our flight landed, I made my way through DIA
like it was a second home to me. Walker, at first, had

trouble keeping up with my pace. But eventually, when we reached the train terminal between the loading docks and the airport itself, I finally leveled out. There was nowhere to go on that train, and with Walker giving me the side eye I knew that I needed to slow down.

Once off the train we picked up our luggage with the rest of the commonwealth. Waiting for your bag to drop onto the conveyor has always been the most excruciating part of the airport experience, in my own opinion. It's like ordering a meal at a restaurant and watching everyone else's meal pass you by in the meantime.

But once we located our suitcases, we hopped in a taxi and left. Our destination was a fine enough four-star hotel just a mile from the Essex where Frankie still stayed. I thought it was appropriate, with me making my millions being put up in luxury, while the man who had been mudslinging me was still rolling the mud like the pig he was. Then I thought, "*Had he always been this way*?" Perhaps I was too blinded by friendship to see it beforehand. Hindsight is twenty-twenty and all that other shit, but this *felt* different. Like, I had known the guy for as long as I could recall. Yet, through some absurdity I had missed the obvious.

They say that your friends are a reflection of you, or something along those lines. If that was the case, then perhaps I was destined to meet Jack, foil with all my follies, and end up where I was today. What I'm saying, I guess, is that I finally had taken out the trash and for more than one instance. Myra, Frankie, Jack, they were all just garbage waiting to be disposed of. And no, friendships cannot be recycled.

Approaching the hotel, Walker had a change of heart.

"Change of plans, I'll make it worth your while." He had shown a few hundo's to the taxi driver, who immediately agreed before knowing what he was agreeing to. Like clicking a box that says you agree to a set of terms and conditions that you've never read and will never read.

"You don't want to settle down at the hotel first?" I asked, I was generally curious.

Walker, with some actual compassion in his eyes, turned to face me. "I can still feel that fire in you. The sooner we get this over with, the sooner we can both move on with our lives. I've been betrayed too. It's not hard when you become a lawyer. So, in a sense, I know how you're feeling. And there's no settling down until this business with Frankie is settled."

I appreciated him for that, more than when he defended me in court and any time between then and now. But could I consider my lawyer as a friend? Was it the same or any different than considering Frankie, the man who insisted on exacting some abstracted revenge on me, a friend? Or had I lost the ability to tell the two apart?"

"Are we -you know- friends, Walker?"

He looked shocked for a moment but smiled and laughed soon afterwards.

"We can be friends, if that's what you want. But more so we're business partners, and professional colleagues. That's what the general public expects out of our own relationship, a friendship, so to speak, would encroach on that."

"I understand." But I really didn't. We tell little white lies to ourselves, to others, just to keep the peace.

Though, if this is what peace meant, then I'd gladly go to war for some actual fucking companionship.

Now was not the time, however. We pulled up to the Essex with a different war to wage. I wasn't just here to express myself. Walker and I had plans, and through my sound and his fury, we'd hopefully have Frankie at a crossroad. One, in which no matter what path he chose would benefit us more than him.

The taxi driver parked right below the same second floor room next to the staircase where I knew Frankie would be. We were early, which would certainly catch him off guard. Any advantage was advantageous, like an oxymoron for a moron like him. Looking around the parking lot, full of potholes and cracks, I happened to see one of his women from before soliciting herself to a young man from the college nearby. I wanted to interfere, but I left it as is. There were more important things at hand. And when reaching the door, Walker pressed an arm against me and, with a single nod, I allowed him to be the one who knocks.

There was rustling behind the door, and a lot of it. As if we had caught Frankie in the middle of filming another flop for the porn hub. We spent nearly ten minutes in front of that door, knocking on occasion, until finally someone answered. And it wasn't fucking Frankie.

It was some Latino who barely spoke English. I not the type of person who gets offended if you don't speak English in America, or even if you're an illegal immigrant. I was much more concerned with the whereabouts of my ex-best friend.

Eventually, through some phone translation, we managed to find Frankie on the opposing side of the

Essex. He had moved from one room into another, something he probably had to do to keep his business discreet. A fact that I was thankful for not being involved with. After leaving the man to his business, I couldn't help but peer inside his room, our old room at that. There was a large bong, numerous lighters scattered around, and a girl who definitely was hiding naked underneath the sheets.

No matter, as we made our way down. Room 218, a corner room. Frankie had moved up in the world, if only by millimeters. Walker knocked once again, and the door flung open violently. At first Frankie was yelling on the way to the door. Something about *not coming back until a deal was made*. And when the door opened, he yelled out a name that only I had recognized, even if I couldn't put the face to the name.

"Amber! Wha' the fu-" he saw Walker first, then me.

His guard was broken, so we were on the attack. As long as his defenses were weak, we could break through and settle the score.

"It's been a minute, ol' friend." I could tell he didn't like me saying that. But it hurt him as much as it hurt me. I guess that's what a hurt person would say. Like "hurt people hurt people" but the fire between us both still carried the flame.

God, it's like I'm talking about a lover more than a friend. And maybe a friend can be more than a lover. But in no way, not now at least, could I ever love Frankie. Not like a bro, a brother, or a childhood friend. He was the enemy, and my eyes grew callus by just looking his way.

He invited us inside, with the word "*invite*" being used loosely. There were beer cans, empty vodka bottles, cigarette butts, and used condoms all over the floor. Frankie, out of some form of mindless courtesy, swept them into a pile in the corner, using his socked foot as a broom. Walker was not impressed and may have finally realized why I held so much resentment for the man, if you could call him one.

The one and only table of the room was dragged over to the bedside where Frankie would pathetically sit, while Walker and I took the two breaking chairs over. It was no wonder that Frankie tried to bring me down and get some notoriety of his own. He lived like an addict, stuck up in some shitty motel with the same two girls from before performing his dirty work. They were all losers, so, how could I lose?

"If we're ready, then my client would like to make his statement." Walker commended, wavering in his chair. Probably at the thought of how many cum stains were consumed into its flattened fabric. But as he moved around in his chair, I caught his hand reaching for something in his pocket, before releasing it back onto the table where his hands remained cuffed.

I couldn't blame him. But, before I could speak, the son-of-a-bitch Frankie just had to say the first word.

"Client, eh?" he chuckled, he was already drunk. I didn't mention that we could smell it from the moment he had opened the door. But with all the empty bottles and cans lying around, both Walker and I must've thought that it was a symptom of the living space. Unfortunately, when Frankie opened his big mouth, the scent of hops overtook the conversation. In fact, the booze spoke louder than the words he was speaking.

"Frankie, buddy, I just want to say a few things and we'll be off."

"Back to that mansion in Beverly Hills I suppose?" with a hiccup at the end.

"You need to let your friend talk to fully understa-" Walker came in, but not before becoming interrupted.

"He has nothing to say that'll shut me up!" my friend's furiousity was as great as mine, if not greater. "This stupid cunt left me hangin' here! He went out of his way to take everything from us both! I was the one talkin' to Jack, and if I had been the one in Cali then I wouldn't've fucked it all up! And even if I did, like this stupid bastard had, then I'd probably be rich and famous and shit. And man," he pointed at Walker, "you'd probably be my legal slut in the courtroom, you intimidating bastard you."

Walker kept his cool though. I could tell that he had more than a few words to say back to Frankie. But he stayed composed and I wondered suddenly if anything could compromise the man sitting next to me. Then after Frankie's outburst, I dropped my eyes to the table as I responded. As if pulling the string to a bow, letting the pressure build before releasing the arrow.

"Frankie . . ." I was saddened. Before, with my rage, I was consumed and swallowed whole. But after seeing my old friend in such a state of decay, I knew that there was no choice but to bring the dog out back and shoot it square between the eyes.

Suddenly, learning through Walker, I kept myself composed. ". . . I always thought of you as my best friend. And when Jack contacted me – I don't think you ever knew that he did – but he did. And it was a last-minute thing. I didn't want to leave you behind, but in Jack's own words, he thought that you weren't cut out for the job."

"That's bullshit . . ." Frankie lapped, like a sorrowful dog dragged across the street, "That's absolute bullshit and you know it!"

"It's not, it's the God damned truth of the matter. He wanted me, my expertise, not just another fuck-boy. He had plenty of those. And when I got to Cali, he hooked me up with cocaine, and later heroin. Then some other opiates, with plenty of high-class booze to wash it all down. Along with the pills, and the girls, and later my own integrity."

"So, what? You're my fucking savior or something? Jesus on the cross and whatnot, keeping me from my sins?" This was as philosophical as Frankie had ever been. "I could'a been great! Anyone can point a camera at these damn whores; I do it every day! They pay me through the videos that they make! And I pay them with whatever keeps their coochies shut, as I plow my cock right down their throats! But here you are, thinking that you're superior to me for running the same damn circus as I am."

"You're circus is a side-act, Frankie." I wasn't listening to him any longer. I should've given up ages ago, but he was a friend. And now, a friend no longer. "With you, there was no future. I can see it in this disgusting room, with scattered trash and one-night regrets. With you, I would've ended up in the same place, plastered by booze and broken by ideas.

With you, I wouldn't of wanted to live another day."

His face turned red, maddingly red, as he jumped from the bed and pushed the table to his beer belly in the process. I had hit a nerve, a deep and discrete artery that would leave him bleeding. But he wasn't done yet, as he gripped the table to turn it over, as both Walker and I rose in time to avoid its crash onto the floor.

"You have everything that I should have! You're everything that I should be! It was your fucking plan, after all! Your fucking idea to fuck every girl we met, put in online and sell it to the masses! I've been picking up girls and boys ever since. Filming them as best I can. But I could never match your numbers . . . I never had the same connections. Because you took it all away from me!"

That's when Walker revealed his smoking gun, with the bullet already having been fired. But it wasn't from my mouth that the gunpowder had ignited, it was from Frankie's, as Walker shone the bright silver tape recorder that he kept inside of his pocket.

Right away, Frankie panicked. At first, he tried grabbing for the recorder, but Walker was a strong man. My fucking lawyer of all people had sent Frankie to the dirty carpet along our feet and shouted to him.

"Right now, I could call the police for aggravated assault! And with my track record in court, you'd be locked up for sure. But that's not what we're going to do." I saw him smirk, and it was a beautiful thing to witness.

"We now have evidence of you committing a conspiracy, as well as soliciting sex as a business opportunity. That court settlement we gave you will be taken back into court through a countersuit, where you will lose more than what you were given. You have no way out of this mess, even if you plea innocent I will ensure that the court finds you guilty!"

That seemed to keep Frankie's mouth shut for a moment. And what a relief it was, standing up from those cum-soaked chairs and outright over him. But then I noticed something that I did not expect, not from

Frankie, not in a lifetime. He began to cry, actual tears and sulks and all.

For a minute in time, watching him crawl along the carpet in tears, did I ever expect to feel sympathy for the friend who I had always considered greater than myself. But as time heals all wounds, hopefully this revelation would heal his own.

"Frankie, you were a good friend . . . but now, I'm digging you a hole so deep that you won't be able to climb out from."

That's all I had left in me, before tailing Walker out from the door. We'd arrive back in Cali, but I'd find a place back home. A small, luxurious cabin set deep in the tree line and mountains of the western slopes in Colorado. I was still on break, and so, I'd spend my time there. And as I was in the process of purchasing my cabin, Walker was in the process of countersuing my good friend. I felt guilty at best, even if I were proven to be innocent. And Frankie, he wouldn't be able to pay us back what he owed.

I guess that was the point.

But even through the struggles, the hardships, and listening to my old friend's bullshit statements, I somehow still resented myself. For the person that I became, for the person that I was and, in dread, for the person I would become.

– 33 –

Myra

I WATCHED THE BARREL IGNITE, but only after the Vietnamese girl had jumped from the bed and laid her own teeth into Jack. As he fired, I felt a quick shock

293

travel through the right side of my chest. At first, I felt no pain at all. The quickly, like a virus, it consumed me from the inside.

Then I woke up, along the floor of my bed. I had almost made it under the sheets before blacking out, I was doing better than before. Rising against the hardwood, I slumped myself along the mattress, hearing the bottle of Jack Daniel's rolling below me. Jack Daniel's, and another nightmare about Jack, how hilarious I thought.

"How fucking fitting." I laughed lightly, before cracking my neck and looking through the window.

It snowed again. I thought maybe, just maybe I could get out of bed and shovel for once, if I felt right enough to do so. But I hadn't in weeks, there must've been three-fucking feet of snow piled outside of my cabin by now. Although it really didn't matter, I wasn't going anywhere any time soon.

But the snow reminded me that my birthday was coming up. December 28th, just a few days away. Then I realized that it was Christmas morning, or at least the afternoon. Though I wouldn't be expecting any calls, nor presents under any trees, the thought of it being Christmas somehow brought back pure memories of mine as a child. And those thoughts alone comforted me.

It had been years since I had seen anyone. Some days, if desperate, I'd drive to the nearest town to purchase more groceries and liquor for the following month. There were no delivery services where I lived. I thought about my fridge and freezer, I was still somewhat certain that I had some salmon filets and potatoes left to cook. But even if there wasn't a crumb left in sight, at least I had that half of bottle of Jack rolling around on the floor. Calories were calories after all.

Yet, for minutes on end I lay in my bed, tossing and turning to the nausea and pain I felt within my beltline. I understood, for many years now, that things could have worked out differently. But this was the path that I had chosen, so there was no turning back.

Shortly after dealing with Frankie, and the countersuit had been settled, I felt awfully bad about myself. Not that sort of thing, like you wake up not wanting to be yourself. Instead, waking up and knowing that you are yourself, and there's no prospect of changing that.

I half-hoped to hear from Steven, or even Walker. Something like a Christmas gift, like a new book deal or interview opportunity. But ever since my documentary series aired, I was all aired out.

One bad interview was all it took.

It was Saturday night, live television for the masses to consume. I was wasted hard and was meant to be the opener for the show. Let's just say that things hadn't gone so swimmingly. The next thing I knew I was blacklisted, abandoned, and facing several live television charges. Frankie had gotten to me, even from the fiscal grave, but I couldn't let it go. On air, I admitted myself to a mistake, proclaiming to the world that I was always the bad guy and that no good could ever come from me. Some real pussy-shit in hindsight, if I ever had sight of a goal.

The money wasn't the issue, it was me. I became a liability, had always been one in a sense. I was amused after the fact that Steven, nor Walker, had realized this after I had clearly betrayed Jack years prior, and Frankie later.

Sometimes I'd go back and watch that episode, just to remind myself that I had fucked up everything in three minutes of airtime. That I chose to fuck things up. Even if I wasn't happy, I still could've been composed. I was composed at a time, but again time was fleeting. And it had fled from my enormous luck as soon as it had arrived. I could have kept calm, minced my words like I always had, kept the stocks to my own performance at an all-time high.

But I couldn't even do that.

"*What can I do*?" I thought aloud, turning again with the nausea flaring with the pain in my liver.

Perhaps today was the day that I'd make my apology video, post it online and garner back my audience. Though, I wasn't dumb enough to believe that I could gain what I had lost in those few minutes. Even my book sales had declined to all-time lows, especially after my publisher and agent had revealed to the world that I wasn't the one writing them. All five of them, in fact, if you could believe that five books could be written based on one life event. Series and shows do worse, stringing out endless seasons of needless content to audiences that had lost interest in the years following. And that was it, the word "*needless*" appearing in thought. That's when I knew, no apology could recover my wealth.

But fuck my wealth. I was practically retired before the age of thirty, the American Dream. God, that American Dream that I had once saw, fully envisioned, fruitful, and obtainable. Oh Hell, had I obtained it, but it didn't come without its costs. And those costs were too high for me to pay off in the short term.

Was I a candle burning far too brightly?

Probably, but I didn't care. I didn't care much for anything, anymore. I got what I wanted, had spent it, and here I was. The same place where many end up due to fame and fortune, although I had streamlined my way down the spiral. Did I miss the journey to the destination?

I thought back to my fans, all the voices that I had convinced, all the minds that I had changed, nearly four years ago. Four fucking years ago.

I got up from the bed and stumbled, walking towards the bathroom I slashed some cold water against my face. For one reason or another, I didn't want to become useless today. But while staring at my own self in the mirror, I noticed my complexion staring back at me.

I was fatter, even if I ate less. Alcohol does wonders to your body fat content. And I was out of shape, with the muscles on my arms becoming weak and sluggish. Then there were the wrinkles underneath my eyes, and the slack to my jaw, and the fucking pimples growing out between the crevasses of my nose. I was an ugly son-of-a-bitch, and it showed all too apparently.

Again, another day where I'd look over myself and wish that I was somebody else. I had the money to become that somebody, but not the will power to do so. And sometimes that fact was more depressing than having always woken up as ugly as shit, hungover, and desperate as before.

I really needed a change in my life.

But that change, it wasn't happening, not right now. I needed to make it happen. So, going downstairs into my living room, I crossed its boundaries into the kitchen, and then towards the garage door. Inside my garage sat an old 1976 Jeep CJ7, a classic, repainted in a striking red. Then beside my Jeep were numerous boxes full of memorabilia, from a time when I was on top of the world.

I opened the garage doors and, sure enough, there was about three feet of snow caving inwards. Taking my shovel, it might as well have been brand new, I began. It felt like shoveling acres of ice, but in my mind, I was throwing away everything that had kept me dormant. With every single sling, I was throwing my regrets behind me. And with every shovel-full of snow, I was paving a way towards redemption.

Sure, it sounds silly while reading about it. But for me, in the lonely place that I was at, it felt like progress. Even the smallest steps we make can lead to something grander.

I no longer wanted popularity or money. Right then there, in twenty-one-degree weather, shoveling three feet of snow from my driveway, I just wanted to live again. Sometimes it's true that you wake up one day and want to change it all. It never happens that fast, but it's a step towards change, nonetheless. And at this point, anything was better than taking one step forward and two steps back.

But just as I had taken another step forward, a phone call sent me back. Not just by two steps, but perhaps by two hundred steps. As I looked at my phone, I saw the caller ID appear. It was Myra.

I was hesitant to answer, but curious, nonetheless. I hadn't heard from the girl since our estranged breakup years prior. As I stared at her name on the caller ID, I began to recall her history. Not just with me, but with others.

She was a victim, an actual victim, unlike me. Maybe that was masochism, considering the scars that I still wore daily across my flesh from Jack's bullet wounds. But I never considered myself the victim, because I had always felt too much guilt in feeling that justified.

But a victim or not, she was on the other line.

And I answered, hesitantly.

"Myra?" I'd speak, not only as a question but as a statement to my past resolves. Whatever she had to say, whatever she wanted, I would deny. Just like Frankie, she probably wanted some sort of settlement as well. I didn't recall Walker ever sending her a settlement, nor did I recall ever mentioning her when speaking with Walker. She was still a guarded secret of my past, one mistake that I couldn't let free. Not to the public, of course, but neither to those closest to me now. She was that grand mistake that, in my mind, I could never forgive or forget.

Until she answered back, "Hey you, it's been awhile. How're doing these days? Pretty well I suppose?"

"What do you want?" I answered, in my terrible sense of cynicism. I wasn't in the mood for games and this felt just like a game. Whether it was chess or checkers, my money could outweigh her bluff, my fame could bury her deep beneath the pieces along the board. But after hearing her, the game changed drastically.

"Nothin' really. Just checking in. I see you're a big shot now. I'm really surprised, really, I am. But . . . I guess I called because I-"

"Because you want something? Because you want my money? Or, maybe, a portion of my fortune?"

Then suddenly, I was obliterated from the inside out, like a red dwarf star succumbing to my intimate demise.

"Because I was thinking of you."

She shattered my world just then. I didn't think that it was possible. There I was, with my slack-jaw and shovel at hand wondering, in deep thought, if she was playing a royal flush to my pair in hand. But from the sound of her voice, she had become serene. And from the methods in which she moved her vocals, with every vowel seeming heavenly in the hearer's presence, it made me more tense.

"Thinking of me?" I thought aloud, as I usually did. And I didn't care any longer, whether she heard me say it or not. I became astounded all the same.

"Yeah, like . . . your in all the headlines these days. I even read about Frankie, and, like, I knew that what he said couldn't be true. I guess I called because, like . . . when I met you, I was afraid. I was a scared little girl looking for comfort, and when I met you and thought that I, well . . . could control you, I thought that I could control my life. And, well . . . that didn't really happen and I'm –"

"You're trying to control me now?"

"I'm really sorry for the way I acted back then."

Then it all came together, like the last letter of a wordle. Like the final piece to a puzzle, like any other fucking metaphor that you could think of, it manifested itself into this one phone call. And instead of feeling accomplished, like all the parts had been put together, instead I felt the hole in my heart growing deeper.

"Wait . . ." I could hardly contend, "you're . . . apologizing? But I was the one tha-"

"You weren't anything other than a man desperate for love too." She let my heart sink further. "My step-father was arrested, actually earlier this year. My mom, I always thought she would resent me for it, but she cried. She cried and cried for days, and I didn't know what to do. I still thought that it was my fault, for making my mother cry so much and all. But she . . . she eventually came around. And explained to me that, no matter what man she h-had in her l-life . . ." I heard her breaking into tears too, "Th-that she loved me more. And that's when I knew th-that I had . . . I just had to call."

And there I was, my own tears freezing in the cold. I was thankful that she hadn't been able to seen me like this. Otherwise, it might've felt like social suicide. Boy, would the press get a kick out of that, for sure. But she was honest, not only with herself but with me. And that level of honesty, I hadn't heard by before since my parents had told me that they loved me. But even that was a long mile away from where I was today.

"Myra . . ." I spoke her name, but didn't give any thought into what it meant. In a way, I felt selfish for that. But in another, I figured I was only covering for my own guilt-ridden insecurities.

"I hope you're happy and . . . well, I hope that you don't think too badly of me. After all, aside from my step-father, you were my first. My real first love, and, I suppose that means that, well . . . I guess I love you."

My heart broke then and there.

"Please, Myra . . . please, I was never a good guy to you. You know that! I never treated you well, I never saw you for more than . . . than a piece of meat! Please, you really can't love me, can you? That isn't true?"

I attempted to justify my own self-sabotage as a way to escape from this dilemma. But if fate were real, as it spoke in actions to our words, then perhaps this was all predestined. Yet, that made me feel even worse.

"I know you pretended. In fact, I know you didn't really like me at all. But I gave up – gave up everything for you. And that was enough to know that I really loved you."

Then, from the crackling of her voice, to the static of my own incessive wavers, I knew that things were coming to a close. But before I could speak another word, the line had been broken and I was left with the sound of a deep ringing in my ear. I had not been able to say my goodbyes, or admit more of my faults. In the end, all that had needed to be said was said, and Myra and I were done.

But it felt wrong.

As I stood there, alone in the snowy driveway, with just my shovel and my phone in either hand, I shook in panic. Never before had I been played so well. But it wasn't like a play with actors along a stage. Rather, it was a stalemate, where both opponents shake on an equal victory.

But this wasn't a victory, how could it be?

I was left alone again, freezing, hungover, defenseless again against the shadows of my past that seemed to haunt my every step. Or was I the ghost, following the former footsteps of places and people that I used to know? Again, perhaps they were calling me back through Ouija boards and candles amongst a seance circle painted in blood.

But the only blood that I saw spilled that day was my own. Almost immediately after the call, I ran through the garage and to the kitchen. I wanted to end it all but was too afraid of death. I say this now because, with my sharpened Misono UX10 8.2-Inch

Gyutou clever, I took a slice across my wrist and hardly felt a thing.

That was until the blood started leaking, and the pain began to settle in. Funny, the word "*settling*". Like settling a dept with Jack or settling a resolve with Frankie. Suddenly, I was settling a fear I hadn't overcome, that had been quieted, that out-of-nowhere appeared and forgave me for all my wrongdoings. Wrongdoings, that I feared, would be the death of me, and so, I cut just a little bit deeper.

– 34 –
Abby

I WATCHED THE BARREL IGNITE, as I felt a quick shock travel through the right side of my chest. At first, I felt no pain at all. The quickly, I became panicked. I had been shot. I always had dreamed of being shot, like in the movies, with my body lunging backwards with the force of the bullet.

But that wasn't the case. Instead, the bullet pierced right through me. No lunge, no fallback, just the point of impact sending me astray, then, as the bullet reached the wall, my blood began to flow. Stricken veins, but no arteries, luckily. It's crazy how a singular metal fragment can cut through the flesh and muscles without hesitation. As if a bullet needed to be hesitant, of course.

The point I was getting at was the fact that an ignited and shot piece of shrapnel could tear through our flesh as if it was paper against a printing press. Like inked letters to a statement that proclaimed independence from tyranny, the bullet could always pass through whatever politician, religious leader, innocent, or bystander that stood in its way.

But I began to wonder, bleeding across the hotel floor once again, for the fifteenth, thirtieth, or hundredth time, whether I was the bystander or the innocent.

When I awoke the next day, after Myra's call, I knew that I was in trouble. Running down my staircase and into the kitchen, I opened the door to the garage to find that I had never closed it since. Snow had poured in, and my head was pounding, along with my heart still racing. But I knew I had to clear it out. And after about ten minutes the job was done, but I was sore and out of breath from it.

Pathetic, I knew it. I could no longer manage the basics along my cabin. I had grown weak, had grown complacent. Myra seemed to have put me in my place, but it was still my place regardless. So then, why was I still blacking out through alcoholic overdoses and short-term dementia the prior day. I had somehow climbed back into bed, but the moments between then and during Myra's call were still a mystery. In my twenties, blacking out didn't mean a thing.

But now, it was a loss of memory, perception, and things you might've said or have done prior.

I knew this all too well, and so I took to my socials. Examining any sort of messaging feed carefully, there was nothing new. All except for one, a platform dedicated to online images and uploads. I had messaged one of my followers, though I knew her well enough before. For a second, I wished that it had been Kimmy. But it was Abby.

It was always Abby.

I saw pictures of her with a man who wasn't Michael. Surprised by the man, I wasn't surprised at all that it wasn't Michael. Recalling what he said way back when, I knew the melancholia would get the better of them. But the new man, he was bigger, taller, with a bushier face, but a smile that was sincere. And after scrolling through their wedding photos for some time, I was happy that she had found the right man.

Though, I was sad that I was never the right man for her.

As I looked down to the gauze that I had sloppily wrapped around my arm just yesterday, I guess that I couldn't have been surprised either. Then, suddenly, there were no surprises. Like in my teenage years and early twenties, when I thought I knew it all.

How to fight the system through porn, beat capitalism by playing the same game, trying so hard to be the person that I thought I was meant to be. But who we see, through images of ourselves through pixel screens and magazine covers, is never truly who we end up becoming. It's all a façade, really, a great delusion that provides us with false hope and fantasy dreams to a happy ending. That happy ending would've come without chasing the dream, I was sure of now more than ever. I could've let life play out, as it does without our consent. Instead, I ignored the consent of others and attempted to manipulate my own predestined outcome.

-God damn, my head . . .-

All this thinking was getting me nowhere, fast. So, I went back to the images on my phone, of happy little Abby now all grown up from who she used to be. Little Abby, as if I had known her since birth. Then there was little ol' me, still looking down on the world, even if I was in the gutter. Maybe my looking down felt like looking down, another oxymoron for the moron.

Perhaps I had always been looking up to the stars and think that I was looking down on them, as if the galaxies and universe were underneath my own two feet. What a cynical way of perceiving things . . .

-Damn . . .-

I couldn't keep thinking, I needed a breather.

But my prescription was the empty bottom of a bottle shattered on the kitchen floor, another mess that I would have to clean up later. There were no drugs left in the cabin, and barely anything I could call food. But I required something to keep me from talking to myself. I was, after all, becoming my own worst enemy.

That's when the devious idea hit me. I had nothing to lose, like repeating history, as if there ever was a thing to lose from the start. Maybe at a time I would've felt differently. Though ever since I held up that sign it seemed like it was all or nothing, do or die. So, I did.

I called Abby.

As the phone began to ring, I felt myself sweat. Though that could've been from the night of black out drinking beforehand. Nonetheless, the phone rang and rang and, for a short second, I thought that maybe her number had changed.

And as I was ready to hang up the call altogether, the line picked up. With one simple word, I knew that it was her. The sweetness of her voice with a scent of bitterness strung its way through the white noise, and I was brought back to that coffee shop we're we first met, alone together.

"Hello?"

God, I was nervous, like the first time a boy calls his crush over the phone kind of nervousness. I didn't know what to say, how to greet or back, or even if I could speak. Then, I could tell that she was hearing me breath heavily against the phone, I knew that my caller ID must've appeared, so I had to answer. But for a man with no answers, how was I suppose to follow through?

That was my life, always starting something and never seeing it through till the end. I was growing tired of it, for sure I was. But like a disease, I hadn't found the cure.

But the cure was in my own words, as I replied, "Is this still Abby?"

I knew it was her, there was no mistaking her voice. It had repeated in my head for years now, ever since she slapped me across the face and left me in a wreck. Then I began to wonder whether she was the cause of my dismissals and every one of my mistakes. But that thought was selfish, much like the voice in my head telling me to call her. The same voice that told me I needed another drink, the same voice that told my parents I was doing well in college. The same fucking voice that somehow taken control.

No longer.

"This is. Whatcha' need, old friend?"

"*Friend*" somehow hurt, but in a comforting way.

"I was, uh . . . I dunno, really. Just, I guess, seeing how you've been, how you're doing and all and I, um . . . it's been a little while hasn't it?"

"Around five years, yeah." She sounded sad, but I could hear a crying baby in the background and her husband asking who was on the line.

"A baby, huh?" That part of her life wasn't posted in her socials. She was a smart woman, after all.

"Listen, I gotta get to work soon so . . . is there something you wanted to say? You're not suing me too, are you?"

"No! I would never . . ." I couldn't believe that she perceived me that way. Then again, a whole lot of people with money obtain the ability to sue for more, so I couldn't blame her. "I just, I don't know. I can let you go, really."

"Yeah . . . well," I heard her steps and then a door close behind her, "I'd really like to know why you're calling me? I'm not interested in being in another book. Though, I guess I should thank you for not using my actual name. I guess."

"I suppose." This wasn't going well and I wanted to hang up right then and there. But I had to see this through, if it was the only thing left that I could see through. And while figgiting with the gauze around my arms, I had loosened it and exposed my dried scars. Those red cuts into my flesh, it was then while staring at those slits at the choice had been made before it was even thought up.

"I wanted to let you know that I was – I was a terrible person to you. Treating women like you like . . . well, that. I didn't have any right to, and I – I'm sorry if I said anything bad about you in the book. Honestly, I didn't even write the damned thing, as I'm sure you know. But, I gues I was just scrolling online and I, like, I happened to come across your profile and stuff and I . . . I want to say I'm sorry."

It was quiet, quiet for a long time. But I could hear her, muffled over the phone on the other line. I think she was sobbing, perhaps, or maybe just fiddling with something like I was with my gauze wraps. Though, after a few minutes of nothingness, she finally returned.

"I – I appreciate that, I really, really do. But . . . I'm not so innocent either and, some days I've thought about calling too, to say that I'm sorry. And I still am, and I accept your apology, even though it was probably the worst constructed apology that I have ever heard!" and we both laughed.

"Yeah, well . . . I didn't really think it through. This call was just . . . kinda' on a whim, you know?"

"I do." I could almost feel her smile through the phone. A certain warmth in her voice, an upbeat in her demeanour, that's how I knew she must've been smiling back at me from hundreds of miles away.

"I guess I was never very good with the girls." I'd joke.

"No, you're wrong. You were kind, if not kind've stupid. But kind enough, and I could tell that you were chasing after something, well . . . it just wasn't you. You know?"

I thought for a moment, and although it still hurt my head to do so, she had confirmed everything that I felt this morning. Just then I wanted to pass through the screen, travel the digital circus, hardwire the circuits until they connected to her own, and leapt out from her phone on the other side and give her a hug. Maybe a kiss, if her husband was still away and if she allowed it. Not on the lips, of course, but a kiss along the cheeks, the kind that friends give on 9mm film reels. I wanted to crash the system, break through every firewall, dismantle every hard drive, punch an AI super computer, and send every sattalite crashing back down to earth to show Abby how much I really cared about her.

But that wasn't my destiny. My destiny was over the phone, alone in my cabin, with a rotting liver and a rotten mind. But like the sunlight in the spring, speaking to her had grown flowers throughout my world. And before the call ended, I could feel myself in bloom.

"I really do have to go but . . . it was nice talking to you again. I hope that you're doing well, truly."

And before my own goodbye, she hung up.

But Abby wasn't gone.

She would always be a part of me, just like Myra, Frankie, and even Jack. They were the roots, but I remained the tree that could stand tall through the winter, into a new year. I had to.

– 35 –

Jack

I WATCHED MYSELF ON THE SCREEN CONSTANTLY. It took twelve months in a rehab program, with help from both Steven and Walker, who at first were hesitant, to rebrand me as a reformed man online. It was a lot of work, as it always was. But it was paying off better than before.

I admitted to my faults and accepted my mistakes. Broken in more ways than one, I had opted to piece myself back together. And outside of the year that it had taken me to get clean and come clean, it took another year of marketing myself to the masses. It was a simple business practice, but I wasn't going to take the easy way out again.

I started writing my own books, before my editor suggested that I simply go with a ghost-writer again. But I wouldn't, I couldn't, based on the public's perception. I would hold live streams everyday of me just typing, proof-reading, editing, formatting, marketing, and the works. Not just to prove to others that I was becoming capable, but more so proving to myself that I was capable of such feats. Sure, one ghost-writer's job had been lost. But it was better than using AI, and so I kept on writing.

Until my editor gave me the green light, and my novel was introduced to the world. It wasn't "Behind A Red Curtain", but it wasn't not that novel either. This one was that, but different, hard to explain, I suppose. I guess the easiest way to describe it would be to take an old CD that you didn't write, take the contents and remix them. It was a remix of my former story, only, it was mine now. Every word ink pressed and printed onto the paper was my own. And this time it didn't have some ridiculous title to it. Even if my editor and publisher both fought me on the same soil. I wanted it to be mine, to be from me.

The book was titled "Looking 4 Amateurs", just like the cardboard sign. I had come full-circle and had accepted my past as being *the past*. I was moving forward.

At first, sales weren't extraordinary. I was making most of my income from the same old spiels, from podcast and television appearances, as well as my online streams and occasional online shorts. I was half as rich as I once was, but far wealthier now that it was all coming from me. That's what mattered now, that it was me.

Not the voice in my head that became quelled. Not the rebellion I had tried to fight against the system. I was the system; I had a system. Whether it was the twelve steps to sobriety or my own intuition, I was a new man.

A *good man*, I thought.

No more lies, little whites or greys. Every question I was asked, I answered with absolute honesty and certainty. I even made numerous public statements online, taking Walker's recommendations with a grain of salt at times. It's funny how with fame one needs to pretend to be or say or act a certain way. But when you're open about it all, nothing stands in your way. I was bulldozing my way through my past to meet a new resolve. And it was here, and whether it made me a dime or lost me a dollar, I was still adamant about keeping it real.

And it felt good.

After those two years of reform, I decided to take a break. Steven fought against it, but I argued with him. Most successes stem from suspense these days. So, while I sat up in my cabin, writing my next book and filming shorts for the internet and my followers to digest, I let the anticipation of my next few moves stir within my gradually growing community. And I loved every second of keeping people in wait.

That's where we are today. Sorry to fast forward my life so much, but most days remained the same, but different of course. More oxymorons, but I was a moron no longer. After giving up the drugs, alcohol, and self-destructive behavior, there was no point in going back to it all. Mai even met up with me on occasion, and not just on the talk shows. We had filmed a few good shorts together, and her English was nearly perfect by now. Like a father, or a brother, I was just as proud of her as I had become with myself. We had both grown immensely, in our own ways.

That felt special to me, as I ended another stream, up in my office in my cabin, still awaiting the news of an upcoming docuseries by the largest streaming platform there was. It was exciting, but not as exciting as knowing that you left your past behind and learned from it to do so.

It was all coming together, not by porn but by being one with oneself. Some hippie-dippy bullshit, I know, but it works. I guess that's how our parents had figured it all out, right before they had kids and their worlds became chaotic again. But I recognized that without chaos there can be no law. And without law, there is only chaos.

Then, when a knock came to my door, somehow, I knew that there was no law.

Only chaos.

I had scheduled any interviews, nor were Mai, Walker, or Steven supposed to drop by. I was on *my break*, not *a break*. Something that took some thought and time to grow used to. So, I walked down the staircase to my front door. The sun was setting; I could see it through my front door's camera as I peered through the live image on my phone.

Whoever it was had been dressed very formally, though they were standing so close to the camera that I couldn't make out their faces. Winding the reel back, they had parked to the side of the cabin and had made their way from the side of my estate. At once, I wondered how they made it past the gates. But they obviously knew that I lived here and, so, weren't just tourists looking for an autograph.

I kept myself a secret during times of suspense, and only those closest to me knew of my whereabouts.

Still, I kept my suspicions and answered through my camera's speaker.

"Can I help you two?"

Yes, if it wasn't obvious, there were two of them. I couldn't see anyone else through the blinds of my windows, just their shady figures at my front door.

313

They were both about the same height and build as one another, and their sizes seemed familiar in a strange way. Then they knocked again, as I approached the door.

"Sorry but, this is private proper-"

Wood shrapnel flew through the door where the handle was placed. I felt myself lunge back, grabbing towards my abdomen in sudden shock and pain.

As I fell to the floor, the door creaked open with smoke leaking inside. Then the two men stepped in and I saw their faces. I couldn't believe who it was.

"Been a awhile, but it's coo." Jack stated, with Frankie following in after.

"How's it goin' bro?"

After all these years I thought that both Jack and Frankie had been dealt with, I was wrong. Unpredicted, unpresidented, now invading my home, I was afraid on the floor, bleeding out with several shards of wood imbedded into me. How did it come to this?

How could it not?

"Gotta' nice place here, cat. Better than the cell they were hold'n me in. Must be nice, eh? All this wealth and power and dogshit." As Jack leaned over me, with the barrel of his sod-off shotgun at my junk. "See here, I had's some time to think in the clinker, all locked up and shit from your telltale lies and all. I mean, I give'ya some credit, most'it was true, to a point. But ya didn't have'tah leave me hangin' for so long. Ain't that right, Frankie'ol'boy?"

"You had this comin' man. Ain't no way out now."

I began to crawl back, but Frankie grabbed me by both ankles and swung me sideways into the wall.

"Hey!" Jack yelled, "Ya'lmost tripped me you dumb bitch!"

"I ain't your whore, Jackie. I gotta' score to settle too!"

"That wasn't the in the fuck'n deal we made pal! Using this cunt as a hazard for me." Then Jack looked back, and I saw the same fury in his eyes as the night I betrayed him. "Is coo though, is all coo." He jutted his gaze to Frankie, who smiled and proceeded to stomp against my right ankle with his big black boot.

I could hear something snap or go out of place. And damn, did that shit hurt. But not as much as seeing my best friend with my greatest nemesis. That shit hurt harder than any cock I ever filmed penetrating a pussy.

Then I began to think of all the ways they'd torture me. Obviously, if they wanted me dead, then they wouldn't be scuffling with one another so casually. Then again, if all went well, it could be a short demise rather than a long dea-

The shotgun fired, but it missed my genitals and the buckshot was sent straight into my uppermost thigh. I cried in panic, holding my leg as more blood spilled across my hardwood oak flooring.

I was becoming an abstract painting by the minute.

"Let me have a fuck'n turn, would'ya? I'm the one who found this son-of-a-bitch after all!"

That's when I realized that the legal papers that Frankie had must've led them both back to my cabin. Idiot, I thought, when I had put my own personal address on those papers. The past was still here, and it was bleeding me dry.

"I didn't see you up at Pelican Bay, bruh. You got paid out, like the bitch that you are. So, I got ever'ight to shoot this mother fucker up."

There was a scuffle, that much was clear. But between their bickering, all I could think about was the life I led. Family, lovers, friends, every single second up to this point. And the seconds were turning faster.

Then soon, Frankie had elbow checked Jack into the wall, sending him onto the floor and grappling with the shotgun. I was slowly crawling into my living room, while reaching for my phone.

As soon as I had pulled it out, I dialed 9-1-1. It was a repeat of before, as I flung the phone beneath the couch so that the two buffoons couldn't find it. I had high hopes that the police would arrive on time, but I was miles out from the nearest town. So, in a way, I laid on my back and waited for their own fight to end, accepting my fate as I could have years and years ago.

Eventually Frankie won, with a few hard hits against Jack, and the back of the shotgun slammed into the man's face. With Jack out cold, Frankie positioned himself above me, raising that shotgun to my face.

"I always hated seeing you on the tele, on every video I watched, your fucking books making the headlines, the stories you were makin' up. I hated it!" He yelled, and I couldn't blame him, not one bit.

I had left him behind; I had betrayed both him and Jack. So, in a way, this was my fitting end.

"Any last words for the press, you fuckin' traitor?"

But I had none left, no words that weren't already written into a book or spoken live on air. In fantasy, we always dream of some symbolic way in which we'll pass on. But when it comes to reality, most of us just die natural deaths, mostly alone in a room without a hand to hold or a face to kiss, or a person to speak to otherwise.

I guess I was lucky enough to have my old best friend with me, even if he was aiming the gun towards me. But it would make for a dramatic headline the following day.

Would I be remembered as a martyer or sorts? Or a new man who had found resolution in the end? Then again, perhaps if all went well in the time after my death, I could be remembered as a good man. I supposed that that's all I ever wanted from the start.

So, without thinking twice, already feeling the impact of the slug to my skull, I answered Frankie.

"I love you man. I did you dirty and you didn't deserve that. And I hope that, after today that you'll-"

"Fuck you!' he screamed out, "Fuck-You-Man, and all of your manipulative bullshit! I've had enough of it! I should'a known sooner than now than to just get rid of you! You were holding me back, always were!"

"Holding you back?" I confusingly answered, "You were the one fucking Abby, you were the one who gave me the pills to fuck Abby, who you decided to fuck anyways. You were the one who got used to being on camera, fucking every whore at our college. But I was holding you back?" The truth came out; I couldn't sustain a lie any longer.

"I – I what?" he was suddenly in shock, pulling the barrel over his shoulder and pressing that damned boot back into my already broken ankle. "I tried to help you! It was your fucking idea! I didn't even know if I wanted to be a part of it, let alone how to work a god damn camera!"

"Well . . ." I huffed out of exhaustion and pain, "it's not too difficult to flip a fucking switch, turn the damn thing on and point it at our genitals, now is it?"

""Excuse me? I never worked a fucking camera before! You act like I just know everything that your artsy-ass knows and went with it!"

"My artsy-ass eh? What were you going to college for? Definitely not some logic degree or philosophy or some shit! Ever since I snuck out with you on the last day of middle school I kinda' knew that you were destined for failure!"

"F – fu – failure? Really? I was still attending my fucking classes you prick! Until you got into my head about this new fangled fucking idea of going into porn and shit. I just liked watching the stuff, I never wanted it to become my life!"

"Well, that's your life Frankie! Not mine. I didn't make the decisions for you! You just fucking *went with it* like you always do, because you don't have a mind of your own!"

"I wanted more than just to be a fuck boy on the side, you dumb bitch! You're really arguing with me as your bleeding out on your own multimillion dollar mansion?"

"This is hardly a mansion, Frank! It's a God damn cabin in the middle of nowhere! And I'd hardly say it'd cost me more than a million at best. You know? The simple life and all that shit!"

"The simple life, man, you are an idiot! You make millions a year and this was the best you could come up with? Some crack-shack in the middle of the mountains away from everyone? That's so sad little bro, so sad."

That's when I noticed Jack in the corner, beginning to sit upright again.

"Frankie! Get your head out of your ass and turn around!"

"Dude, oldest trick in the book, like, you think I'm really that stupid? You've always looked down on me, man!"

As I saw Jack drawing a knife from his pocket.

"You always treated me like I was lesser to you!"

As I watched Jack lift himself up, stumbling towards Frankie.

"You always have had this superiority complex and never thought that, maybe one time, I happened to notice it?"

I was Jack's inhibition.

"Frankie! Turn the fuck around!"

But it was too late.

Jack had begun stabbing Frankie, not once, not twice, but until his energy had run low. With over ten stab wounds inflicted, Frankie finally was able, on the floor and underneath Jack and all, to aim the shotgun and fire its last shell into Jack's skull, spreading fragments of his head across the open space of my cabin's entry.

After that last impact, with Jack's remaining body falling over him, Frankie carefully pressed the corpse off his own bleeding body and ended up beside me. And there we were, two old friends, bleeding out in the same house that time had built at both of our expense.

"I tried to tell you, man." I admitted, as if I needed one more win before the end.

"Shut it, man." He said while holding a hand against the blood flow rushing through his side.

But at that moment, I couldn't help but laugh, with the pain lapping with each convulsion. "We had all these years, and all these things to say to one another. And we just let it stew until the end. That fucking sucks, man."

"For the first time in a while," he spoke through a cough of blood, "I agree with you."

"What was your favorite part in all this?"

"Favorite part? Dude, we're both gonna' die here."

"I know. Bu at least we can die happy. Right?"

So, we reminisced with the time we had. And I hate to say it but, Frankie died first, mid-sentence in fact. We had made amends, and that was enough to forgive the old chum for doing what he did.

And as I awaited death, beside my best friend, I thought back to everything that had come before now. Then, as I heard sirens and saw flashing lights outside of my cabin, I knew it was too late for me. But I was happy.

That's what I always wanted to be. But it wasn't until my end that I somehow had found true happiness.

As the police and paramedics entered, I was already seeing the white lights. You know, the one's they always talk about through biblical infomercials and the like? It's true that you see that white light.

But there were no pearly gates, or God and his son waiting to greet me like a Walmart employee on the way out from the registers. Instead, every nerve in my body surged, my endorphins were rising rapidly, and it felt like the greatest drug trip were told. That part about your life flashing before your eyes, in came in waves, really. And it was all so pleasant at the time.

Until the white began to fade to black, and the voices and sounds surrounding me drowned out into an indisputable silence that overtook all of my senses. Before my taste and touch and smell disappeared, and all that I was left with was a warm blanket of black.

Hoping that this life would bleed into my next.

And thinking that, just maybe in my next life, I would've learned something out of this one.

www.ingramcontent.com/pod-product-compliance
Lightning Source LLC
Chambersburg PA
CBHW021456240626
47154CB00002B/393